The Last Line

The Last Line

Stephen Ronson

HODDER &
STOUGHTON

First published in Great Britain in 2023 by Hodder & Stoughton
An Hachette UK company

1

Copyright © Stephen Ronson 2023

A CIP catalogue record for this title is available from the British Library

Hardback ISBN 978 1 399 72123 3
Trade Paperback ISBN 978 1 399 72124 0
eBook ISBN 978 1 399 72125 7

Typeset in Plantin light by Manipal Technologies Limited

Printed and bound in Great Britain by Clays Ltd, Elcograf S.p.A.

Hodder & Stoughton policy is to use papers that are natural, renewable and
recyclable products and made from wood grown in sustainable forests. The logging
and manufacturing processes are expected to conform to the environmental
regulations of the country of origin.

Hodder & Stoughton Ltd
Carmelite House
50 Victoria Embankment
London EC4Y 0DZ

www.hodder.co.uk

Dedicated to the memory of my grandparents
Bessie, Eric, Peter and Vera
all of whom served their country on the home front.

I

Friday, 10 May 1940

I was walking in the meadow between the woods when I saw the Spitfire. At first, just a speck in the sky. The engine sounded wrong, the revs falling, spluttering, then finally cutting off with a last cough.

My meadow must have looked like a godsend. Flanked by the woods on either side, running south to north from his perspective, quarter of a mile long. Big enough for me to get a useful amount of hay come haymaking time. Not much distance to slow a fighter plane from flight speed to full stop. Maybe enough. Maybe not. At the northern end of the meadow, a row of ancient chestnuts was a dark wall in the bright early morning. If he hit those trees at speed, there wouldn't be much left of him.

He came in fast, trying to line it up without any power. Behind him, up in the sun, a speck – another plane.

I was halfway along the meadow, inside the treeline. If he survived the landing, he'd need help getting out of the plane. I ran towards those chestnut trees, keeping close to the edge of the field in case the plane suddenly came my way. I did my best to run through the long grass in my heavy boots but it must have been quite a sight – a forty-year-old farmer running flat out like a boy on sports day.

The Spitfire clipped the big oak at the far end of the meadow, breaking off a branch with a loud crack, then he blew past me, hitting the ground hard. The left wheel ripped off and the wing dipped and caught the grass. He got it back up again but only for thirty yards before the wing dipped again and dug in.

I struck out diagonally across the meadow, following him towards the trees, barely registering the sound of another plane passing close overhead.

With the wing dragging, the Spitfire kept turning, bringing it back towards me. I stopped running and watched it complete a tight circle before coming to an abrupt stop.

The plane that had buzzed me came around again, lining up for its own landing. I hoped he could make a better job of it than the man on the ground.

I hurried towards the downed Spitfire. The canopy slid back and the pilot climbed out, shaking himself out of his restraints. He jumped down onto the grass and stood with his hands on his knees, shaking like a racehorse that's been worked too hard.

'Are you all right?' I asked.

He looked beyond me to the plane coming in to land, his face screwed up in anger.

The second plane was a Messerschmitt. Unmistakable, with the yellow nose and black cross of the German Luftwaffe. It touched down lightly and bumped towards the north end of the field, deftly turning and taxiing towards us. He cut the engine and let it roll to within twenty yards of us before he pushed his canopy open. He was grinning.

He was a young chap. He had a weathered face and a white silk scarf tucked into his shirt. As he climbed out of his cockpit, I put myself between him and the English pilot.

'I think I caught your coolant line,' he said to the English pilot behind me.

'There,' he nodded, 'I see my bullet holes.' He gestured in a diagonal with his flattened hand, sketching out the path his bullets must have traced. 'I wanted to make sure you're all right, but it looks like you are,' he said, confirming his own diagnosis. 'I think we'll see each other again over France in the coming days.'

The German stepped past me and held out his hand. But the English pilot refused his offer to shake.

'Get away from me, you fucking Kraut,' spat the English pilot, taking a step backwards.

The German stood with his hand held out. He smiled ruefully and took it back.

'That's OK. The adrenaline. I get it. How many flying hours for you in the Spitfire? Twenty? Twenty-five? I was the same.'

He turned to me.

'I'm sorry if we damaged your field.' He looked around appreciatively. 'It's a beautiful place. Maybe when all this is over, I'll become a farmer. It must be good to spend your life growing things, after a war.'

I nodded.

'My boys will be wondering where I got to,' he said, turning back to his plane.

'Fucking Kraut,' muttered the English boy, more to himself than to the German. He fumbled with a lanyard around his neck and pulled an Enfield revolver from the front pocket of his jacket. His arm shook as he raised the gun, his muscles spent from bringing down the plane in one piece. I stepped out of the way. I've had a lot of guns pointed at me and it's an experience I try to avoid. The boy pointed his gun at the back of the German. A symbolic gesture, or so I thought.

The gun fired with a shocking loudness, echoing back off the trees. If this had been a Jimmy Cagney flick, the German would have turned round and uttered a final thought, perhaps a curse on England. But it wasn't a film. He didn't turn around to wrap things up like a gentleman. He dropped to the ground like a puppet with its strings cut.

The English pilot walked stiffly to the body and fired again.

'Fucking Kraut.'

He grinned at me like a boy who's hit a six.

'I got him,' he said.

He knelt by the body and turned it face up. I knew what he was doing and I turned away, wanting nothing to do with it. I'd seen it too often in the last war: men trading their honour for a souvenir. I guessed he'd take the scarf unless it was too bloody. Maybe he'd take it *because* it was bloody.

I studied the Messerschmitt. It was a beautiful machine, second only to our Spitfire in its speed and manoeuvrability, or so they said. I put my hand on the fuselage and felt the glossy paintwork. It was warm from the May sun.

'Their guns are much better than ours,' the pilot said, joining me and circling around the front to examine the propeller. 'They don't tell you that on the newsreels. It's not a fair fight.'

He peered underneath.

'Fighter-bomber,' he said, nodding at a hefty-looking bomb strapped to the undercarriage. 'Two hundred and fifty kilograms. They're using them to take out our ships in the Channel. Pretty nervy of him to land with that still attached.'

I took a step back, wondering how the bomb was detonated. Presumably some kind of impact trigger.

'They're coming,' he said. 'The sky over France is thick with them.'

'It was on the news,' I said. 'They said Belgium and Holland.'

'It's not like last time,' he said. 'They're already overrunning us. You can see it on the roads. They're jammed with people evacuating. It's a mess.'

He looked around.

'They'll be here in a few weeks.'

★

A bright red sports car turned onto the lane in the distance, accelerating down the straight half-mile towards my farm.

We waited in front of the house, leaning against the stone wall separating the garden from the lane. Bees buzzed lazily around the blossoming lilacs.

The pilot was rehearsing the story in his mind, his face previewing some of the emotions he was going to get across, bagging his first Hun and all that. I didn't judge him for it. In war, everything you do is obscene to anyone who wasn't there. I wouldn't have shot the German in the back if it had been me, but it hadn't been me. When it had been me, a long time ago, I'd done things, and I'd told people stories afterwards. I'd told myself stories afterwards.

'He was right,' he said, 'twenty hours flying. And I'm one of the experienced ones in our squadron.'

I looked up at the sky, clear blue.

'From what you said about the situation over there, it sounds like you'll get a few more hours under your belt before you know it.'

'I wonder how many I'll get before my luck runs out,' he said, following my gaze upwards.

*

A clipboard-wielding NCO took my details in preparation for the salvage operation. It would be three or four weeks at least. Planes were falling out of the sky over Sussex faster than they could haul them away to the scrapyard.

'We've taken the Jerry,' he said, offering me the clipboard.

'Will you get word back to his unit?' I asked.

'We've got a pretty good line of communication with them,' he said. 'We'll let them know what happened and they can notify his family.'

I signed in triplicate. Good to see the armed forces hadn't lost their taste for paperwork.

'You should cover up the planes,' he said. 'Get some camouflage over them until we get them hauled away. Herr Goering might send you a nice, personalised bombing raid. They try not to leave operational planes behind.'

2

Tea was sausages and boiled potatoes. It was one of two dishes Mum made, so we ate it three or four times a week. That suited me fine, I've always been a creature of habit. Nob always ate it, so we had to assume he didn't have any complaints. Luckily for us, neither sausages nor potatoes were rationed, at least not yet.

Uncle Nob didn't do well in the last war. The Great War: always capitalised, always thick with meaning. I'd done my bit – couldn't wait to sign up, told them I was sixteen. I spent my time at the front, but I got off lightly, more of a Boys' Own adventure than the horror stories others experienced. Nob was there for the duration. Ypres, the Somme, Passchendaele. Every big push. Hundreds of thousands of boys and men at a time, both sides of the field. Nob never really came back. When he was pushed out of a taxi at the end of the lane, dressed in his demob suit and clutching an empty cardboard suitcase, he walked up to the house, found his old armchair by the fire, and sat quietly, his hands shaking. More than twenty years ago. He hasn't said a word since.

We sat at the old oak table in the kitchen, where the oven kept things warm all day every day. The rest of the house was cold and damp, even in summer, so the kitchen got the most use.

'This is the BBC,' said the newsreader on the wireless. 'The Prime Minister, Neville Chamberlain, travelled this afternoon to Buckingham Palace, where he met with the King and delivered his resignation. A government spokesman said there will be an announcement later this evening naming his successor. It is widely expected that Lord Halifax will take the role.'

'Told you,' Mum said. 'He should have gone straight after Munich.'

It was a commonly held view. Chamberlain and Hitler had met in Munich in 1938 to negotiate the future of Czechoslovakia. Chamberlain had bent over backwards to appease Hitler, turning four million Czechs into Germans with a signature. Chamberlain returned home triumphant, proclaiming 'peace for our time', and thirty-six German divisions rolled across the border with the blessing of the international community. Within six months Czechoslovakia didn't exist. Turned out those thirty-six divisions didn't stop rolling once they'd taken the bit we'd allowed them. Playground politics. Give in to a bully today and he'll be back tomorrow wanting more.

'In further news, German bombers have attacked Rotterdam,' the BBC newsreader continued. 'This unprovoked attack on a city of civilians is seen as an early indicator of the tactics that Hitler's Reich intends to pursue across Europe. Eyewitnesses report thousands of casualties, with much of the population of the city fleeing in advance of the expected German invasion force.'

Mum switched over to Radio Hamburg. Their news was nonsense of course, but they had better music in the evening.

3

The Cross wasn't the closest pub to my house, but it was my local. Half an hour's walk across the dusty fields. The first pub I'd walked into with my friends when we were fourteen, desperate to get rid of the money we'd earned from a hot day of baling hay, and even more desperate to be men. All we knew was that men worked hard in the fields all day, then spent their pay that evening in the pub. Most of my friends were gone, as was the boy I'd been. Only the pub was still there, slowly sinking into the ground under a rotting thatch that was almost all black moss. I often daydreamed about buying the place, pulling it down, and replacing it with a smart brick and concrete building.

Without needing to be asked, Jim pulled me a pint of best, and a porter for Doc Graham. I put the change in the jar for the Spitfire Fund and carried the drinks to my usual place in the corner, instinctively ducking under the ceiling beams. I always sat with my back against the wall, which gave me a full view of the small public bar. I was facing the fireplace, blackened firebricks reeking of woodsmoke throughout the year, the mantel hung with brasses and now littered with leaflets exhorting us to 'make do and mend', 'keep our spirits up', and report our neighbours if we thought they were up to no good.

I kept an eye on the front door, and beyond that the lounge bar, where the gentry gathered to talk about foxhunting and politics. The public bar where I sat was for farm workers and labourers. An unwritten rule that never needed enforcing.

When I'd left the army, I'd put all my savings into our dying farm. I'd turned it around, and bought land from my neighbours. Now I owned the largest farm in the area. I would have been allowed into the lounge bar, but I wouldn't have been welcomed. Doc Graham was the only man I knew who moved with ease between the lounge and the public bar. He said he had to drop into the lounge every now and then to keep his paying customers onside.

'Quite a day,' Doc said, taking a long swallow of beer as he took his seat. Doc drank like most people breathe.

'We knew it was coming,' I said.

Since the start of the war the previous year, we'd been waiting for the real action to start. They'd called it 'the phony war' because we'd been 'at war' but there hadn't been any fighting, at least not for us. A lot of people had been willing it to start. Get it over with. Face your fears. That kind of thing.

'He'll sweep through the Netherlands without too much trouble,' he said. 'Then Belgium. What do you reckon until he's in France? Christmas?'

'That sounds fast,' I said. 'Our boys and the French are ready for him. They'll start digging in and he'll get bogged down. Same as last time.'

'Is your mind still made up?' he asked. 'Now it's happening?'

'I've got nothing to lose. No wife, no children, nobody to mourn me except Mum and Nob. Better me than anyone else I know.'

We'd had this discussion all through winter, and the logic hadn't changed. When Germany turned west, England would need another few million bodies to soak up their attack. The last war had almost finished us off, and those of us who survived had grown up in a country missing a generation. If it was going to happen again, the least I could do was to take the place of a young man who could otherwise stay at home and raise a family.

'Well, you know what I think,' he said.

'I know what you think about everything,' I replied.

'What am I thinking right now?'

It was too easy. While we'd been talking, he'd absently drunk most of his pint. Like breathing, as I said. I'd caught the quick flick of his eye towards his glass.

'You're thinking it's your round,' I said, 'and you're wondering whether to switch to whisky to speed things up.'

Doc's eyes twitched. He was embarrassed. He didn't like to think anyone knew about his drinking. There were things you were meant to pretend not to notice.

I pushed it. I was annoyed. At him. At Germany. At the stupid boy who'd shot that brave German pilot in the back.

'You're thinking of getting a quick shot on the side while you're up at the bar, but you'll drink it while I'm not looking and come back with the beers.'

'That's ridiculous,' he said, but I could tell he was hurt, and I felt a brief flare of triumph before it died away to leave the inevitable regret.

'I don't care what you do as long as you come back with two pints in your hand,' I joked, giving him a way out.

★

Two airmen spilled into the bar, wrapped up like they were slotting into a scrum. They were both tall and aristocratic, and in their fine blue uniforms they stood out like royalty in the gloom.

Their arrival had been heralded by the sound of wheels sliding on gravel and a high-powered engine gunned with an unnecessary flourish before being cut out, then doors slamming.

Behind them, the pilot who'd crash-landed in my meadow staggered in, a young woman hanging on his arm. He was flushed and unsteady. Looked like he'd started drinking the minute he got back to the airfield.

I recognised the girl. Harold Staunton's daughter Mary, from Newick. Staunton did my books, and he used to bring his little girl to the farm to see the animals. It was a shock to see her grown up, dressed to the nines, face made up like a Hollywood starlet.

The airmen passed out their drinks, including a pint for Mary. She took it and glanced around the pub, self-consciously. She caught my eye and smiled. I didn't think she'd have remembered me. I nodded in reply and raised my glass. It was unorthodox, having a bright young girl like that in the public bar, but that was how things were going. The war was shaking things up everywhere you looked.

The airman who'd bought the drinks proposed a toast.

'Pilot Officer Billy Baxter, the living legend! The first of our unit to bag his very own Jerry.'

The pilot did his best to ignore his friend. He cast his eyes around the pub and noticed me, sitting in the corner.

'Shut up, Geoffrey,' he muttered.

'Said Jerry having doggedly pursued said pilot officer all the way across the Channel, on a one-man invasion mission you might say, trying all the while to finish off our good friend, until our friend outclassed his enemy, getting behind him and shooting him out of the sky.'

The pilot's eyes were locked on mine, and I held his gaze. I sombrely raised my glass to him and nodded.

'That's not what happened,' Mary said. She hung on his arm, and I realised she was drunk.

'Shut up,' he said.

'That's not what you told me, Billy,' she said loudly, pulling away from him and staggering. 'You said he landed—'

The loud crack of his hand on her face was shockingly loud in the small bar.

The pub fell quiet. Even Mary was silent – the pain hadn't arrived yet. She raised her hand to her face, already turning a livid red.

I stood up, with a scrape of oak on the stone floor, and put myself between the girl and the pilot. 'I think you've had enough,' I said, looking him in the eye, 'and you owe the lady an apology.'

It wouldn't have been a fair fight. All he saw was a farmer, an old man whose fighting days were long behind him. He didn't see the apprenticeship I'd served in some of the most hostile environments in the world, learning hand-to-hand combat against men who didn't know the meaning of the word prisoner. I wanted the pilot to hit me, so I could do to him far worse than he'd done to Mary.

He glared at me, but he picked up something from my confidence and backed away, trying to be nonchalant. He gulped down the rest of his beer.

The door slammed behind me, Mary running out of the pub.

'Let's get you another drink,' said Geoffrey, putting his arm around the pilot.

'Going outside,' the pilot mumbled, shrugging off his friend's arm and following Mary out through the door.

I sat down, vibrating with adrenaline, my stomach churning. A long time since I'd felt like that. The way the body took over, girding itself for the fight. I tried a breathing exercise one of the doctors had taught me. By the time I finished, Doc was back with two more pints.

4

Closing time. Last pints swiftly downed. Good nights said. Doc and I stepped out into the car park and I was struck by the fact that it wasn't completely dark. May's arrival had brought long evenings.

Doc's house was in the opposite direction to mine. We stood in the cool air for a customary pause between the evening and the walk home.

There was one car at the far side of the car park, almost hidden in the gloom under an old yew tree. The driver's door opened and the pilot stepped out. He walked unsteadily towards me and Doc, a glint of something metal concealed in his hand.

The passenger door opened, and Mary climbed out.

'Billy, leave it alone will you?' she said. 'I'm sorry, Mr Cook. I've been trying to calm him down. He's not usually like this.' There was an edge of panic in her voice.

'I think you've got a problem with me,' Billy said.

'Hold on a minute, let's be sensible,' Doc said.

I kept my eye on Billy's trailing hand. He had something hidden. A knife or a gun. I don't like knives, but I certainly hoped it wasn't a gun. I'd already seen him shoot one person that day, so I knew he had it in him. Now he was drunk and angry, and I'd humiliated him in front of his girl.

My best option would have been to run. One thing I learnt in the trenches – you win every fight you don't have. But I wasn't alone. I didn't think Billy would turn on Doc or the girl, but I wasn't sure. Billy didn't seem all that stable; he was drunk, and he was having an interesting day.

The next best option would have been to take out Billy. Leave him unconscious on the gravel, immobilised, his right arm broken to ward off future surprise attacks. But I didn't want to hurt him too badly. It wasn't entirely his fault he was worked up. It was the war. He deserved a day to blow off steam, even if that included a brawl in a pub car park. And he was a trained Spitfire pilot. We needed every one of those we could get. If I damaged him, I might as well be fighting on Hitler's side.

'What have you got in your hand?' I asked, calm, trying to keep things civil.

Billy raised his hand sheepishly to show me a flick knife.

'That's not very sporting,' I said. 'Drop the knife and I'll fight you, fair and square.' I used my best command voice. I'd known a lot of young men like him. Shipped off to boarding school and raised in a strict hierarchy. They always responded to authority.

He dropped the knife on the gravel and Doc picked it up. I nodded and rolled up my shirt sleeves. It was a pantomime of what you were meant to do before starting a fight. I'd been in lots of fights, some for show like this one, most real. In a real fight there wouldn't have been any verbal warnings, no dropping of knives or rolling of sleeves. If this had been a real fight, one of us would have been dead or immobilised by now.

Billy rushed at me, and I made a big fuss of raising my arms in front of my face, like a boxer. I didn't want him to break his hand on my skull.

He thumped me in the stomach, right where I'd led him. I knew it was coming, and I'd tensed my muscles, but I acted like I'd been poleaxed. I went down and moaned. I stayed

down, keeping one eye on him in case he wanted to follow up
with a kick. I wouldn't allow that.

'Cook! Are you all right?' said Doc, as he knelt down by my
side.

I groaned, giving the performance all I had.

Mary caught up with Billy and grabbed him.

'Billy!' she cried. 'Leave him alone, you've half killed him.'

She draped herself on him, as if she were a prize he'd won.
It was a clever move, and it worked.

'See?' he said. 'Told you I'd sort him out.'

'You did,' she said. 'Now let's get you back before they put
you on report.'

★

The car roared out of the car park with a shower of gravel.
Doc and I stood, waiting for the quiet to return.

Doc threw something into the air, catching it deftly. Billy's
knife. He turned it in the moonlight to read an inscription.

'Pilot Officer Billy Baxter.'

'Baxter,' I asked. 'From over at The Grange?'

'Thought he looked familiar,' Doc said.

Billy Baxter. From The Grange. The kind of place where
domestic girls didn't last very long. The kind of place that
casts a long shadow. Growing up in a place like that, I almost
felt sorry for the boy. Still, he'd got out and signed up. He was
doing his bit.

5

I'd called my old regiment as soon as I heard the news of Hitler's westward invasion. After a year of talking about it with Doc, it was finally time. If I'd had any doubts about the urgency, the arrival of the Messerschmitt put paid to that.

There was a train to London at eleven. Mum was in the kitchen, pretending I wasn't going. She'd been through this before, back in '15 when I wasn't more than a boy. Nobody thought we'd have to do it all again.

Nob sat at the kitchen table, watching silently.

I grabbed my hat and gave Mum a kiss, turning to leave before either of us could show any emotion. Better that way. I clapped Nob on the shoulder and pretended not to notice his face was wet with tears.

I pulled open the front door and was surprised to find someone standing there. One of those moments. It was Charlie Neesham. Neesham had hung around with me and Doc when we were boys, never quite fitting in. We'd played cricket together on and off. Friendly as adults, but always something there, both of us caught up in the roles we'd set in stone when we were still running around in short trousers.

We walked into the yard while he went through the pleasantries. Hot for the time of year. Garden looking nice. Young wife. New baby on the way.

His police car was parked in the yard.

'I'm doing the rounds,' he said, nodding to my delivery van, 'making sure everyone's disconnecting their distributor caps overnight.'

There'd been a leaflet. One of many. We were meant to disable our vehicles when we left them at night, so German parachutists couldn't use them. Not a terrible idea.

He opened the door and felt inside for the bonnet release. He seemed familiar with the make. Probably been doing this all week. Probably thoroughly bored with it.

The bonnet popped. He lifted it up and propped it with the stand.

The distributor cap was still attached. He looked at me and sighed, disappointed. He'd thought better of me.

'Sorry,' I said. 'Had a few last night. Wasn't thinking straight.'

He slammed the bonnet shut.

'Let's call it a warning this time,' he said.

'Thanks, Charlie,' I said. 'Appreciate it.'

I held out my hand and he shook it.

'That's what friends are for, right?' he said, with a grin.

A flash of white caught my eye. At the far end of the lane. A cyclist, heading our way. Neesham followed my look.

'Who's that?' Neesham asked.

I watched as the cyclist got closer, lit intermittently by chinks of sun where it broke through the leafy canopy that covered most of the lane.

'Harold Staunton's girl, Mary,' I said. She was dressed for tennis, as if it was a normal May day.

'She's grown up fast,' he said, watching her.

I knew what he meant. She was like one of those pictures they painted on the bombers in the newsreels, all curves and smiles and rosy cheeks. She could have had her pick of the young men, I thought. Billy Baxter was a lucky young man.

She freewheeled into the yard, her bike chain clicking and the brakes squealing. She smiled when she saw me. A slight wince from the bruise on her face.

'Miss,' Neesham said, raising his hat to her. He stood by his car, showing no sign of wanting to leave. It was his job to be curious.

'Hello!' she said. 'Sorry, am I interrupting something? Is Mr Cook in trouble?' She smiled.

'Not at all,' Neesham said.

Mary looked around.

'Where are the cows?' she asked. It was milking time. Back when we kept livestock.

'All gone,' I said. 'Orders from the War Ag. The Ministry of Food tells the War Ag less meat, more veg. The War Ag tells me what to grow. We're all going to be eating a lot more potatoes and bread, and a lot less meat.'

'That's a shame,' she said. 'Seems like a farm should have cows.'

'I'll let the Minister know, next time he asks,' I said.

'I wanted to see if you're all right, after last night,' she said. 'Billy was crowing about it all the way home. He said you thought you were better than him. I told him he was being stupid of course, but you know what boys are like.'

She turned to Neesham. 'Mr Cook was such a gentleman. He stood up for me yesterday. My boyfriend was a bit hot under the collar.'

Neesham nodded.

'He got me a lucky one,' I said. 'I can't promise he'll be so lucky if he tries it again.'

'I made sure to tell him he was in the wrong,' she said, unconsciously touching the bruise on her face.

'What did your mum and dad say when they saw that?' I asked.

'Dad's in France with the BEF,' she said. 'He was too young last time so . . .'

She didn't need to finish the thought. A whole generation of men had grown up in the shadows of their fathers and elder brothers. Hard to live in a country where the only story is honour and sacrifice, and you didn't get to do your bit.

'Mum doesn't know,' she said. 'So it's our secret if you don't mind. I ducked out before breakfast. Told her I had an early match. Anyway . . . I just wanted to make sure you're all right.'

She was sweating. Despite the heat, she was wearing a wool cardigan over her blouse.

'Do you want a glass of water?' I asked.

'That would be lovely,' she said.

I held out my hand to Neesham. The universal sign for the end of a meeting.

6

'It'll be another hot one, I should think,' Mary said. She pulled her blouse away from her neck.

'Must get warm on that bike,' Mum said, holding out a glass of water.

'I'll say,' Mary said. She fingered the cardigan. 'I have to wear this when I'm out. You don't know what it's like. Every boy in town undressing you with his eyes. Not you, of course, Mr Cook. I didn't mean—' She flushed bright red.

She was right. I didn't know what it was like.

She gulped down her water.

'Billy's father has these men working for him,' she said. 'They give me the right creeps. You'd think they've never seen a woman before.'

'I'd go and have a word with them,' I said, 'but I won't be around after today.'

'You're not going too?' Mary asked.

'John thinks the army can't do without him,' Mum said.

★

Neesham had gone by the time we walked out into the yard. Mary teetered on her bike, one foot just about reaching the ground. She looked around at the empty cattle sheds.

'Shame about the cows,' she said. 'I would have liked to come and visit them.'

'There's lots of rabbits,' I said. 'Come around in the evening and you'll see plenty of them.'

'I'd like that,' she said.

I was expecting her to set off, so I waited politely to see her go, but she paused. It looked like she had something on her mind.

'I should get going,' I said. 'Everything all right?'

'Oh it's nothing really,' she said.

I waited. Nothing was clearly something.

'You were drinking with Doctor Graham last night,' she said.

'I was,' I said.

She paused, trying to find the right words.

'Is he a good man?' she asked.

'No man's all good,' I said, 'but Doc's about as good as they come. Do you need to see him about something?'

'Oh it's not me,' she said, rather too quickly. 'It's my friend, from tennis. Elizabeth. She's an evacuee so she doesn't know anyone round here. She's in a bit of trouble, and I don't think she knows who to turn to.'

She looked at her wristwatch.

'Look at me, taking up half the morning talking,' she said.

'Mary,' I said, 'do you need help? Did you want to see Doc?'

'It's not me,' she said, again. 'But thank you.'

'Well, tell your friend Doc's a good man,' I said.

7

Half an hour's walk to the station. It would be tight, but I'd make it. Across the fields to the church, then down Belmont Lane, leafy and cool in a month that felt more like August than May.

I had my gas mask with me, pristine in its cardboard box. We'd been issued them the year before, told to take them everywhere we went. Mine had sat in the cupboard, untouched. I didn't imagine the Germans would be interested in gassing my farm. But now I was heading up to London, I clutched it like a schoolboy on an outing.

The train from Brighton pulled in at precisely ten fifty-eight, and I took a last look around before boarding. I said my goodbyes to Uckfield and wondered if I'd ever see it again.

★

As I stepped out of Victoria Station, it was evident we were at war, every building buttressed with sandbags, and every person in uniform. The newspaper sellers were barking the latest headlines – Whitsun bank holiday was cancelled so we could all work an extra day. A kick in the teeth from an elite who would no doubt be taking their own holidays, war or no war. Perhaps it was supposed to make us hate the Germans more.

From the bridge in St James's Park, I looked back at Buckingham Palace and the swarm of barrage balloons high overhead, their thick tether cables forming a screen to prevent strafing runs from low-flying aircraft.

Nobody was carrying a gas mask.

I was due to meet Blakeney for lunch at the Yorkshire Grey, around the corner from the War Office. I arrived five minutes early, got myself a pint, and sat in the corner by the dark fireplace. The pub was quiet, with only a few other drinkers reading their papers and smoking.

By the time I finished the pint, Blakeney was ten minutes late. Uncharacteristic, but I knew I wasn't his top priority. I could wait. I was in a pleasant pub, in the heart of the capital, perhaps for the last time.

Returning to my table with another pint, I caught the eye of one of the other drinkers. He'd been sitting across from me, reading his paper, and he gave me a nod as I sat down. I returned the nod, our social interaction concluded, and was surprised when he got up and came to sit across from me.

'John Cook?' he asked.

I nodded.

'General Blakeney sends his apologies, but he won't be able to join you. He asked me to come and talk to you instead.'

He was a military man. Probably in his sixties, so he would have been an officer last time, back at HQ, or blowing a whistle in a trench. He was as thin as a rake, and his suit looked like he'd slept in it.

'I'm sorry,' he said, 'I'm Bunny.' We shook hands.

He reached into his briefcase and pulled out a scuffed file. I recognised the number, printed pedantically on the front cover twenty-five years earlier by a bored clerk, while I'd stood to attention in front of him, desperate to impress. It was my service record. It had been through a lot since that day.

'I understand you want to be useful,' Bunny said, opening and reading my file. 'Signed up age fifteen in time to help out at the Somme. Distinguished Conduct Medal. Re-enlisted after the armistice. Sent to the Khyber Line, North-West Frontier. Specialist training in . . .' he peered at the file, 'unconventional warfare and close-quarters combat.'

He looked up at me. 'What did you make of Afghanistan?'

'Not enough pubs,' I said.

He laughed politely.

'His Majesty's government thanks you for your offer of further military service, but respectfully declines,' he said, closing the file.

I was shocked. The army had been my home from the age of fifteen to twenty-four. Eight years, five months. Since then, another sixteen years had passed, but I'd never doubted that one day I'd be back in.

'It's not because of Kandahar,' he said, 'it's quite clear you acted in the best interests of your men, even if your methods were rather unconventional.'

He leant in closer and kept his voice low.

'We've got a group of chaps in war plans,' he said, 'Oxford Dons. Slide rules and all that. They've been studying Hitler's plans.' He looked around to make sure we weren't being overheard. 'They think he'll take France quickly. Very quickly. Then come for us.'

I tried to keep the shock off my face. The last time we'd faced Germany, advances of hundreds of yards cost thousands of lives, even hundreds of thousands, and weeks or months of combat.

'But the French have spent twenty years building their defences,' I said. 'What do the slide rules say about that?'

'They like the Maginot Line,' he said. 'They say it can't be breached.'

'I imagine that's why he's going through Holland,' I said, 'where we've got a million men lined up, with twenty years' worth of artillery production.'

'Of course, but Hitler knows that. Despite being a raving lunatic, he's not stupid,' Bunny said. 'So, what's his plan?'

I pictured a map of Europe. From Germany to the English Channel, Holland and the Low Countries were the obvious route around the top, if the French had the majority of their border defended.

'He's got the Nordics already,' I said. 'He could go straight from there to us, missing out France entirely. Not a bad idea after how badly that went for them last time. Stage an invasion from Copenhagen or Gothenburg, but that leaves him crossing the North Sea.'

'It worked for the Vikings,' Bunny said.

I shook my head. 'The Vikings weren't going up against the largest navy in the world,' I said.

I thought more. Drank more beer. Apparently I wasn't as clever as I thought.

'What about the Ardennes?' Bunny asked.

'Too hilly, too wooded,' I said. 'Narrow country lanes. You couldn't get an invasion force through that.'

'That's what everyone's told themselves for the last twenty years,' Bunny said. 'But it turns out nobody told Mr Hitler.'

He pulled a photo from the back of the file. It was taken from the air and showed a country lane jammed with tanks.

'A hundred and sixty miles of tanks, artillery and support vehicles backed up all the way to the Rhine. Every road through those hills. Twenty divisions, ten armoured, minimum. Half a million infantry, all aimed at Sedan, a quiet river town just north of where the Maginot Line ends.'

'So redirect the French,' I said.

Bunny laughed. 'Here's how that works. We tell the French. The French don't believe us. We get the PM on a plane over to Paris to tell them and show them the pictures. Their PM tells their generals. The generals don't believe him. They've been building their line in the wrong place. A lot of people invested in not believing him. But let's say they believe him; they'd need to send the message out to their units closest to Sedan. Do you know how the French send messages?'

I shook my head.

'They lay telephone lines between their front lines and their battle command centres. But what happens if you want to get a message to somewhere that doesn't have a telephone line? You have to get Paris to requisition a line crew to go out and put in a new one.'

'No radios?' I asked.

'Apparently they don't believe in radios,' he replied. 'Lower-quality sound.'

'More mobile,' I said, but as I was talking, I was thinking through the horrifying logic of what he was saying.

'Why would they need mobile?' he asked. 'Everybody knows this war will be the same as the last one. Massive armies lined up against each other, moving inches in a week.'

'Unless . . .' I said.

'Unless, indeed,' he said. 'We calculate that if the Germans get through Sedan they've got a free run across France, all the way to the English Channel. Once they're at the coast, they build up airfields, re-supply, then two weeks later they're ready for the final push and suddenly we've got half a million paratroopers floating down out of the sky over London and the South-East.'

We both looked up, as if we could see the sky from inside the pub. All I saw was an ornate plaster ceiling, stained brown with centuries of tobacco smoke.

8

'They'll come by air, and by sea,' Bunny said, shouting over the noise of the traffic as we pushed through the crowds approaching Trafalgar Square. 'We'll do what we can to slow them down of course, but once they establish a beachhead where they can safely unload, we'll be down to the final overs. We're thinking Newhaven, maybe Cuckmere Haven – that gives them a straight shot north to London. Which puts you in the bull's-eye. You could have German tanks rolling across your fields in three or four weeks' time.'

He stopped in a clear patch of the square, far enough from the crowds that we were safe from being overheard. There was a work crew building an above-ground shelter against the north wall of the square, nestled into the slope in front of the National Gallery. None of the workmen gave us a glance.

'When Jerry comes rolling over your farm, you're going to let him,' Bunny said, keeping his voice low. 'You'll feel an overwhelming urge to defend your country, but you won't give in to it. You'll meekly raise your hands and shout your "Heil Hitler" along with anyone else left alive. They'll probably kill you anyway, but they might not. They're going to need people like you to keep farming, so they can send the food back to the Fatherland. While you're doing this, we'll be evacuating the royal family and as much gold as we can stuff in our pockets to Canada.'

'You don't want me to fight back?' I asked. 'Give me a few good men and I could probably hold them for a day or two. Maybe more if we had some armour. I've had some experience fighting men who are defending their homeland. Seems to motivate them quite powerfully. I expect we'd be the same.'

'Not on invasion day,' he said. 'You and your shotgun versus a Panzer regiment? I give you about two seconds before you're a cloud of red mist. No. You lie low. You stay alive. You let us do our bit. And then, when the dust has settled and the German brass have gone back to Bavaria, *then* you get to work. Wreak as much havoc, kill as many Jerry as you can. Judging by what I saw in your file, I'd imagine that could be quite a few.'

'Just me?' I asked.

Bunny shook his head. 'I want you to form a small team, I'm calling them Auxiliary Units. Someone local will make contact with you. Work with them to pick a few more men you can trust. Ex-army probably. Men who take the initiative, who can find their way around the country, who know the woods. Men who get things done without being told how to do it. Men like you.'

'How do I communicate with you?' I asked.

'You don't,' he said. 'This isn't regular army. No chain of command. No safety net. If you get caught with a machine-gun and a pound of TNT under your bed next week, you'll be shot as a German spy. No crying to Mother.'

9

Three or four weeks, he'd said. The country wasn't ready. We'd spent a year preparing for aerial bombardment, digging bomb shelters and evacuating children from the cities, but everyone had assumed the real action would be in the trenches, across the Channel.

The journey home was a blur. The train was packed with schoolchildren being evacuated from London, all with luggage labels tied to their wrists. I kept to myself, watching the scenery as it unrolled: livestock in the fields where there should have been defensive lines being established; cyclists and drivers travelling winding lanes unchecked; bridges sitting vulnerable to aerial attack, without any ack-ack gun emplacements or camouflage. We'd placed all our chips on the defence of France.

When I got off the train at Uckfield, I hurried up the high street, picturing it from an invader's point of view. At the top of the hill, I stood on the steps of the cinema, ignoring the crowds coming out of the afternoon's flick, and looked back the way I'd walked, down the length of the high street to the Downs on the horizon.

Uckfield high street runs north to south, from the cinema to the train station. Ten miles further south, you come to Lewes, guarding one of the few gaps in the rolling chalk hills of the South Downs, then it's the coast. Most of the coast is tall white cliffs where the sea is slowly eating away at the Downs.

If you ever see a picture of a row of white cliffs, that's the Seven Sisters at Cuckmere Haven, where the hills dip down to form a welcoming landing stage: the most likely place to land an army, as Bunny had said. If you took a map and a ruler and drew a straight line from Cuckmere Haven to London, you'd draw a line up Uckfield high street.

I imagined the screech of tank tracks on the tarmac road. I could take up a sniper position in the tower of the cinema, or in the church further up the road, do my best to slow down the advance. I pictured a tank aiming its cannon and firing. Bunny was right. Any one man trying to slow down the advance of a regiment of tanks would last as long as it took the German gunner to swivel the turret, aim, and pull the trigger. I'd need artillery, at the very least an anti-tank rifle, capable of piercing the steel sides of German Panzers.

The problem was, our artillery and our tanks were in France, headed for Holland, along with most of our infantry, and if the Germans got to the coast, they'd have the whole lot of them surrounded. They'd have our men, our tanks, and our guns.

10

I told Mum and Uncle Nob the army had declined my offer of service. We all pretended it was nothing.

The six o'clock news from the BBC was grim. Duff Cooper, the new Minister of Information, told us that the greatest battle in history was in progress and we should expect bad news more so than good. We listened as we rushed our tea, Mum fussing around, hurrying us along.

Some of the evacuees on my train had been allotted to Uckfield, and word had gone out for volunteers. Mum had her heart set on a girl, with a sunny disposition and bows in her hair. There'd been a big wave of evacuations the previous year, when it all started. The papers had been full of dire predictions. They'd expected over two hundred thousand deaths from bombing in the first days of the war, but once it became clear that the bombers weren't coming, a lot of the children had returned home. The basic human inability to believe that the worst is really on its way.

That first time round I'd put my foot down and said the last thing we needed was a city kid under our feet. Mum had sulked for weeks, and even Nob had given me the cold shoulder. I hadn't realised how much they'd wanted some young blood about the place. Now that the second wave of evacuations had been announced Mum had been the first to sign up. I'd told her I'd go along and help her pick.

Nob sat in his armchair with a small piece of wood in his hand. I'd seen him carving it in the evenings, sitting by the fire.

I asked what he was hiding. He pretended not to hear me, but opened up his hand a bit, so I could see. It was an owl. It seemed Nob had also kept his hopes up.

We'd been told the matching process would start at half six, so we got to the church hall for twenty past. There was quite a queue outside, huddled in the early-evening shade along the side of the vicarage. Good for Uckfield, I thought, turning out to help the city kids.

One of the teachers from the Saunders School, a young girl not long out of school herself, opened the door, introduced herself as Miss Spencer, and described the process to us as if we were her pupils. We were to file in, in an orderly fashion, and fill out a form listing our details and the size of accommodation we could offer. Then, and only then, would we be introduced to the children who might be the best match.

That was the theory. The queue had other ideas. As soon as Miss Spencer finished talking, everyone surged into the hall.

There were about forty children, lined up in the middle of the dusty, wood-panelled hall like a couple of football teams before kick-off. They were all trying to put a brave face on it, give them credit, but you could smell the fear coming off them. The queue swarmed them, like shoppers in a bazaar.

I guided Mum to the trestle table set up for filling in paperwork, as we'd been instructed. We were the only ones. The next time I looked up, the line of kids was decimated.

The girls went quickly. The sweetest ones went first, then the plain ones, then the sour-faced ones. Everyone had the same idea as Mum – a pretty surrogate daughter, or else an unpaid domestic servant, someone who'd 'do' for them about the house, without eating too much.

An argument broke out between Miss Spencer and a prospective host, Mrs Burton. Mrs Burton, who was known throughout the town for always getting the best price, wanted the last girl. Miss Spencer bravely informed her the girl had to be kept with her brother. They came as a matching set. Mrs Burton, who hadn't come out to get two, grabbed the girl and tried to pull her out of the line. The girl was clutching her brother and sobbing, while Mrs Burton told Miss Spencer she should be ashamed of herself for letting the children dictate terms to her. Miss Spencer, showing more spine than I'd expected, kept a smile on her face, and insisted that the offer on the table was two or none. Mrs Burton left with the pair, but I didn't fancy the boy's chances of getting a decent berth.

Once the girls were taken, the strong boys were next. Mr and Mrs Shepherd, who struggled to get by with a rather lacklustre twenty acres and an even more lacklustre daughter and son-in-law, made a beeline for two strapping lads who looked like they could pull a plough without breaking sweat. I heard them telling the boys there'd be as much rabbit and eggs as they could eat – neglecting to mention that the boys would have to supply said rabbit and eggs by means not strictly legal. Everyone in the transaction seemed happy, so who was I to judge?

That left me and Mum, standing with our properly completed forms, eyeing a pasty-faced boy of about ten. Grey shorts, grey shirt, everything threadbare. His neck was livid with what looked like a nasty parasite. His pale face was a mask, eyes betraying nothing. Miss Spencer watched us hopefully, and I nodded to her, prompting a sigh of relief.

The transaction was completed. We had what we'd come for, after a fashion, and Miss Spencer had done her job of placing the hopes and dreams of England's future with generous and well-meaning hosts. The best thing that could happen to these lucky children, all of whom would end up rosy-cheeked from the pure country air and the good life on the farm. At least, that's what the newsreels would say.

The boy's name was Frankie, according to the luggage label around his wrist.

'Right, Frankie, you'll be coming with us,' Mum said.

Mum took him by the hand but he squirmed away.

'Have you ever been on a farm before?' Mum asked.

Frankie glared at her.

'Come on then,' she said, guiding him out of the hall, her hand on his shoulder.

I took a last look round. Miss Spencer was mopping up a puddle of urine. She caught my eye and blew a lock of hair out of her face, grinning.

★

We were fifty yards away when the door burst open and Miss Spencer hurried out.

'Mr Cook!' she shouted.

I walked back to meet her.

'I was meaning to ask,' she said. 'Would you mind volunteering your tractor to help us dig our victory garden at school? We're going to plough up the cricket pitch.'

'I'm not sure I could be part of that,' I said. I was joking, but her face fell. 'Sorry, I didn't mean to make fun,' I said, 'I'd be happy to help.'

She brightened. 'You could take a look when you bring Frankie to school.'

★

We walked home, past the church, across the fields. Swallows and swifts wheeled above us. The boy didn't say a word. I kept an eye on him, wondering what he made of it all. Had he ever been to the countryside? You heard stories that some of these kids hadn't ever left the slums they'd been born in.

He didn't even look up from his feet.

★

As we got close to the farm, I saw a black car parked halfway down the lane, almost invisible in the twilight. An odd place to stop. I left Mum with the boy and cut across the field to see what was going on.

It was a police car. Two men stood in the field, looking at something in the long grass. Neesham and a constable.

'Neesham?' I called out. 'What's going on?'

Neesham said something I didn't catch to the constable, a young lad who looked like he'd been crying. The lad pulled out his handcuffs and walked towards me nervously, like a young farm hand approaching a bull. I ignored him and walked to Neesham. As I got closer, I saw there was a new gap in the hedge between the field and my lane. There were tyre marks in the mud, and a lot of the grass was trodden down.

Neesham was looking at something in the grass.

It was Mary Staunton. She was dead, lying in a patch of grass stained black with her blood. Her cardigan was gone. Her tennis blouse was ripped open and her bare chest was covered with livid scratches. Her skirt and her slip were pushed up over her waist and her underwear was gone. Her face was a mess of blood.

I've seen a lot of death. I've seen bodies left to rot in the mud of no-man's-land. I once saw a rat dragging away a man's hand, his wedding band still glinting on the ring finger. I saw a boy disappear into vapour when a bomb exploded next to him. I've seen almost every way a man can think of to kill another man in war, but this was worse. The last time I'd seen Mary Staunton she'd been off to play tennis, wobbling away down the lane on her bike. Now she was on display like a freakish exhibit at a carnival. I could hear cars pulling up in the lane. More men coming to see the show. I heard Mum and Frankie behind me. The constable intercepted them but not before Mum caught a glimpse of the body. I heard her call for Frankie, protecting him.

I took off my jacket. It would cover some of Mary's nakedness. It wasn't enough, but it was something. I stepped towards her, but the constable restrained me.

'Keep him back,' Neesham said.

He looked at me in disgust.

'For Christ's sake, Cook, what have you done?'

I I

They took me to the station and threw me into a cell that smelt of piss and vomit. They left me cuffed. I sat on a concrete platform built into the wall and tried to make sense of what had happened.

Mary had come to see me in the morning, and by the evening she was dead. Neesham's deductions led to me as the killer. I couldn't fault his logic. A pretty young woman shows up at the home of an unmarried man. The man's an old soldier, ergo has a history of violence. The young woman and the man were last seen disappearing into the man's house, after they made sure the policeman was on his way.

But Mary had left. She'd been going to play tennis. There would be witnesses. You can't play tennis by yourself. Neesham would find those witnesses, if he hadn't already.

She'd been killed next to the lane to my house. Had it happened immediately after she left, or had she been coming back?

I pictured Neesham. He'd be thinking it through, sitting at home, glass of whisky in hand, the paper unread on his lap. He'd be sorting the evidence, trying to come to the right conclusion. But his thinking would be unbalanced by the way he probably thought of me – John Cook, the man who chose war over his fiancée and his farm. The man who drinks too much, goes for lots of long walks, doesn't go to church, avoids his neighbours. Never married. What was that girl doing turning up on his doorstep all blousy and flustered?

It must have been Billy. I'd seen it happen with men in combat. You strip away the rules of civilisation so a man will go out and kill on command, but once those layers are gone, it's hard to put them back again. At least in combat you're away from home. This new way of waging war, flying over to the front by day and back with your girl in the evening, didn't allow for the same separation. Add sex into the mix and you've got even more hormones and adrenaline. You end up with a young man trained as a killer, his bloodlust up, versus a girl trying to fend off his advances.

Young Billy Baxter and I would be meeting again, and the next time I wouldn't be holding back. England would have to fight the Luftwaffe with one less fighter pilot.

12

Late evening. I heard the front door bolted shut. I heard voices. Urgent whispers. Arguing. Urging. Then resolve. Then footsteps, making their way back through the booking room, to the cells. Two policemen, both young, both angry.

I lay on my concrete platform, hands cuffed in front of me, staring at the ceiling. I watched them out of the corner of my eye. Curious.

The taller of the two had a makeshift noose in his hands, made from a pair of trousers that vaguely matched the ones I was wearing.

His partner stood behind him, red-faced, holding a shotgun.

'Supper time,' the tall man said.

'Not hungry,' I said. 'Come back tomorrow. Tea and toast for breakfast at seven. Real butter, not margarine.'

'Mick here's Mary's cousin,' he said. 'Bet you didn't know that.'

The keys rattled in the lock, and the door opened with a screech. I watched the tall man approach. He had the noose in his left hand, and his truncheon in his right. He'd be planning to hit me with it, knock me out cold, so he could get me into the noose and string me up. A lot easier to do that if I wasn't struggling and fighting back. It would put a bruise on me that the coroner might question, but it was the best option under the circumstances.

In my favour, his entering the room took the shotgun out of the equation. Not the most subtle weapon. Unsuitable for killing one man and leaving the other man standing, when both men were in a small brick room.

I sat up as he approached, and he brightened. Perhaps he'd been worried about the prospect of striking a man who was lying down. Probably went against his sense of right and wrong.

'This is for Mary,' said the shotgun-wielding man, from his position behind the bars. It wasn't a bad tactic. If I turned to look at him, the tall man could swing his truncheon and take me out. End of innings.

So, I looked at him. But I planted my feet firmly on the ground and tensed my legs.

I tracked the swinging truncheon in my peripheral vision. The tall man extended himself, using his long arm to bring the weapon around in an arc. He wasn't holding back, and if he hit me, it would crush my temple. No need for any fancy story about hanging. The prisoner tried to escape and he was subdued by force. Must have had a weak skull, your honour, we've all seen it before.

I pushed up from the ground, head first. Unexpected, from the tall man's perspective. You're swinging at a man's head, you expect him to defend it, maybe hold up an ineffective forearm. You don't expect the head to come rocketing towards you.

My head hit his face and his nose disintegrated with a spray of blood. I kept going, pushing with my legs through the obstacle, no backing off. I lost balance, my cuffed arms no use, and committed to the fall. As he went down under me, I tucked my head in and went into a roll, landing on my back and using the momentum to end up back on my feet, in a crouch, against the opposite wall.

The other man tried to track me with his shotgun, which he'd half poked into the cell, but the barrel knocked against the edge of the door. I was too far to the side of the cell for him. I improved my position by darting forwards, into the front corner of the cell. Now he'd have to step inside and swing the gun round to get me in his line of fire. It would take a brave man to step into the cell, and he hesitated.

The barrel of the gun was still proud of the door, sticking through the bars like a dog's snout, so I kicked it, hard, making a solid connection right against the end of the barrel. The gun rocketed backwards. It clattered to the ground and he ran.

I ran after him, barging through the outer door as he tried to shut it, slamming him against the wall and cracking his head on the painted wall. He went down on the floor, out for the count. I stood above him, my boot above his neck, the fury and the adrenaline telling me to end it, to crush him.

I counted to ten, giving my civilised mind a chance to counter the rage. I'd be justified in killing a man who'd just tried to kill me. On the other hand, the fewer policemen I killed in my home town, the more likely I'd be able to protect my country from the invasion force. Added to that, perhaps he really was Mary's cousin. If I'd been in his shoes, I'd have probably done the same thing.

I sided with logic, with a nod towards revenge. Instead of ending his life, I stamped down hard on his right hand, crunching the bones between the heavy sole of my boot and the concrete floor. I did the same with his left hand, just in case, then took the keys from his belt and unlocked my cuffs. I dragged him back to my cell and locked him in with his partner. I left them on their sides so they wouldn't choke, and retreated to the reception area. I needed to decide what to do next.

If I left, there'd be a manhunt. They'd come for me with shotguns. The man who killed Mary Staunton and attacked two policemen. No chance they'd even try to take me alive a second time.

If I stayed, I'd be headed for the gallows. In theory I'd get my day in court. Perhaps I'd be able to tell my side of the story. But it was largely a story I couldn't tell. I'd spent the day in London talking with Bunny, sworn to secrecy.

Not an ideal set of options, all things considered.

13

'Tell me about your relationship with Mary Staunton,' Neesham said. He opened his notebook and stared at me. This wasn't the man who'd forgiven my mistake with the distributor cap the day before. He'd made up his mind. He waited impatiently for my reply, pencil at the ready.

Neesham had been first in, ready to clear up the case with a confession from the guilty man. I'd told him about the overnight attack. Underplayed it a bit, didn't want to get the men in too much trouble if they really were Mary's cousins. He'd locked me in the office while he worked out what had happened. There'd been a lot of shouting and slamming of doors.

I wondered what kind of story they'd come up with. I'd have claimed significant memory loss. Always worked for me in the army.

He came back for me at eight and took me to an interview room, the walls and floor painted an institutional pea-green. His rhythm was off. He'd come in with a plan to get me confessing, one that started with me simmering in a cell, not spending the night in his office, sitting in his chair, my feet on his desk. It changed the power dynamic.

'Why d'you do it?' he asked.

'You're meant to tell me what I'm accused of,' I said. I wanted to establish a solid grounding of facts. Wanted him to tell me what he knew, and what he thought.

'Constable, please remind the prisoner what he did.'

It was the same young constable who'd tried to handcuff me in the field, now freshly scrubbed, his uniform stiff with starch. I pictured his mum up late, ironing it for the big day ahead.

He nervously thumbed his notebook.

'At quarter to six p.m. on the eleventh of May, an anonymous caller telephoned to report a young woman had been murdered and could be found at the farm of Mr John Cook. The caller stated that the girl had been the victim of a crime of a particularly violent nature, having been violated and beaten until she was dead.'

Neesham watched me as the constable spoke.

'Upon the police constable's arrival, the young woman was found to be dead. Her clothes were ripped from her body, leaving her exposed. Detective Sergeant Neesham observed that the land was owned by John Cook, who had been seen with the young woman that morning. Detective Sergeant Neesham said, "It's that maniac Cook. He's not been right in the head since he came back." '

'Did Miss Staunton come to visit you yesterday morning?' Neesham asked. He kept his voice light. Casual. Just making conversation.

'You know she did,' I said.

He wrote my answer in his notebook. Took his time. Careful to get it right.

'She was pleased to see you. Flustered, you could say.'

'It was a warm morning. She'd been cycling,' I said.

More writing.

'Why did she visit you yesterday morning?'

'She wanted to see if I was all right. I'd been in a fight with her boyfriend the night before outside the pub.'

'Tell me more about that,' said Neesham, nodding. 'What was the fight about?'

'I'd embarrassed her boyfriend in front of his flying chums. They were all rather the worse for wear. He slapped Mary. I stepped in to defend her.'

Neesham wrote more, and then showed his notebook to the constable.

'Friday evening at The Cross,' the constable said. 'Gets busy down there. But you're the one who steps in to defend a girl who gets out of line with her boyfriend?'

'Out of line?' I asked.

Neesham turned to the constable. 'Mr Cook's a war hero, you see. In fact, he was so heroic, he stayed in the army when everyone else came home, because he'd got the taste for killing, and went off to India where they turned him into a . . . what's the word they use?'

He turned to me, but I didn't rise to the bait. 'A commando, I think they call it,' he said, 'which is a fancy way of saying killer. They say he can kill a man just by looking at him. Or a girl. Never been married, not like a normal man. Lives with his mum, all alone in that big farm. Makes you wonder.'

He paused for a minute. Thinking about which way to go with the interrogation.

'Why were you fighting over a pretty young girl, Mr Cook?'

I didn't answer.

'What do you think, Constable? Why would a man get into a fight over a girl?'

'Perhaps he had a reason,' the constable said, 'some kind of relationship.'

Neesham wrote in his notebook. 'Relationship,' he said.

'You're being absurd, Neesham,' I said. 'She's a beautiful young girl and I'm old enough to be her father.'

'Beautiful,' he said, looking me in the eye, then writing in his notebook. His pencil paused.

'B. E. A. U.,' I said, glad to see his cheeks flush with embarrassment.

'Look, we're wasting time while there's a killer out there,' I said. 'It was her boyfriend. His name's Billy Baxter, from The Grange. He's got a history of being violent with her.'

Neesham wrote the name in his notebook. He paused to rub his temples, like the name gave him a headache.

'What were you doing yesterday?' he asked.

'I was with Mum at the church hall,' I said. 'Picking up an evacuee.'

Neesham consulted his notes.

'That started at half six, I understand,' he said. 'How about the rest of the day?'

'Forestry work. Coppicing.'

'Don't you have men to do the work for you?'

'The men are off fighting,' I said. 'Most of them anyway.'

I saw the constable flush. My remark had hit home.

'Besides,' I said, 'I like the work.'

'I think you're lying,' Neesham said.

I counted to ten. It didn't help. I counted to twenty. Reminded myself I was hanging by a thread. Better help him come to the right answer.

'If I'd attacked her, why would I leave her in my field, right on the way to my house? I've got over a hundred acres of land. If I wanted to get rid of a body, you think I'd leave it on my front porch?'

I could see him thinking it through.

'You saw us together that morning,' I said, 'I'd have to be stupid to go and attack her a few hours later. I'd have known you'd come for me. I'm not stupid.'

'Perhaps you weren't thinking straight,' he said. 'Shell-shock. Isn't that what they call it? Like your Uncle Nob. Another freak.'

'There were tyre tracks through the hedge. Her attacker was following her in a car. He crashed through the hedge. Why would I do that?'

Neesham shook his head.

'If you're asking me to put myself in your head and come up with a perfectly logical, reasonable account for why you raped and murdered a young woman, you're wasting your time,' he said. 'A normal man wouldn't have driven his car through a hedge. A normal man wouldn't have raped and murdered a young woman. In our line of business we don't look for normal men. We're looking for criminals. We don't need to find a justification for every sick and depraved thing they do.'

'You should be looking at Billy Baxter,' I said. 'He's at war. You know what that's like, Neesham. We both do. Think about when you were at the front. How long did it take you to calm down after a raid? How long 'til the adrenaline went away and you felt like yourself? These pilots are in the thick of it one minute, then the next they're back in the real world, at the pub with their girls. You've seen the way they behave. It's a wonder there aren't more cases like this.'

'That's your position?' he asked.

'There's something else,' I said. 'She said something to me yesterday. I didn't pay attention at the time. She said some of the men at The Grange had been looking at her.'

I didn't mention our conversation about Doc. About the girl in trouble. Mary had probably been talking about herself, so I considered that conversation private. If Neesham wanted to find out about Mary's problem, let him do his job and detect it.

'She said Baxter's men had been making her feel uncomfortable,' I said.

Neesham's hands went to his face again, this time brushing across his eyes. He knew something but didn't want to admit it. Didn't want to see it.

14

The young constable sat with his arms crossed, watching me in case I decided to break down and confess. His big moment, cracking his first case. Neesham had stepped out, letting me stew. No doubt a trick learnt at a training conference for up-and-coming detective sergeants.

I heard raised voices from a distant room. Then footsteps.

The door opened. A new man. Older. Clearly senior from the way he strode in, taking charge. Neesham stepped in behind him.

'Cook,' the new man said, holding out his hand for me to shake. 'Sergeant Major, isn't it?'

'It was,' I said.

'Royal Sussex?'

'Eleventh Battalion.'

He grunted with approval.

'Major Armstrong,' he said. 'Somerset Light Infantry. First Battalion.'

He looked around at the room with distaste.

'Chief Constable nowadays, Crowborough and Uckfield District.'

I don't like men who cling on to their rank. In large part, that rank was a recognition of the amount of money and social standing they'd had when they joined up. The Chief Constable interested me, though. He had a roughness, a thickness in his neck and arms that suggested he'd fought his way up.

He looked meaningfully at the young constable, who got the hint and sprung up out of his seat.

'Let's hear it then,' the Chief Constable said, taking the vacated seat.

I told him the story from the beginning, starting from the plane landing in my field. I told him about Billy shooting the pilot, and about the fight at The Cross. I left out the trip to London. He listened without interrupting.

'So you think it was this young pilot?'

'He's moving from combat to peacetime every day, and then back again. That sort of thing has an effect on a man. I saw signs of it at The Cross.'

He sat in silence, thinking.

'Troubling,' he said, eventually.

'We can have the pilot brought in, sir,' Neesham volunteered.

The Chief Constable shook his head.

'No need,' he said. 'I've talked to his father. Mr Baxter told me his son was flying all day yesterday.'

'I'll confirm it with his unit,' Neesham said, opening his notebook.

'I'll do it,' the Chief Constable said. 'You've got enough on your hands with the evacuees.'

I watched the two of them. A common enough power dynamic. The senior man had decided the outcome, and the junior man didn't like it, but knew he wasn't going to fight it.

'It's quite clear what's going on here,' the Chief Constable said. 'We've got two local men. Both war heroes. Two of the most respected landowners in the area.'

'Sir—'

The Chief Constable held up his hand, cutting Neesham off.

'Two honourable men,' the Chief Constable continued. 'There's a fight at a pub, two decent chaps blowing off steam.'

Neesham closed his notebook.

'But murder?' The Chief Constable shook his head. 'I don't see it. I don't see that at all. If either Sergeant Major Cook or Pilot Officer Baxter had committed the crime, why would they leave the body out in the open, in their home town? Apart from the fact that it's a monstrous suggestion in the first place, both men have got land to spare, they could hide her away somewhere quiet. No. This is an outsider, someone passing through. Someone of a lower order I'd say, who saw one of our young ladies out enjoying a spring day and took advantage.'

The Chief Constable stood up.

'Neesham got a bit over-excited bringing you in,' the Chief Constable said, 'but we can't fault him for that. Ask forgiveness rather than permission, that's what I drill into my men.'

He offered me his hand again.

'Thanks for clearing things up,' he said.

I stood up and we shook hands.

'We're rounding up all the Germans in the area,' the Chief Constable said to me. 'Shipping them out to the Isle of Man. I think we'll find the crime rate drops considerably once they're safely out of the way.'

He took a last look at me, nodded, then left. Efficient. Quick decisions, quick actions. Presumably characteristics that had served him well in the army. I wondered whether those same qualities were just as effective when it came to police work.

He paused at the door.

'Neesham, get your men back out on the streets. Reassure the population.'

The door slammed behind him.

15

Doc's wife met me at the front door with a sombre smile practised on countless patients and their relatives. Her eyes met mine for a second then flicked away. Jane and I had been engaged before I'd gone away to war. When it was all over I wasn't ready to come home so I volunteered for more and they shipped me out to India to keep the tribesmen out of our tea plantations on the North-West Frontier. By the time I eventually returned, Jane and Doc were married with their first child on the way. Water under the bridge.

'They let you go,' she said. 'We were worried.'

I let myself through to Doc's office, an oak-panelled library where he saw most of his patients. He wasn't there, but I heard movement in the far room through a discreet door almost lost amid the bookcases. I followed the noise and found him in the treatment room – a utilitarian space with a tiled floor and an examination table where he did his more serious procedures. He had Mary's body laid out on the table.

'Come in,' Doc said, 'I want your opinion on something.'

When I'd got home from the police station, there'd been a message waiting. Doc wanted my help.

'You're the expert,' I said.

'I'm the medical expert,' he said. 'You're the expert in violence.'

It was indecent, us two men being there with her. She should have been with her family. She should have been playing tennis, or shopping, or anywhere doing anything other than lying on an examination table. It was hard to believe only yesterday we'd been talking. She'd had a life ahead of her. Now she was a body laid out on a table.

Doc moved the sheet to show me her arm, the pallid skin marred by a set of livid bruises.

'She was held, tightly,' he said.

I nodded and took a close look.

'You see bruising like this with a lot of rape victims,' he said. 'The attacker holds his victim down, keeping her hands immobile.'

I looked at her face. It was a mess. Barely recognisable. She'd been hit hard, again and again. I've seen a lot of victims of violence. This was worse than most.

'What do you think happened?' he asked.

'It could have been punishment,' I said, 'the attacker's handing out something proportional to the offence, and in his mind here the offence was significant. He'd probably already decided how many blows, like a headmaster doling out fifty stripes with the cane.'

'It would explain the overkill,' Doc said.

'Could be something else,' I said. 'Could be torture. Used to make her talk. Repeated blows, repeated pain. Tell me what I want to know, and the pain will stop, otherwise there'll be more.'

There was something about the hand marks on her wrists. I looked at them closely.

'Stand in front of me,' I said to Doc.

I stood behind him and held his wrists. I looked closely at where my fingers would have been. I checked with the bruises on Mary's arms. They matched.

'Two men,' I said. 'One man held her from behind. The second was in front of her, beating her.'

I pictured the pilot beating her. He would have done as much damage to his own hands as to her face, which would mean he wouldn't be able to fly. After I'd been so thoughtful with him the day before. If it was him, we'd find him grounded, nursing bruised hands.

'She came to see me yesterday morning,' I said.

'That's old news,' Doc said, 'half the town's talking about it. I think Neesham's hoping for a conviction in the court of public opinion.'

'She was asking about you,' I said. 'Checking your credentials. She said something about a friend being in trouble. I think she was talking about herself.'

Doc looked down at Mary.

'Christ,' he said.

There was a soft knock on the surgery door.

'What is it?' asked Doc loudly.

'Mrs Staunton,' Jane said, through the door.

*

Betty Staunton was sitting in the waiting room, an old copy of *Punch* unread in her lap. She rose as Doc entered. I hung back, not wanting to intrude, but she came to me and hugged me tightly, like a drowning woman grasping a floating timber. I stood and held her as she sobbed, until she was ready to let go.

Jane brought tea and passed it out, the simple ritual giving everyone things to do, passing cups and saucers, and milk and sugar.

'Mary came to see me yesterday,' I said. 'She'd got in a fight with her boyfriend the night before.'

'She tried to hide it from me,' Betty said. 'As if I wouldn't notice.'

'Has he hit her before?' I asked.

Betty shook her head. 'He's been a good lad. Always taking her to the pictures and the tennis. She had him wrapped around her little finger. Used to get him to treat her to the best seats, buy her chocolates, all of it. If it weren't for the war, I'd expect they'd be engaged by now.'

'Was he pressuring her?' Doc asked. 'Young men can get frustrated when they're courting.'

'No,' she said. 'We'd talked. He wasn't frustrated.' She flushed. She looked just like her daughter. 'They weren't, you know, but they were intimate.'

Doc caught my eye. He was worried I'd say the wrong thing. It made me realise how many of these conversations he must have had over the years. Breaking the news.

'She said something about the men at The Grange,' I said. 'Were they bothering her?'

'She's had something on her mind, but she wouldn't tell me,' Betty said. 'She was a happy girl until a few weeks ago. Spent most of her time reading, or out courting with Billy. Honestly, the lives these young people lead. You wouldn't know there's a war on sometimes. But something changed. I don't know what it was.'

'She said she was worried about a friend,' I said.

Betty nodded.

'There was a girl she played tennis with. Elizabeth, an evacuee. She idolised Mary by all accounts. Mary said she'd run away. Went to see the police, all proper. They said they'd keep an eye out.'

'She played tennis up at the pleasure ground?' I asked.

Betty dabbed her nose with her hankie. 'She was always up there, if she wasn't with Billy,' she said.

Interesting that Neesham hadn't mentioned a report about a missing evacuee. Fair enough, he wasn't obliged to show me all his cards.

'Did she suffer?' Betty asked Doc.

'No,' Doc said. Always the right answer.

'Mr Cook,' Betty said, 'Harold always says you know almost everyone in Uckfield. Maybe you'll hear something, about who did it.'

'I'll keep my ear to the ground,' I said.

She looked at me directly. 'You were a soldier?' she asked.

'Yes,' I said.

She didn't finish the thought. She didn't have to.

16

Some things are complicated. Some things aren't. I'd seen Billy Baxter shoot a man in the back and then gleefully search the body for souvenirs. I'd seen him strike Mary without a second thought because she'd threatened to embarrass him. When he identified me as another threat, he did his best to put me on the ground. If I was looking for Mary's killer, I didn't need to look any further.

Doc drove. A short trip up to the high ground of Ashdown Forest. Misnamed, almost bare of trees, it was a large expanse of heathland covering a dome of sandstone. We could see the North Downs far off, a line of green hills in the distance between us and London. Behind us, the South Downs formed the southern horizon. The forest was a natural viewpoint, with commanding vistas in all directions. A perfect spot for an air-field, part of the RAF's strategy of dispersing the fighter force across the country.

We took the right fork at Nutley, past Pippingford, and then onto the Roman road, a dead-straight stretch of road laid out by an invading army, two thousand years ago.

'Up here on the left,' I said, peering through my side of the divided windscreen. Doc slowed, looking for the entrance amidst the scrub. A sentry guarded a counterweighted bar painted white with red stripes.

Doc pulled in. He rolled down his window and snapped at the sentry.

'Doctor Graham. Come on, man, it's urgent.'

The sentry got to it without question, generations in his past of people who opened gates and took orders from men a few steps up the hierarchy.

Doc put the car back into gear, and we nosed through the gate. We bumped along a gravel track, flanked by shoulder-height gorse bushes, their sharp thorns scratching the car every time we had to detour around one of the frequent, deep potholes. After half a mile of manoeuvring, bouncing and scratching, we reached the airfield.

After being hemmed in by the gorse, it was jarring to emerge into the wide-open expanse of the makeshift airfield – a cleared area of about ten acres. It had been done hastily, by bulldozer. Piles of tree stumps, gorse, and topsoil made mounds at the eastern edge, leaving behind a scraped landscape of sandstone and mud.

Back on the road we'd been in Sussex. Now we were at the front. I felt like I'd stepped through a hole in time. The last twenty years had been a daydream. The war hadn't ever been over. Only the planes had changed.

A Spitfire buzzed us, close overhead, trailing smoke as it circled the airfield. I looked ahead, straight down the length of the landing strip. It was blocked by the wreckage of a burning Hurricane. A crew of engineers was trying to get a cable around it so they could tow it out of the way, but they were being beaten back by the fire.

Overhead, the Spitfire circled urgently.

'Pull up by that bulldozer,' I said to Doc. He bumped the car over the rutted ground.

I jumped out and climbed up into the cab of the bulldozer. I'd never driven this model before but had put in quite a few hours on others like it. I hoped the controls were recognisable.

I primed the ignition, then hit the switch to turn over the starter motor. It whined, and the engine caught with a roar, then a growl, as I feathered the choke. I felt for the blade control. The blade lifted off the ground, and the whole machine leant forward as it took up the weight. Everything seemed in order. I took a quick look behind me to check I was clear, then reversed it out in a tight turn. I shoved it into first, and set off towards the burning plane.

The shouting engineers didn't hear me coming at first. They were too busy, trying in vain to throw their cable over the burning wreckage. They were just boys, none of them older than twenty, shouting at each other, lost in panic.

I gunned the engine and kept the bulldozer pointed at the burning plane. I didn't know whether the power and torque of the bulldozer would be enough to win over the mass of the plane. I was worried about the wings. If I hit the plane in the centre of its fuselage, there was a risk the wings would break off as I pushed. Best case I'd come back for them on a second and third sweep. Worst case they caught on the bulldozer blade and enveloped me in fire as I pushed through. Too late to worry now. The boys scattered, and I lowered the blade to just above the ground and hit the plane.

The plane dug in at first, as the blade lifted the body and the far wing buried itself deeper into the ground. I floored the accelerator, keeping a careful feel on the clutch so I didn't stall. I felt the caterpillar tracks of the bulldozer start to spin on the solid sandstone, then they dug in and we jolted forward, with a screech of metal as the blade peeled the left wing off the plane.

The remaining wing, bracing the plane like a prop in a rugby scrum, buckled as I moved forward, and then suddenly the fuselage was free and I was pushing it to the side of the narrow landing strip, into a pile of gorse. The last thing I saw, before I looked back to reposition for a second run at the wings, was the blackened remains of the pilot. I hoped he'd been dead before the fire took him.

The circling Spitfire lined up for its approach. He was going to try and make it down despite the burning debris on the landing strip. I thought I could make one more pass before he got there, so I headed back, painfully slowly compared to his approach at what must have been close to a hundred miles an hour. I tried to work out the geometry of what was about to happen, but that part of my mind was shut down, focusing all my efforts on keeping the bulldozer under control and pointed in the right direction.

I reached the burning wing and this time there wasn't any mass to slow me down, just a shower of flames as the whole thing disintegrated against the blade of the bulldozer. I kept it moving forward and ducked down behind the small windscreen. Behind me I felt a blast of air as the Spitfire touched down.

17

'Where the bloody hell have you been?'

As the newly arrived Spitfire taxied towards a row of Nissen huts, a man strode towards me. He had the bearing of a man in charge and I braced for further abuse. In my experience, when a senior officer approaches you at speed, they're about to scream at you for something you've done wrong, or to tell you you've volunteered for something unpleasant.

He was about my age, his face brown and deeply lined from a lifetime of squinting in the sun. He held out his hand.

'Squadron Leader Johnson,' he said.

'John Cook,' I replied.

'Please tell me you're my new man from Biggin Hill?'

'Just visiting Billy Baxter.'

'Fucking hell,' he said, 'I thought they'd finally sent someone who doesn't need to be shown how to tie his own shoelaces. You've no idea the shambles they're sending me.'

'There's a man still in the cockpit,' I said, nodding to the smouldering wreckage on the far side of the airstrip. 'What's left of him.'

'We're losing them faster than we can train them,' he said.

'Is Billy around? I asked.

'Just got in,' he said. 'Let me buy you a cup of tea in the meantime.'

We walked together to the makeshift barracks, joined by Doc as we neared the mess tent. Doc and the squadron leader shook hands and introduced themselves.

'The PM's promised the French we'll base our fighters over there, but Air Chief Marshal Dowding doesn't think that's such a good idea, so we're slow-walking it. In the meantime, we fly over to help out and then back home for tea. If we're lucky.'

'You fly all the way to Sedan?' I asked.

Johnson shook his head.

'Sedan was yesterday,' he said. 'They've broken through. From the air it's like watching a dam breaking. They're pouring through the breach and if we're not careful they'll cut right through to the coast.'

I looked down the length of the airstrip. The English Channel was about fifteen miles south of us. If the Germans reached the French coast, they'd be about forty miles away, closer than we were to London and about five minutes' flying time in a Stuka dive bomber.

Johnson's batman emerged from the mess.

'Three teas, quick as you like,' Johnson snapped, 'and tell Baxter he's got visitors.'

The young man disappeared back into the tent, and Johnson motioned to a group of camp chairs, set up facing the airstrip.

'I didn't catch what brings you chaps here,' he said.

Doc answered. 'I'm afraid we've got some bad news,' he said, 'there's been some trouble with a girl Billy was courting.'

'You're not here to march him to the altar, are you?' joked Johnson. 'You won't get permission, you know. They're not allowed to marry until they've had a year in service, and he hasn't.'

'I'm afraid it's worse than that,' I said. 'His girlfriend was killed yesterday.'

I wanted to see his reaction. A good commander knows his men, and knows what they're capable of.

'Looks like she had an argument with someone,' I said, 'someone who's been under a lot of pressure.'

Johnson caught on. He looked at me carefully.

'Who are you?' he asked.

'We're friends of the girl's family,' I said. 'They asked us to talk with Billy.'

Johnson thought before he answered. 'Listen,' he said, 'Baxter's an arrogant prick. Thought he was God's gift when he got here. We disabused him of that notion pretty quickly, and he didn't take too kindly to it. If you're asking me if he could blow his top, I'd say probably. But he loves that girl. He's got an engagement ring. Been showing all the chaps. Was going to pop the question any day.'

'Where was he yesterday?' I asked.

'France,' he said. 'Wheels up at about ten. Straight over to the front. Either flying or refuelling.'

He looked along the length of the runway.

'We tell them, bring the bloody bird home or die trying. Every one we lose over France or ditched in the Channel is a hole in our defences, and the boys at Supermarine can't turn them out as fast as we lose them.'

'Is there any chance he could have flown home during the day?' I asked. 'Ducked out without being missed?'

Johnson thought about it, as his batman brought out our tea. When he was gone, he replied. 'That would be desertion,' he said. 'Possible? Yes. Do I think he'd do it? No.'

We drank our tea and sat in the morning sun. It was going to be another hot day. The gorse bushes smelt like vanilla, heating up in the sun.

'No,' Johnson said again. 'Flying back like that. Why would he? He sees her a few times a week as it is. Not like last time.

These boys have it easy. Go to work shooting Jerry then out to the pub with your girl in the evening.'

He stood up and threw the dregs of his tea on the grass.

'I'll send him out. You chaps stay here,' he said. 'Go easy on him, will you? He's devoted to that girl. Had it all planned out. Marriage, kids, the lot.'

18

'What are you doing here?' Billy said.

I watched him carefully. It was very likely we were in the presence of a violent killer, someone capable of beating a young woman to a pulp. I didn't buy the commander's logic about Billy not flying home. I thought a man who wanted to see his girlfriend, who thought the rules didn't apply to him, could very easily award himself a few hours' leave, and nobody would be any the wiser.

'We're here to talk about Mary,' Doc said.

'Mary?' said Billy. 'What's she to you?'

I looked closely at his hands. No cuts or bruises. He hadn't been the one punching her in the face. He would have been the one standing behind her, holding her arms behind her back so tightly he left livid bruises.

I wondered which of them had raped her, and whether it was before she died, or after. Maybe they took turns.

'What happened?' I asked. 'Did she step out of line again, like she did at the pub? Was she leading you on then saying no? Playing the blushing virgin?'

'Listen,' he said, 'I'm sorry I hit her. I really am. I've already told her I feel miserable about it.'

'When did you leave for France?' asked Doc.

'I'm not allowed to talk about it,' he said.

'Has anyone spoken to you about Mary since you left?' I asked.

He looked confused. If it was an act, it was a good one. It threw me. I was expecting angry denial. I was expecting him to swing at me. I'd respond in kind. We'd fight. I'd win. He'd admit he'd done it and I'd finish him off.

'Look, I know I shouldn't have shot the German. I was cut up about it when I talked with Mary, and I told her the truth. When she blurted it out at the pub I panicked. I'll never hit her again. I'm going to ask her to marry me, for Christ's sake.'

'Billy,' Doc said, 'Mary's dead.'

Billy looked at Doc in disbelief. He turned to me, expecting some kind of punchline.

'Yesterday afternoon,' I said.

The colour drained from his face, and he collapsed into a deck chair. It was a convincing display.

'That's impossible,' he said.

Doc put his hand on Billy's knee.

'This must be a shock,' Doc said.

'What happened?' Billy asked. He looked at me. His jaw set. Trying to hold it all in.

'We don't know,' Doc said. 'The police are looking into it.'

'The police?'

'She was attacked,' I said.

Billy put his head in his hands.

'Does her mother know?'

'We were just with her,' Doc said.

'This isn't real,' he said. 'What happened?'

I looked at Doc. It felt like he would be the right person to give the details. Billy caught our look.

'Tell me,' he said.

'She was attacked,' Doc said. 'Probably two men. They took advantage of her, and then they beat her, and then they killed her.'

We let him sit with that. He turned from Doc to me, looking for someone to tell him this was a bad dream.

'She said she was in trouble,' I said. 'Needed to see a doctor.'

That got his attention. His face flushed.

'That's impossible,' he said.

'Why impossible?' I asked.

'We didn't . . .' He buried his face in his hands. 'We were waiting until we got married,' he said, softly. If he was acting, it was a first-class job.

'She said something else. About your father's men giving her the creeps,' I said.

'What?' he said.

'What do you think that could have been about?'

'I don't know,' he said, looking me firmly in the eye. 'I really don't. She was a lovely girl. Everybody loved her.'

'I think you know something,' I said.

He looked at me. He was trying to decide whether to trust me.

He decided. He shook his head.

'I'm sorry,' he said, 'I don't know.'

19

'Tell me again what she said to you,' Doc said, as he pushed his way through the hedge to the place where Mary had been killed.

I followed him through. There'd always been a small gap, big enough for a person to push through and cut the corner of my land. People used it when they were walking from town to The Cross.

Now the gap was bigger. Tyre tracks showed a car had left the tarmac and destroyed a section of the hedge. Quite an extreme thing to do. Maybe they were swerving to avoid something. Or to hit something.

'She said she had a friend who was in trouble. I assumed it was a way of talking about herself. She asked if you were a good man. I lied and said you were.'

He ignored my attempt at lightening the mood. Quite right. It wasn't the time.

'Did you tell the police?' he asked.

'No. It felt like it wasn't my secret to tell.'

I followed the tyre tracks into the field. They ran at an angle to the road. The car had been driving towards my farm, then cut through the hedge.

I pictured Mary cycling along the lane, stealing glances behind at a car getting too close. Ahead, the safety of my farm. She didn't know I wasn't there.

She'd crashed through the small gap, the car following her. The bike wouldn't have got very far in the long grass. She

would have leapt off and started running. Car doors opening
and slamming closed behind her. She only got about twenty
yards into the field. She would have been tackled from behind.
Brought down. Rolled over. She would have screamed. I
would have heard, if I'd been there.

'What did you think about the pilot?' I asked.

'I don't think that was an act,' Doc said. 'It's theoretically
possible he did it and he's blocked it out, but I doubt it.'

The grass had been trampled by the men, the police, and
every other person who dropped by to have a look. There was
a patch of black where it had happened. Blood.

Doc knelt down in the grass.

'It could have been strangers,' I said. 'Someone sees her
cycling around town. Attractive girl, on her own. They follow
her.'

'Where's the bike?' he asked, standing up and looking
around. An obvious question. The best questions usually are.
'I presume the police took it,' he said, answering himself.

'No,' I said. 'It wasn't here.'

'Why would they take the bike but not the body?'

We both looked around, as if we'd suddenly notice a bike
that had been overlooked.

'Mary said something about men working for Billy's father,'
I said. 'I'll go and talk to them.'

I knew what I'd find. Men who'd seen her around the farm.
Undressing her with their eyes. Wanting more. Discussing it
between themselves. Testing the idea in their heads. Moving
from planning to action. Escalation.

20

Bill Taylor, my farm manager, was waiting for me in the yard. I was late for our weekly meeting. We usually walked the fields and discussed priorities for the coming week. Sundays didn't mean much to Bill. He didn't have any family and as far as I knew didn't have any hobbies outside of work, apart from going up to Lords to watch the cricket once a year.

Bill was the reason the farm was a success. When I'd taken the place on, I'd been by myself, with Nob doing what he could, and local labourers hired in when we needed them. I'd done a middling job of it, enough to pay off the debts that Dad had let mount up before the war and then to start expanding the place, buying up nearby land as other farms failed – either because the men in the family hadn't come back, or as a result of the crash in cereal prices, as grain from Canada and America had flooded the market. A tough time to make a go of a farm.

I'd been stretched so thin it looked like the whole thing was going to collapse. I'd been determined to do it all by myself, without asking for help, when Bill had knocked on the door, asking for work. Nobody else would hire him. He'd been a conchy in the first war, refusing to pick up a gun and kill another man, even if it meant sitting out the war in prison. You'd think that mark would wear off over time, forgive and forget and all that, but no. I didn't share his views, but I respected his taking a stand for his beliefs. I'd hired him as a labourer and within the first week he was improving the way we did things. He had an eye for improving processes, often little tweaks that didn't seem like they'd make any difference, but that resulted in an hour saved here, another saved there. Soon it became obvious he should be managing the place, with me taking the role of gentleman farmer, meaning he would kindly tolerate me helping him out whenever I wanted the satisfaction of getting my hands dirty. Most of the time, though, I knew enough to stay out of his way.

We walked out to the far meadow to look at the planes. We found the spot where the German had fallen, and once again I found myself looking at bloodstains on the grass. I wondered how much more blood these fields would soak up before the whole thing was over.

Bill pulled the tarpaulin back from the Messerschmitt.

'Amazing how inventive we can be when it comes to creating new ways to kill each other,' Bill said, dropping the cover and shrouding the plane.

'How about being inventive to defend ourselves?' I asked. 'Where does that fit into your philosophy?'

'What've you got in mind?' he asked.

I strode out into the middle of the meadow.

'We've got to make this less of an attractive place to land,' I said. 'I'm thinking a deep ditch cutting across from there,' I pointed behind him to the edge of the trees, 'to over there.'

He joined me in the field and looked around, weighing my idea.

'If we're digging ditches, perhaps we should make them effective against tanks, as well as planes.'

We batted the idea back and forth, ending with a design six feet deep and eight feet wide, shored up on the northern edge with timbers, making a vertical wall that a tank would be unable to climb. We could take down one of the old barns for the timbers, and if we needed more we could knock down some of the mature pines in the woods.

'What do you know about Baxter's place?' I asked, as we walked back across the fields. He stopped and leant on a gate, looking out over twenty acres of wheat, still green in the late spring.

'The Grange?' he asked.

I nodded.

'It's like a lot of the old places,' he said. 'The farm buildings are on their way out. The house needs a new roof, and the ivy should have been taken off a couple of decades ago. Probably the best thing that could happen to it would be if the Germans dropped a bomb on it, and they collected the insurance. If I owned it, I'd accidentally leave a light on, maybe on the roof, every night. Maybe a set of lights, in a bull's-eye formation.'

It sounded like he'd appraised the place with the eye of a potential owner. I wondered if he'd done the same for all the local farms.

'What about the people?' I asked.

'Nobody knows much about them,' he said. 'Keep to themselves. There was a wife but she died young. There was talk but I wouldn't put any weight on it. I think there's a son. Is he the one . . .' Bill nodded back towards the meadow.

'Pilot,' I said, 'yes. He was courting the girl who died. Mary.'

Bill looked out across the wheat, waving in the breeze. On the horizon, the Downs were silhouettes against the afternoon sun.

'You think they'll make it to the Channel?' he asked.

We both stared south, trying to imagine an invasion force fighting its way up from the coast. It was too easy to picture.

'They'd better not,' I said. 'All of our boys are over in France, with all of our equipment. If the worst happens and our boys are outmanoeuvred, it's going to be me with my shotgun and you with whatever your conscience allows, facing off against the most modern, mechanised army the world's ever seen.'

Bill spat out the stalk of wheat he'd been chewing.

'You'd better clean up that shotgun, then,' he said. 'I don't think you've had it out since before last Christmas.'

We walked on.

'You should come over to the White Hart this evening. Have a pint,' he said.

'I was thinking of looking up some of Baxter's men,' I said. 'Mary said something about them. Worth taking a look.'

'They drink at the Red Lion,' he said. 'They're not very friendly, if I remember rightly. You might want to take that shotgun.'

21

The crash of a plate smashing on the floor told me something was up, even before I opened the kitchen door.

'Don't you dare!' shouted Mum. The object of her fury, Frankie, stood on a chair, holding a mug in his hand as if he were ready to throw it at her. 'Get down from there and clean up this mess you've made,' she said.

Mum was standing by the sink, red-faced and angry. The floor was littered with shards of a shattered plate and discarded slices of bread.

The boy looked like a cornered animal. He looked at me, saw I was blocking his escape route, and desperately looked around the rest of the room. I realised it was the first time since we'd picked him up that I'd had a good look at him. He was even thinner than I'd first thought. His face was pulled tight over his skull as if he'd never had enough to eat. He was dressed in his grey, threadbare clothes. His gas mask box bumped against his chest, its strap around his neck.

'I want to go home!' he shouted.

'That's enough,' I said. 'Come down from there and help clean up this mess.' I used my best command-presence voice, battle-tested and proven to get Tommies to run towards almost certain death just because I combined the right vocal tone with the right level of self-confidence.

The boy threw the mug at my head. I only just dodged it, he had a good eye and a useful throwing arm. It smashed against the wall behind me. Evidently nobody had yet instilled in him the desire to obey a superior officer.

I needed to get him out of the kitchen. It was where we kept all our breakable things, and he seemed intent on working his way through them. I strode towards him, ignoring the surprisingly effective punches he threw at my arms, and grabbed him around the waist. I threw him onto my shoulder like a sack of flour, and marched him out of the kitchen, through the front hall and out the front door. His arms beat my back. I did my best to pin his legs against my chest, so he couldn't get any serious kicks in.

I looked around. I had a feeling he'd run away if I just put him down, and he looked like he'd outrun me. I needed somewhere he could wear himself out.

I strode across the farmyard to one of the smaller barns. There was some old threshing machinery in there, destined for scrap. I put him in there as gently as I could under the circumstances.

'If you want to kick or throw something, feel free,' I said, and backed out. I slid the top loop of the padlock through the catch to keep the door closed. There were enough chinks in the old wood walls that he'd have plenty of light.

I stood by the door, wondering if I was being cruel, or kind. When I was a boy I'd have loved to be left to play in a barn, but this was a city boy who'd just been taken from his home and shipped to the country.

Mum joined me at the barn door. She looked at the padlock, and I shrugged. We both stood in silence, listening. There was a thump as something heavy hit the wall.

'How long have we got him?' I asked.

'They didn't say,' she said.

That was about right for the government, I thought. All fanfare and headlines, but only half the job done. Worry about how to get them home later, if there was a home to go back to. Of course, sending them here, dead centre of the invasion route, was a lot like out of the frying pan and into the fire. But that was a nuance I wouldn't have expected a bunch of civil servants to understand.

'How many plates have we got left?' I asked.

'We can buy more plates,' she said. That was rich, I thought, coming from a woman who never spent a penny when she could get by without.

'Get some tin ones, in case he wants to throw more of them,' I said.

'Don't you worry,' she said.

She stepped to the barn door and put her mouth to a crack between the door panels.

'Frankie?' she shouted. 'Me and John are going inside for a cup of tea. You play in the barn and I'll come and get you in a bit. I'll fry up some sausages.'

We listened for a response, or a sign that she'd been heard. The door rattled as it was hit by something heavy.

22

I had a quick sandwich and a cup of tea with Mum and Nob, listening to the news at six.

The BBC was still making a brave face of it, but if you knew what to listen out for, it was a worrying situation. German Panzers, led by General Guderian, were through Sedan with all of France ahead of them. The French Ninth Army had surrendered *en masse*. If you believed the newsreader, our boys were spoiling for a fight and the Germans would be slinking home with their tails between their legs before you knew it. The problem was, even the newsreader didn't sound like he believed it. I could imagine him, sitting in Broadcasting House in his best suit, planning what train to catch out of London when the paratroopers started falling out of the sky.

I grabbed my hat and wallet. Time to go and talk to Baxter's men, see what I could find out, but I heard a knock at the door. It was Neesham. Showing up like a bad penny.

'Where did you hide the bike?' he asked, as we walked out into the yard.

'I presume it wasn't there when you arrived at the crime scene?' I countered.

'I'll need to look around,' he said.

'I'll warn Mum and Uncle Nob so they don't mistake you for a thief. Good way of getting shot.'

If he'd been expecting me to be worried about the prospect of him searching the barns and outhouses, he would have been disappointed.

'Have you found out who she was playing tennis with?' I asked.

'She didn't play tennis after she was here,' Neesham said. 'I checked. She wasn't booked for a court, and nobody who played saw her. I believe that was the one piece of evidence you were offering as proof she ever left here.'

'Her mum said she had a regular match with a girl called Elizabeth. She said she's run away. Apparently Mary came to you lot and tried to make a report.'

There was a thump from the barn. Neesham heard it, and gave me a quizzical look.

'Our evacuee,' I said. 'He's playing in the barn.'

Neesham strolled over to the barn door.

'The padlock part of the game?' he asked.

I unlocked the door and pulled it open.

'Frankie,' I shouted, 'get your gas mask, we're going to the pictures.'

23

We walked across the fields. The soil was dry. Everything was dry. If we didn't get a good rain soon we'd lose the sugar beet. With Hitler blockading the Atlantic, we'd be stuck without sugar for our tea. I wondered how desperate things would have to get before Churchill would sue for peace.

Frankie followed behind me, like a dog that's been beaten.

He clutched a piece of paper in his hand like I was liable to steal it from him any minute.

'What's that in your hand?' I asked.

'Nothing,' he said.

I felt ashamed of myself. Locking up a boy who'd been sent away from his home. No wonder he didn't trust me.

'Who's your favourite film star?' I asked. 'You like George Formby?'

He ignored me, kicking up clouds of dust.

'No,' I said. 'Me neither.'

'Why aren't you in prison?' the boy asked.

'What do you mean?'

'You're a murderer,' he said.

'I didn't kill Mary,' I said. 'She was a friend.'

'Why does the policeman think you did it?' he asked.

'She came to see me yesterday morning,' I said. 'She wanted my help.'

'What with?' he asked.

I thought about what to say.

'She was worried about a friend,' I said. 'An evacuee, like you.'

'Says you,' he said.

'She said the girl's name was Elizabeth. They played tennis together. Maybe you'll see her at school.'

'They told us they're keeping us with our own class,' he said. 'Don't want us mixing.'

'I'm sure that's not it,' I said.

He didn't reply.

*

It was busy and we had to queue, the late-afternoon sun bouncing off the white painted wall of the cinema. Every time someone came out, squinting in the light, they let someone in. After twenty minutes of silent waiting, I got two tickets and we headed upstairs to the circle. We found two seats where we could sit with our backs against the projection box. I don't like having people sit behind me.

According to the poster outside, the main feature was *Night Train to Munich*. Some kind of action adventure, no doubt in which brave English chaps would defeat the bumbling Germans.

Frankie settled in with a bag of gobstoppers I'd bought him. A cheap trick to prove I wasn't a notorious murderer. His precious bit of paper was stuffed in his pocket.

I told him I had to step out for a minute. See a man about a dog. He didn't look away from the screen.

24

The Red Lion was right across from the cinema, where Grange Road led east from the high street out towards Buxted.

Pubs were supposed to be closed on Sunday afternoon, to protect our moral character, and re-opened at six. When I pushed open the door and walked in, it was busy, and nobody looked like they were only just getting started. Most of the patrons were successfully accomplishing their weekly goal of drinking last week's wages before the next week came around. Marx called religion the opium of the masses. Most of the masses I know are too busy drinking to go to church. Perhaps Marx mixed with a different class of working man than I did.

I found a place at the bar and ordered a pint of best. I knew the landlord. Bert had been a few years behind me at school and had been an effective fast-bowler, so we'd played together a few times both then and since.

'Haven't seen you for a while, John,' he said. 'They kicked you out of The Cross again?'

I took the beer, savouring that first taste.

'Fancied a walk into town,' I said. 'How's business?'

He looked around at the busy room.

'Can't complain,' he said. 'As long as Churchill doesn't call up all my customers.'

'You heard the German tanks are through the line at Sedan?' I asked.

'Try to ignore the news,' he said. 'What's the point? It'll be bad, then it'll be worse, then one day it'll be good again and we can get back to normal.'

'Could get a lot worse than last time,' I said. 'As in, us all speaking German worse.'

Bert shrugged.

'They say the Germans have got it pretty good since Hitler,' he said. 'They lost the last war, but now they're the ones with all the jobs and the money.'

I was surprised, not by the pro-Nazi sentiment, which was pretty common, but by the fact that he felt comfortable enough to say it out loud. That's what comes of being the landlord in your own pub. You get used to being king of the castle.

'I went to Munich a few years ago,' he said. 'Took the train all the way. Went for the beer festival. Beautiful. You'd like it.'

'What's the beer like over there?' I asked, looking for a subject we could talk about safely.

'Lovely,' he said. 'You drink in these huge pubs where they bring you gallons of the stuff. You just sit there at your table while birds with their tits falling out of their shirts keep topping up your glass.'

He looked around at his own pub. No birds with tits falling out of their shirts. No revelry. I almost felt sorry for him.

'Maybe the birds with the tits will follow behind the tanks,' I said, raising my glass as a toast.

Bert shook his head.

'I should have stayed there,' he said. The refrain of a man who'd seen a better life for a brief second but had lacked the vision or the courage to do anything about it.

I looked around at the drinkers. I was looking for anyone with bruised hands, like you'd get from repeatedly smashing your hand into an undefended human skull. But it was too dark and smoky.

'Any of the lads from The Grange in tonight?' I asked.

Bert nodded towards the dartboard.

'Toby and Jack have been in all day. Toby's the ugly cunt throwing darts,' he said. No love lost there.

I felt in my pocket for the right change and left half a crown on the bar.

'I'll have another one,' I said, 'and whatever you're drinking.'

★

I took my beer over to the corner where a darts match was working towards its conclusion. Toby threw his three darts, then walked to the board. He'd left himself with fifty-seven to go. Toby was a bull of a man. Thick neck. Thick arms. All he wanted was a ring through his nose.

He turned from the blackboard with a smug look of satisfaction that melted when he saw me.

'This is our board. We've got it for the night,' he said. 'So, you can fuck off back to The Cross.'

The other man was sitting at a small table cluttered with empties and an overflowing ashtray. He finished his pint and stood up to take the darts. Jack, I presumed. If Toby was a bull, Jack was a farmyard dog – long nose, darting eyes. Looking for a master to obey.

If I were looking for two men strong enough to hold and beat a young girl, I'd found them.

'I'm looking to buy some land out your way. Wanted to get your thoughts about the best way to approach Mr Baxter. There might be a few bob in it for you if things work out my way.'

'Offer cash, and I reckon he'll take your hand off,' Jack said, as he took his darts.

I watched him throw, which made him self-conscious. His first dart hit the metal frame and bounced off. He tried to be nonchalant about picking it up. He was trying not to look at me but failing.

The way he was throwing his darts, he knew why I was there, and he knew he was in trouble. His next two darts found the board, but his score had suffered.

Toby took back the darts, spat a flake of tobacco from the tip of his tongue, and threw his first. He hit a triple nineteen with a thud.

'You're buying,' he said to Jack, before turning to me and rolling up his sleeves for dramatic effect.

'You going to fuck off, or are we going to take things outside?'

A valuable opportunity. I wanted to put on a show for Jack. He was clearly the smarter of the two, but subservient. The kind of man who doesn't do his shoelace without getting permission. I had a suspicion he knew something, but he wouldn't tell me without a bit of encouragement. Toby had just volunteered to be the encouragement.

'I was drinking with young Billy and his girl on Friday,' I said. 'Pretty young girl. Mary, wasn't it?'

Toby spat again. He looked at me, calmly.

'Fuck off, or outside. Up to you.'

'She seemed like a nice girl,' I said. 'She came to me and asked for my help. Told me what's been going on.'

Toby stepped forward, crowding me and putting his face close to mine.

'Mr Cook,' Jack said, 'everyone's cut up about what happened to her.'

'Shut up, Jack,' Toby said.

'Are you cut up about what happened to Mary, Toby?'
I asked. 'Did she used to come around the farm when you
were working?'

I watched Toby for reactions but got nothing.

'Not really fair that Billy got to roll in the hay with her, but
you didn't,' I said.

Still nothing. Maybe the information was still making its
way from his ears to his brain. Either that or he didn't know
what I was talking about.

'You follow her home? Knock her off her bike, just as a
laugh?'

I'd come here with some kind of daydream about finding
out who had killed Mary. Good Sir John, defending the honour
of the fair lady. But instead, I was in a dingy pub, inches away
from a farm hand who stank of sweat and cigarette smoke.

'Did you rape her before you killed her? Or did you do it
afterwards? Is that the only way you can get a woman to let
you fuck her?'

This time the pathways in his brain did their job, albeit at a
sluggish pace. His eyes registered the fury first, then his jaw
clenched, ready for battle.

Everything slowed down. My body flooded with adrenaline. My senses heightened, as my body prepared itself for
fight or flight. I was tired of being the gentleman, so I chose
fight.

Toby's neck tensed. He was going for a head-butt. It was
the smartest move. He presumably had a long and successful
track record of bar fights, and I'd have bet this move worked
for him every time. He launched his forehead at my face, aiming to crush my nose. Even with the adrenaline, I barely had
time to move, but I managed to get my own head to the side,
receiving a glancing blow that felt as if one of the timbers
from the ceiling had cracked me on the side of the head.

His momentum carried him forward, and he stumbled, confused. He didn't have a script for what would happen after his head-butt failed.

I took a quick step to the side to give myself room. I heard the clatter of chairs hitting the floor.

He was taller than I was, and about twice the weight, mostly muscle. A punch to any part of his body would be like hitting the side of a barn. That sort of thing works in the pictures, but not in real life. His weight was still on his front foot, as he tried to right himself. By instinct, I targeted his knee, the joint holding all his weight, but thought better of it. If I destroyed his knee, he'd be out of work for six months, and that wouldn't just be him, it would be his wife and kids suffering without an income. I raised my aim and kicked his thigh, giving it all I had. It took out his leg without crippling him, and he went down in a crash of broken glass.

Bert shouted over at us.

'You're paying for that, Cook!'

Toby was on the ground, down but not out. I knelt on his back and reached my right arm around his neck. I slid my left arm behind his neck and grabbed the back of his head, then locked my right arm into the crook of my left elbow. I squeezed, cutting off the flow of blood to his head.

We practised this move in our commando unit, so I know what it feels like to be the victim. It feels like someone has their arms wrapped around your neck, killing you by cutting off the blood supply to your brain. Not a nice feeling at all.

He fought back, of course. I used to do the same every time it was me. But his range of movement was limited. His muscles were all developed for strength and leverage in front of his body, not behind. He got a few backhand swipes in, but they were weak enough that I could ignore them. I focused on keeping the pressure on his neck.

His friend Jack ran at me and tried to pull me off, grabbing me by the shoulders. When he didn't get a reaction, he tried to get me by the neck, so I jerked my head back and felt his nose crunch. He backed away, swearing but defeated. He'd done his duty and he'd have his story to tell. I turned to fix him with a stare.

'Stay out of this,' I said.

Jack backed away, holding his hand to his nose, now streaming with blood.

Toby wasn't giving up.

'Stay down,' I ordered him.

I counted to ten. Usually your opponent is unconscious by the count of eight or nine. Toby was a big man. He took twelve seconds, then he went limp. I let go instantly. Time it wrong and you're holding a corpse.

I stood up and used my foot to roll him onto his side. No point in him choking after I'd been so gentlemanly about letting him live.

Bert came over and peered down at Toby.

'Is he dead?' he asked. He seemed more curious than concerned.

'He'll be all right. If he wakes up wanting more, tell him I won't be so gentle next time.'

I turned to Jack.

'Tell me what happened with Mary,' I said.

Jack shook his head, his eyes wide.

'It wasn't us,' he said.

'But you know who did it?'

He flicked his eyes around the pub, trapped. If he knew anything, he couldn't admit it, especially now that everyone had seen us fight.

25

Jack knew something. The first rule you learn in the playground: don't grass. He'd be more open to a frank exchange of opinions if I got him by himself.

I stepped across the road, back into the cinema, following a young couple dressed in their Sunday best.

Frankie was still there, engrossed in the action. The film was reaching its climax – Rex Harrison jumping from one cable car to another over a high Alpine ravine while being shot at by Nazis – so we sat quietly until it finished and then watched the newsreels.

They already had film of the early action at Sedan. German tanks were streaming across temporary bridges over the river Meuse. It was an awe-inspiring sight. Even more so, the screaming Stukas, dive bombers equipped with sirens to instil the fear of God into onlookers. The newsreader, with a hint of panic in his voice, said it was the heaviest air bombardment the world had ever seen. It looked it.

We were the onlookers. These dive bombers, with their eerie screams, were designed and manufactured expressly to be filmed and shown in cinemas around the world. Look what we're capable of, they were saying. We're coming for you and we won't rest until our flag is flying over the whole world. I sat there with Frankie, surrounded by the people of Uckfield, and I bet we were all thinking the same thing, that the English Channel had never looked so good, but also so narrow.

26

'I need a post box,' Frankie said, as we walked back to the farm.

'We can go past The Rocks,' I said. They've got one there. What are you posting?'

He pulled out his bit of paper and held it up. It was a flimsy postcard.

'I've got to send this to Mum so she knows where I am,' he said. 'She won't be happy 'til she gets it.'

He walked next to me, instead of behind me. Progress of sorts.

*

Mum had a late supper laid out for us. Sausages. I put two in a sandwich and told her not to wait up. Told Frankie to play in the barn if he wasn't ready for bed.

I got back into town at ten and waited in the alley beside the cinema, where I could keep an eye on the drinkers stumbling out of the Red Lion. Toby and Jack were the last out. Toby didn't seem any the worse for his experience, like a bull that stuns himself by running into a post, then gets up and shakes it off. Jack had plugs of toilet paper stuffed into his nose, black with blood. I was hoping they'd separate. I needed Jack by himself.

Toby headed downhill, and Jack crossed the road, passing close by and heading down Church Street. I slipped out of the alley and followed him. As soon as we were out of sight of the high street, I caught up.

'You've got something to tell me,' I said.

He ignored me.

'You said it wasn't you,' I said, 'I don't believe you. If you had a clear conscience you'd look me in the eye. You'd protest. You'd say it's crazy for me to even think it.'

'Not here,' he murmured.

I walked with him. It was one of those rare evenings when the warmth stuck around. Everyone would have trouble sleeping and wake up the next day sticky and groggy.

As we reached Holy Cross church, Jack looked up and down the street. He stopped, and we stood quietly, listening. Nothing.

He stepped into the lychgate, pitch-dark under the tiled roof. I followed him in. He sat on the stone bench on one side and I sat opposite him. We were both completely enveloped in darkness. Even someone walking past on the street wouldn't have seen us.

He lit a cigarette. It destroyed his cover, but I let him have it. It would loosen his tongue. With his nose blocked by the toilet paper and dried blood, he breathed noisily through his mouth as he smoked.

'It wasn't us,' he said.

'So who was it?'

Silence.

'Do you know what they did to her?' I asked.

We sat in the silence and the dark. It was a fitting place. The last stop on a man's journey from the cradle to the grave, where the pallbearers would pause, resting the coffins across the gap between the stone benches if they'd mistimed their arrival at the service.

'I've got a daughter,' he said.

I understood.

'If they knew I talked to you . . .'

It was hard to keep quiet. I had a lot of questions, and I had a lot of logical points that I wanted to put forward in defence of why he'd be better off with me on his side. But the silence was working, and I forced myself to stick with it.

'Mr Baxter's got money trouble,' he said. 'About a year ago he leased out one of the barns to some bloke in Brighton, for storage he told us. Two spivs used to come around every now and then, delivering or collecting. They've been around more the last few months. Now they've got stuff coming and going every day. Dress in suits like they're trying to look respectable. Spivs, like I said.'

'Why would they hurt Mary?' I asked.

He let out a long, ragged breath.

'Please leave me out of this, Mr Cook. If they thought I'd talked to you they'd do the same to my girl, and then they'd brag about it.'

'Why do you think they'd hurt Mary?' I repeated. He needed to understand – I wasn't going away.

He shook his head. Silence, then – 'Maybe she asked Mr Baxter about what they were up to in the barn,' he said. 'Nobody talks about it, and everybody knows you're not supposed to talk about it. But maybe nobody told her. Or maybe they just liked the look of her. She was a beautiful girl, maybe they just . . . you know . . .'

'What's in the barn?'

'I don't know,' he said, looking away from me.

'Yes, you do,' I said.

I left it at that. A challenge. Calling him a liar.

Silence.

'What kind of lorry brings the deliveries?' I asked.

'Nothing unusual. Just a lorry.'

'Five ton?' I asked.

He nodded.

'Any markings?' I asked.

He shook his head.

'What times?'

'All different times, coming and going.'

'They've never asked you to help unload?' I asked.

'I told you. The two spivs are the only ones who go near it. We don't even go in the yard any more.'

I let him smoke his cigarette.

'Always the same two men,' I asked, 'or different?'

'Always the same,' he said.

'All right,' I said.

The gate banged shut behind him as he hurried away, leaving me sitting in the darkness.

Every part of me demanded I march out to Baxter's place, but I thought of what my old CO would have said. Failing to prepare is preparing to fail. First thing, I'd go and have a look. Do some reconnaissance. Maybe I'd decide to pass it on to Neesham as a complete package. Much as I'd have liked to finish things off myself, I had an invasion to prepare for, and handing an answer to Neesham would get me off the hook.

27

'Out late on a school night, Cook,' said a voice from the shadows of the farmyard as I reached for the kitchen door. It was full dark. Bats wheeled above me in the muggy air. I opened the door and stepped in, knowing he'd follow.

Blakeney. My old CO. The man who'd trained me to survive, who'd kept me alive through the strength of his own will, who'd also sent me out on more suicide missions than a man had a right to survive. The man who'd been a father to me, after mine had died in the trenches. The man I'd hated more than any man in the world for much of my life.

'Tea?' I asked. He took a seat at the kitchen table, the chair scraping on the stone floor.

I didn't wait for an answer but filled the kettle and put it on the stove. We waited in silence.

'I was surprised you didn't show,' he said.

I made the tea. No hurry.

'I sent a messenger boy to the Yorkshire Grey when I was ready to see you. He said you weren't there. Chickened out.'

'I was there,' I said, sitting down opposite him.

He sipped his tea. We both thought it through.

'I take it you met one of my colleagues from MI?'

'I don't know what you mean, sir.'

He sighed.

'If you're getting into bed with those freaks in so-called intelligence, you want to be careful.'

I didn't answer. I'd got the strong impression from Bunny that our chat had been something I wouldn't want to discuss with anyone.

'I'm meant to be with the PM over at Chartwell,' Blakeney said. 'Slipped out after dinner. Got to get back for cigars and brandy.'

'What's he like?' I asked.

Blakeney sat in silence, and I thought he wouldn't answer. It wasn't my place to ask questions, let alone ask about someone higher up in the chain of command.

He answered eventually.

'I think he's one of us,' he said. High praise.

He drank his tea and I waited. He'd come here for a reason, and he'd get to that in his own time.

'Bunny's not someone you want to put your faith in,' Blakeney said, eventually. 'He's got a rather shambolic crew, children of the aristocracy playing at war. They'd give up the location of the crown jewels if it would get them a better table at the Café de Paris. I wouldn't want my life to be hanging on that lot keeping a secret. Last I heard they're passing out old explosives past their sell-by date. You wouldn't want to be relying on any of their kit to get you out of trouble.'

'Do you think we'll be invaded?' I asked.

Another long pause. Blakeney wasn't afraid of silence, and he liked to think before he spoke.

'Hitler doesn't want to fight us. His dream scenario is him and us, shoulder to shoulder, against the Bolsheviks and the Jews and all the other bogeymen that keep him awake at night. If we still had Chamberlain, we'd have a truce by now. But we don't.'

'You don't think he'll stop at the Channel,' I asked.

'No,' he said. 'The big fight is going to be him against Stalin, but he can't focus on that with an enemy over his shoulder, not an enemy with an Empire.'

He stood up, his chair scraping out, then back as he put it neatly in its place under the table. A place for everything and all that. He threw the remnants of his tea into the sink, then rinsed the mug.

'Keep your eyes peeled, Cook. You know what to do if you see something you don't like the look of,' he said.

'Sir,' I said.

'They're going to give me Southern Command,' he said. 'There won't be much to command if our lads across the Channel get trapped, but we'll do our best when the time comes. I might have to call on you.'

'Yes, sir,' I replied.

He paused at the door.

'I hear you've been making a nuisance of yourself. Getting involved with the police.'

I kept quiet. Always best when your superior officer thinks you've done something wrong.

'Don't get distracted, Cook,' he said. 'Hitler's on our door-step. Forget about the girl.'

28

Baxter's place was on the other side of town. I didn't want to be seen walking there so I planned a route that kept me out in the country, turning a two-mile straight line into six miles up and over the north end of town. It was a perfect day to be walking, and it would give me a chance to do some thinking.

I told Mum I'd be gone for the day so she'd have to worry about getting Frankie to and from school. She made me a round of fish-paste sandwiches and a flask of tea and I packed them into my rucksack along with a pair of binoculars, a note-book, and a couple of pencils. I could have been a birdwatcher, out to sketch his finds.

I cut across the outer reaches of The Rocks, keeping out of view of the grand old house, skirting their ornamental lake with its genteel paths laid out amongst specimen rhododendrons. Then I was out in the fields, looping around the top of the town, skirting Buxted Park. More rhododendrons. Finally, I met up with the railway line and the river, and followed them back towards town.

The Grange was a large, sandstone manor house, owned by the same family since Henry VIII had given it as a reward for loyalty. Something to do with getting some letters back from Anne Boleyn's family up at Hever after her execution. The house sat in a grassy valley, about half a mile across. The valley formed a large, natural amphitheatre around the prop-erty. Down in the bowl, the house was surrounded by formal grounds – a walled kitchen garden, an orchard and an over-grown croquet lawn, all of which were going to seed. There was a tennis court, the close-mown grass a lighter green and the net a strip of white. Further down the valley, downstream so it wouldn't pollute the river flowing past the house, was the farm, with its collection of barns and outhouses in equally sorry states.

The valley gave me an excellent vantage point to observe the house. I stayed high up on the hillside, a few yards back into the treeline. I was invisible to anyone down at the house, but I had a perfect view, like sitting in the upper circle at the theatre.

I set out my flask and my packet of sandwiches amongst the bluebells covering the ground, found my notebook and a pencil, and got comfortable with my back against the smooth bark of a beech tree. My goal was to spend the day watching the comings and goings of the house. I didn't know what I'd see, but that's the point of reconnaissance, before you do it you don't know what you're going to learn, and if you don't do it, you don't learn anything.

The house was quiet. Smoke rose lazily from the kitchen chimney, but it was too warm for fires in the rest of the house. I sketched the house, taking care to note key entry points and likely defensive positions. I had a good view of the back, one side, and most of the front. I'd have to circle around to the far side of the valley to get to the other side. It wasn't strictly an academic exercise. Once the Germans swept through, this kind of place would likely be given to an up-and-coming tank commander as a reward for services rendered. By autumn, perhaps, I'd be back here with my unit, ready for action.

Shortly after midday, a housekeeper emerged from a back door and carried a basket of laundry out to a line strung in a yard behind the house. I watched her hanging up the laundry – mostly men's clothes mixed in with some dresses and girls' underwear. I assumed the pilot had a younger sister, or perhaps they had an evacuee.

I heard a car in the distance, beyond the farm. It grew louder as it neared the house, the sound of its engine amplified in the bowl of the valley. It was a police car, grander than the one Neesham used. It drew up in front of the house, wheels crunching on the gravel. The Chief Constable climbed out from the driver's side.

He walked to the door and waited. I imagined I heard the doorbell, but it could well have been my mind filling in the detail. He stood and waited, longer than I expected. I knew there was at least one person in the house, so I was surprised. Perhaps the housekeeper hadn't heard the bell.

The Chief Constable walked back to his car and looked up at the house, trying to see if there was anybody at home.

He waited by the car, in the silent valley. If I were him, I'd be wondering whether to try the doorbell again. If there was nobody at home it would be a waste of time, but then there'd be no downside to trying. But if there was somebody at home, he'd been snubbed. If he rang again and the door was answered there'd be an admission, some kind of desperation on his side, and a subtle exasperation on the side of the person who answered or gave the order for the answer. A Chief Constable had to be very sensitive to such things. His position in the town was tenuous. His job title gave him power, and quite a high rung on the town ladder, but his profession was still that of a servant, and his background accordingly tainted with work. To most of the people in the town, he was a success. To the lords of the manor, he was a tradesman.

I made a bet with myself that the reason for his trip out here was more compelling than his pride, and that would drive him to try the door once more.

I was right. He walked to the door again and rang the bell, this time insistently. It wasn't my imagination, but the acoustics of the valley, amplifying the noise and carrying it to my position a quarter of a mile away and several hundred feet higher up.

He was rewarded for his persistence. The door opened, and he stepped inside, and then all was still again.

Good to see he was investigating Baxter and his men. It didn't concern me that it had taken him a day or so to get here. Better to take the time to do the job right.

I wondered why he'd come himself instead of sending Neesham, like they did for me. Presumably that was a perk of being a lord of the manor, you got the top man even when you were a murder suspect. I imagined them sitting in a genteel sitting room, drinking tea from a bone-china set, and skirting around the fact that they were discussing the death of a young woman.

I wanted to get a closer look at the house, but it would be impossible to walk down into the valley from my position without being seen. The grassy valley, clear of trees or hedgerows, was like no-man's-land between the safety of the wooded lip of the valley and the house far below. It was a good set-up if you wanted a secure position. If I wanted to get closer, it would have to be under the cover of darkness.

Staying up in the shelter of the trees at the top of the slope, I worked my way downstream to overlook the farm. The farm was similar to mine in the number of barns and outbuildings. Compared to mine, though, this was on its last legs. The main barn roof was sagging, and entire patches of slates were missing. Weeds grew everywhere. Every farm has its share of old, unused equipment lying around, but this was like a junkyard. It didn't look like much actual farming had been going on for a long time. This was what my farm would have looked like if I hadn't come back from the war.

As I watched, a man came out of a long, low barn, probably a row of livestock stalls. He wasn't dressed like a farmer, and I picked up the binoculars to get a closer look. Jack had described the new men as spivs, and he'd got it right – this one wore grey trousers, braces, white shirt, gaudy tie, city shoes, trilby hat. An urban uniform of a man with money in his pocket and no taste to temper his spending.

I watched him, careful to keep my binoculars in the shade to avoid any sun flashes that might alert him to my presence. He stood in the yard and lit a cigarette. As he stood and smoked, he looked at his wristwatch, like he was expecting something at a certain time. I checked my own watch. Five past one. I presumed an event had been scheduled for one, and now it was overdue, hence his appearance outside and his time check. This kind of expectation just five minutes after the delivery time spoke of a high degree of organisation. When one of my suppliers says one, they really mean sometime in the middle of the day, closer to dinner than tea, but not always.

He walked to the open farm gate that led into the small lane. To his left, the lane carried on up the valley to the house, and to his right it led back towards the woods between the estate and the town. He turned to his right and stood in the lane, waiting.

Eventually he gave up, flicked his butt into the road, and turned back into the farmyard.

I took out my notepad and made a sketch of the farm buildings, noting the one the man had come from. I presumed it was the barn that Jack had mentioned, the one you weren't meant to ask about.

29

Doc and I sat at our usual table at The Cross, a few pints into the evening. I thought of all the conversations we'd had in that spot. Everything from the theory of evolution to the correct technique for bowling a googly. Now I looked back, it felt like all of those discussions were just killing time, waiting for something to happen.

I told him about my conversation with Toby and Jack at The Red Lion, and my reconnaissance at The Grange.

'You think these spivs are the ones who killed Mary?' he asked.

'Jack thinks so,' I said, 'and it fits with what she said about Baxter's men giving her the creeps. They must have seen her around town and taken their chance. Chased her almost all the way back to my place.'

Doc took a drink, trying to slow his pace to match my own.

'She wasn't pregnant,' he said. 'I checked.'

I thought of Doc cutting her open. Just a dead body. But it didn't feel right. None of this felt right.

'That means she was telling the truth about a friend in trouble,' I said. 'An evacuee she played tennis with.'

We drank. We were both used to sitting in silence. Thinking.

'Mary wanted to help her friend, and now she's dead,' I said. 'She came to me for help and I sent her on her way.'

'There wasn't anything else you could have done,' Doc said. It was the kind of thing you say to a friend, regardless of the truth. The kind of thing that helps the evening along.

'There's always something you can do,' I said, 'I just didn't want to do it. I thought my own concerns were more important.'

30

The tennis club was at the far side of town, tucked away in a leafy corner of the Victoria Pleasure Ground. A green corrugated-iron clubhouse baked in the morning sun. Both courts were in use and a foursome of elderly women sat on the clubhouse veranda, waiting their turn.

The couple on the nearest court were Mary's age. They'd be the most likely to know about her evacuee friend. It was a pleasant morning. I could spare half an hour or whatever it took while they finished their game.

The matrons on the veranda had other ideas.

'You there,' called the oldest one. I turned and nodded politely.

'You're not allowed to loiter here. Members only.'

I took my hat off and approached my assailant. Always best to start with diplomacy.

'I'm looking for a friend of Mary Staunton.'

'You're not welcome here, Mr Cook,' she said.

I must have looked surprised that she knew who I was.

'We know about your sort,' she said. 'One minute you're fighting over a young lady, the next minute she's dead in a field. Well, you're not welcome here, so be on your way or I'll run you off myself.'

I've faced enemies of many nations, armed with pretty much every weapon man can invent, and I've fought my way through each of those situations. But this had me at a loss.

'Go on,' she said. 'You may have fooled those soft-headed policemen, but you don't fool us.'

I looked at the young couple on the court. They were still playing, and there was no way of knowing how long they'd be. Best to make a strategic retreat.

I left the tennis club and walked slowly around the perimeter of the pleasure ground, in the shade of rows of towering lime trees. When I got to the road, in the far corner of the park, I leant on the gate and waited. It was the only way out.

A car pulled up behind me and I heard a welcome voice. It was Jane.

'Thinking of joining the club?' she asked, teasing.

I knelt down to look through the open car window. I nodded through the windscreen, to the tennis club on the horizon. It felt companionable, my head next to hers. The two of us on the same team.

'Doing some reconnaissance,' I said. 'Mary said she had a friend at the tennis club who might be in trouble. Thought I'd ask around.'

'How'd you get on?' she asked.

'Seen off by an old dragon,' I said.

'That's about right,' she said. 'Leave it with me. Some things require a woman's touch. Anything I should know?'

'Mary said the girl's an evacuee,' I said. 'Her name's Elizabeth. Don't know her second name. She ran away. See if you can find out who she was staying with.'

Jane saluted me as I stood up. 'Yes sir,' she joked.

She drove on, and I watched the car make its way around the edge of the park, over to the tennis club.

Not for the first time, I cursed the stupidity of the young man who'd turned his back on such a wonderful woman, choosing war instead. I wished I could go back in time and talk to that young man. Give him a piece of my mind.

31

Bunny had said someone local would come and find me to talk about the unit. It had been a couple of days and I was getting tired of waiting. I took my tea to the parlour – two ancient armchairs in front of an unused fireplace, and a big oak trestle table behind the chairs, covered with books and newspapers. I cleared off the table and spread out my Ordnance Survey map of Uckfield and the surrounding villages.

I studied the map and as always felt a twinge of pride. My land filled a significant portion of the space west of town. Probably one of the reasons Bunny had chosen me. Owning land gave me reason to be out in the fields and the woods. It gave me licence to show up in pubs and markets around town. Bunny would have used similar criteria for his other recruits.

Strip away some of the modern elements like train lines and recently built housing estates, and England's feudal history was very much on display. The countryside was a jigsaw puzzle, where every odd-shaped piece was centred on a manor house or, at a grander level, a palatial country house. Each one had its farmlands, and its woodlands kept aside for hunting. Almost every big house had a 'home farm', and a 'park wood'. Between these estates were villages and market towns, places where the farm workers lived, and where commerce took place.

It would make sense to form a unit with one agent per town or village. Surrounding Uckfield was a ring of villages, aligned with the key points on a compass. Newick to the west, Heathfield and Cross in Hand to the east, and Isfield to the south.

I turned the map around, imagining myself reading it with the eye of an invading general, planning the route the Panzers would take from the coast to London. If Uckfield was right on the route, then Isfield, to the south, was also directly in the line of fire. That made it a priority, for Bunny and hence for me too. The villages to my flanks were nice to have, but Isfield was my vanguard. Bunny would have wanted his strongest recruit there.

There were a couple of pubs in Isfield, as there were in every village, but there was no question which was the central one. The White Hart sat right at the crossroads in the middle of the village, next to the train station on the line between the coast and London. Bill Taylor's local.

★

Three miles walk across the fields to the White Hart. It would have been five minutes on the train, just one stop, but I wanted the time to think. The weather was holding up, and it was another warm, dry evening when I set out, across the fields, down to the river, and then south along the riverbank.

The last mile took me across the outer edge of Isfield Park, one of the largest estates in Sussex. They said it was owned by a distant cousin of the King, although I'd never seen him. Probably didn't move in the same circles.

It had been a long time since I'd been to the White Hart, back when I was a boy, when every pub in the area was exotic territory to be conquered. Bill Taylor saw me, and his face lit up. He stood up from his barstool and hurried over to usher me in. He turned to the men he'd been drinking with.

'Lads, this is my boss, John Cook,' he said. The men gave me a brief glance, and nodded to me, not friendly but not unfriendly.

I ordered a pint of Harvey's, plus another round of whatever Bill and his mates were drinking. That earned me slightly more appreciative glances.

Once the beers were passed out and sipped, I took a minute to look around.

'Nice place,' I said to Bill, who brushed off my compliment but was obviously pleased. I looked at the other drinkers in the place. Most of the tables were taken by farm workers. One table was a boisterous group of youngsters too young to join up. I was invisible to them, just another old man.

In the far corner, where I would have been sitting if this were The Cross, was a man about my age. His tanned face showed he worked outdoors, but his clothes were slightly better quality than those of the labourers. His days of shouldering timbers or bales of hay were behind him. He had an air of self-confidence I recognised. He noticed me looking and met my eye for a brief second. If Bunny had done what he'd said and put an agent into each town and village, I'd just located my counterpart. I pretended to finish my scan before turning my back on the room and facing the bar, mimicking Bill's posture.

'If I were you, I'd be thinking of buying my own place sooner or later,' I said.

'That's a long way off, even without the war.'

We both drank our beer, thinking.

'If we could come up with a way for you and me to be partners, is that something you'd be interested in?' I asked.

Bill studied the bottles lined up behind the barmaid. He drank more of his beer. We were there for the evening, so there was no hurry.

'Assuming the Germans don't invade and cock it all up, of course,' he said.

'Assuming that,' I agreed.

'We'd have to talk about it,' he said.

'All right,' I said.

Talking about it meant sitting quietly and drinking and talking about everything and anything else. Bill told me about his plans for the anti-aircraft defences. We were on track to have every field intersected by deep ditches by the end of the week. He said he'd leave the meadow with the planes until last, in case the RAF wanted to fly the German plane out. That hadn't occurred to me. It was a good idea.

We were interrupted when the barmaid turned up the wireless so everyone could listen to the new Prime Minister's inaugural speech.

'I have nothing to offer but blood, toil, tears, and sweat,' Winston Churchill said, his voice distorted by the distance and radio interference. Everyone in the pub looked at the radio intently.

'We have before us an ordeal of the most grievous kind. We have before us many, many long months of struggle and suffering.' I thought it a bold thing to say, and I looked around to see how it was being received.

'You ask, what is our policy? I say it is to wage war by land, sea, and air. War with all our might and with all the strength God has given us, and to wage war against a monstrous tyranny never surpassed in the dark and lamentable catalogue of human crime. That is our policy.

'You ask, what is our aim? I can answer in one word. It is victory. Victory at all costs – victory in spite of all terrors – victory, however long and hard the road may be, for without victory there is no survival.'

There was a long pause as everyone looked at the radio. Finally, the newscaster broke the silence, promising a return to the scheduled programme, and the barmaid reached up and turned it off.

One of the labourers sitting at a nearby table, an old man whose hand shook as he held up his pint, offered a toast.

'Victory,' he said.

Everyone in the pub raised their glasses and responded, each in his own way. For some of us it was a sombre commitment. For the young lads it was a boisterous cheer.

I turned to Bill and he nodded to me.

'Victory at all costs,' he said. Bill was always precise. He'd heard the nuance that was lost on the crowd. Churchill hadn't been promising victory. He'd been promising that we'd pay any price in our fight to achieve it. It was a masterful speech from a masterful politician. He had just told us we were all expendable, that there would be no negotiation, no peace talks, until we either had total victory, or we were all dead and everything destroyed, and yet everyone in the pub was cheering.

We passed the evening talking and drinking, until the barmaid rang the bell for last orders. Bill drank up his pint and checked his watch.

'I'd best be off,' he said. 'I told my landlady I was only dropping in for a quick one.'

Bill's relationship with his landlady was a subject of great conjecture among the men on the farm. Nobody had met her, but she often featured in his stories.

I raised my glass and drained it.

'Who's the chap in the corner?' I asked. 'I don't recognise him.'

Bill turned around to check.

'That's Alfred Berry, he's the gamekeeper up at Isfield Park.'

'What's he like?' I asked.

Alfred noticed Bill's attention and met our gaze. Bill waved him over.

'Alfred, come and meet my boss, I've been telling you enough about him over the years!' Bill said.

Alfred got up from his solitary position in the corner and came over to join us. He hung back, keeping his distance.

'Alfred, this is Mr Cook,' Bill said.

I held out my hand and we shook, firmly. It wasn't lost on me that Bill hadn't properly answered my question. As I said, Bill was a precise man. If he didn't answer a question, his silence was an answer.

'Good to meet you,' Alfred said. Up close I could see he was a few years younger than me. I didn't think he was a military man; nothing in his bearing spoke of the training that never quite leaves you, and the way he held himself in front of me was polite, but not deferential.

'Bill says you're over at Isfield Park,' I said.

He nodded.

'What did you think about Churchill's speech?' I asked. 'Quite inspiring I thought.'

He shrugged.

'How long have you been at Isfield Park?' I asked him.

'Just a few years,' he said. 'I was over at Wakehurst Place before that. Came over for the head gamekeeper position.'

'What's it like? You've got a lot of land to look after.'

Alfred shrugged. 'It's all right. It's a job,' he said. 'Boss is a cunt, excuse my French, but the pay's all right, and the lads are a good bunch.'

I nodded sagely. I was a boss myself, and Alfred knew that. Maybe he was annoyed he'd been made to leave his spot in the corner.

'My round,' I said. 'What can I get you?'

He put his empty glass on the bar.

'I've got to get back to work,' he said. 'These long evenings everyone gets the notion they'd like to go for an evening constitutional across our land, bringing their shotgun with them just for luck I suppose.'

He left us, heading to the toilets.

'He's not the smoothest talker,' Bill said, 'but he's all right.'

Bill shrugged on his coat.

'I meant what I said about the partnership,' I said.

He grinned, and we shook hands.

'Apologise to your landlady,' I said. 'Blame it on me.'

'I intend to,' he said.

Once Bill was gone, I turned back to the bar and the attractions of the young barmaid. I weighed up the pros and cons of staying for one more pint and found only pros.

32

A woman pushed her way between me and my neighbour at the bar, crowding me but giving me a nice waft of perfume, covering up a faint smell of the stables.

'Box of matches please, Vera,' said the woman, leaning into me ever so slightly. I shifted back to give her space and she turned to me.

'I'm sorry,' she said, 'I'll just be a second.'

The barmaid slid a box of matches across the bar, while the woman stepped back to pull a pack of cigarettes from her handbag. I picked up the matchbox, ever the gentleman, and struck a light. She brought her face close to mine, the cigarette between her lips, meeting the flame.

'Thanks!' she said, blowing a stream of smoke sideways to avoid me. She turned back to the barmaid.

'Vee, can you call Arthur and ask him if he can give me a lift home?'

'Arthur's off tonight,' Vera called back as she pulled a pint for another customer. 'Looks like you're walking,' she said.

'Give me a brandy for the road then.'

'Right you are,' replied Vera.

The woman opened her purse and fumbled through her loose change.

'I'll get it,' I said. It wasn't fully altruistic. She was a beautiful woman, and every man in the pub was looking at her. Her summer dress had seen better days, but it clung to her in the hot pub and showed off her full figure. Her hair was cut short, showing her neck and shoulders, although even with my untrained eye I could see the cut had been done cheaply. I pictured her sitting at home with a girlfriend, giving each other a trim, making do. Probably in her late twenties I guessed. Too young for me, but a man could enjoy the thought.

She held out her hand to me and we shook, formally.

'I'm sorry,' she said, 'how rude of me. I'm Margaret.'

'John Cook,' I said, 'from Uckfield. I work with Bill Taylor.'

'I know who you are,' she said, 'Bill idolises you. You built your place up from nothing and you'll soon own all of Sussex, if Bill's to be believed.'

'Bill's a good man,' I said. 'Our success is at least ninety per cent his doing. What do you do?'

'I'm at Isfield Park, up at the main house,' she said.

I nodded.

'I was just talking to your gamekeeper. I don't think we hit it off.'

She smirked.

'I don't think Alfred hits it off with many people.'

'He said your boss is a bit of a tyrant,' I said, 'although his language was a bit more colourful.'

She considered this, tilting her head to the side as she thought.

'He's probably right,' she said, 'although he should be a bit more discreet when talking to strangers. Not good for morale if we're all out there in the world criticising each other.'

'Quite right,' I said.

Her brandy arrived, and I paid. She knocked it back in one, watching me the whole time.

'Fancy walking me home?' she asked.

33

'So you're trying to poach our gamekeeper?' Margaret said. Straight to the point. I perked up. I'd been anticipating a quiet stroll with meaningless small talk. Her confrontational approach was much more interesting.

We were walking along what passed for Isfield High Street. One village shop, ten farm workers' cottages, a shabby cricket pavilion, then out onto the lane as it twisted its way towards Isfield Park. The sky was dark, but the moon was almost full, casting the street and the surrounding fields with a glow almost as bright as the sun. The papers called it a bomber's moon, gleeful in their anticipation.

'You can keep him,' I said.

'But you're looking for someone?' she asked. 'I thought Bill Taylor was your man for all seasons.'

'Bill's superb,' I said, 'I'm going to take him on as a partner. We'll need someone to take on some of his work.'

'What kind of person are you looking for? Maybe I know someone.'

'Actually, I can't decide if I'm looking for someone or not. I've been told I tend to try to do it all myself. Most of the time that's the best way of getting things done. But sometimes you need other people.'

'If you *were* looking for someone, what kind of qualities would your ideal candidate have? Maybe I can keep an eye out for you.'

'Someone who knows the land. Someone who gets things done without being given directions. Someone who likes doing something because it's a challenge.'

'I can't think of anyone,' she said, 'apart from me, of course. But I'm not looking for a new job.'

I laughed.

'What's so funny?' she asked.

'I thought you were joking,' I said.

'You're not as smart as Bill Taylor thinks you are,' she said.

'What do you mean?'

'You're out walking in the moonlight with a passably attractive woman who let you buy her a drink. The Germans are a few weeks away so she's probably thinking she may as well have a fling with a handsome stranger, before the world ends, and you go and insult her.'

She took my hand in hers. Maybe the insult wasn't fatal.

We walked along the road towards the estate's gatehouse, itself a significant building where the gatekeeper and his family lived and kept an eye on the comings and goings.

'Let's go round the back way,' she said. 'All hell would break loose if I walked through the gatehouse with you on my arm.'

We took a left turn, down the quiet, dark lane towards the church, a lot darker under the trees.

We reached the church, stuck on the outskirts of the village, its polite distance from the big estate a remnant of the plague days when you wanted your dead buried as far away from the living as possible. We picked our way through the graveyard, to a gate in the back wall.

We stopped at the gate and she paused and turned, I presumed to say goodbye.

'There's more we need to talk about, and I've got something to show you,' she said, 'but we need to get something clear.'

'All right,' I said.

Her face was close to mine, softly lit in the moonlight. She leant forward and kissed me. It was a brief brush of a kiss, but it sent an electric shock right through me.

'We're not going to make love tonight,' she said. 'I know what it looks like – I came on to you at the pub and asked you to walk me home, but that was for show, for all those beady eyes watching us.'

She kissed me again, longer this time. I took her in my arms, running my hands over the small of her back.

34

She led me across sheep-cropped grass overshadowed by giant redwoods. The house loomed up to our left. As big as Buckingham Palace but in considerably worse shape, or perhaps that was just the effect of the blackout making it seem unlived in.

We skirted the open ground directly surrounding the house, heading to a cluster of workers' cottages and farm buildings. Margaret opened a gate into the stable yard and ushered me through. A horse stepped forward in its stall to greet her and she walked to it. I followed her over to the stable.

'When I came here to be with my aunt, nobody really knew what to do with me,' she said, stroking the horse, 'so I made myself useful in the stables. Then my aunt died, and I've tried to stay useful.'

She led me across the yard to a flint-walled barn. We were only a few miles south of Uckfield, but the architecture here was different – walls of black flint embedded in chalk mortar. She put her finger to her lips, like a child miming to be quiet, and pulled back the barn door enough that we could squeeze inside.

It was pitch-black inside until she struck a match and lit a nearby oil lamp.

At the back of the barn, she knelt down to grab the twine wrapped around a large bale of hay.

'Help me with this,' she said.

I took my place at the other end of the hay bale, and we worked together, sliding it across the dusty floor. In the space left behind, the metal glint of a circular handle. Margaret grabbed it, gave me a smile, then pulled up the trapdoor. She sat on the edge of the square of darkness, and eased herself down, feeling with her foot for purchase. When she found it, she turned around and grabbed the lamp.

'Come on,' she said.

I followed her down into the barn's cellar, a surprisingly large space with peeling white walls that dripped with damp.

Margaret put the lamp on top of a large crate. She pulled off the lid like she was conducting a magic trick. She clearly wanted me to look inside, so I obeyed. My reaction was no doubt the reward she was looking for.

Inside the crate, nestled in straw, were two Bren machine-guns.

I looked at Margaret and she grinned.

'Looks like you're planning to rob a bank,' I said, looking around the cellar. There were about twenty boxes, covered in cobwebs and shipping labels. The closest one said New Jersey. 'What's in the rest?'

'Be my guest,' she said.

I rummaged through the crates. There were a lot of smaller submachine-guns I hadn't seen before. The boxes were marked 'S.T.E.N.' and had a stamp from the Enfield arms factory. The guns were an austere design, presumably based on turning them out with as little metal or machining as possible – make do and all that. The metalwork had rough seams, as if the parts had been stamped out on a production line. I hoped they fired better than they looked.

There were handguns – boxes of .455 Webley Mark VI revolvers. Nothing to write home about, but they got the job done. What was curious was the country of origin. It looked like these had come from Spain. The boxes were rather the worse for wear.

Then there was the real action. TNT. Explosive packs the size of small bags of flour, designed to be used individually or grouped. They'd be paired with pencil detonators, thin tubes that were designed to be stuck into the TNT, then snapped. A chemical reaction would set off a charge after a set delay. Most of the detonators were ten-minute delays, colour-coded green. Enough time to get some distance.

The last crate I looked in made me smile. It had been assembled by someone like me. A practical man, thinking of the recipient. A set of Fairbairn-Sykes knives, seven-inch double-edged blades, purposely designed for killing. Several fine pairs of Kershaw prism binoculars, each in a black, leather case. Camouflage netting. Garrotte wire.

I looked up at the trapdoor.

'How did you get all this down here?' I asked.

'I rigged up a pulley in the barn. I did it by myself. Nobody knows about this apart from you.'

'What happens if you have to leave here?'

'Why would that happen?'

'What if you lose your job?' I said.

She looked at me curiously.

'I thought you knew,' she said.

'Knew what?'

'About me,' she said.

I looked around at the collection of secret weaponry.

'Well, I only met you an hour ago.'

'I live here. This is my property. I'm Lady Margaret of Isfield Park. I assumed that was why you wanted to walk me home. And all the other stuff.'

I didn't know how to respond.

'I'm glad you didn't know,' she said. 'I'm sorry I said that. About the other stuff. And I'm glad you kissed me when you didn't know who I was.'

I was about to reply when we heard the rising wail of an air-raid siren.

We both looked around, sharing the same thought. Not an ideal place to be in the event of a direct hit.

35

Margaret led me into the main house, moving quickly through a maze of corridors, thick with darkness in the blackout.

'Where's your shelter?' I asked.

'We don't have one, haven't got round to it,' she said. 'This way.'

We took a narrow, dark staircase up to the second floor, and kept climbing. At the very top of the stairs, she opened a door. From my vantage point below her on the stairs it looked like a door to the sky.

'If your number's up, your number's up,' she said. It was a popular sentiment. A lot of people were saying they'd rather stay in bed than go down to a dingy shelter.

'Besides,' she said, 'they wouldn't dare hit this place, my family's related to half the German aristocracy.'

I presumed she was joking, but I couldn't tell. I didn't know her well enough yet.

'The royal family are much worse,' she said. 'They speak German when they're at home, did you know that?'

'You speak German?' I asked.

'*Natürlich!*'

The roof was a perfect place to watch the sky. To the south, the Downs were silhouettes against moonlit clouds. From beyond the Downs, searchlights from Brighton panned back and forth. The siren still wailed, and I listened for bombers.

'I wonder how they know the planes are coming,' she said. 'I suppose on a bright night you could see them if you looked hard enough.'

The official line was that our night flyers ate lots of carrots, giving them enhanced night vision. It was propaganda aimed at making carrots seem more appealing to children, instead of sweets. But it struck me it was also a way of covering the fact that we had some kind of invention that allowed us to see planes in the darkness. At least, I hoped we did.

I stood next to Margaret, leaning against a waist-high stone parapet. Three storeys straight down was the gravel turning-circle in front of the house.

She looked out at the night sky, scanning for planes.

'Last year, I was having lunch with a girlfriend at my club when I bumped into an old friend of my father's. He was looking for landowners. People who knew the country. People who were happy to take the initiative. That's what he said, anyway. I think he knew I was there and had come specifically to meet me. He asked me if I was interested in helping my country and of course I said yes. Next thing you know they pack me off for a week of explosives training at a place in Oxfordshire, and when I get back I've got a lorry load of guns parked in my stable yard.'

The siren changed from its up-and-down wail to a set of shorter pips – the warning that a bomber was close. I pointed out towards the horizon. A low plane headed directly towards us out of the east, as if we were reeling it in. Somewhere out in front of us a Bofors anti-aircraft gun started up. Pom pom pom pom, firing in bursts of four. Flak burst in the sky like fireworks. It didn't seem to trouble the plane. It continued its steady flight directly towards us.

I pictured the bombardier, lining up his sights. The plane flew closer, the roar of its massive engines filling the sky. It flew up the grand avenue towards the big house, and I realised how massive these machines were.

Margaret turned to me and buried her face against my chest. I braced myself for the impact of the bomb. Would we feel it? Would we know we were in our last seconds of life?

It flew over our heads with what must have been only yards to spare, with a deafening roar and a blast of wind.

As it passed over, and the bomb didn't come, Margaret looked up at me. Her hair was wild, pulled out of shape by the slipstream of the plane. I pushed strands away from her face and she smiled. I kissed her. She wrapped her arms around me. The first kiss in the churchyard had been a surprise. This time we meant it. I pulled her body to mine.

The air-raid siren stopped its wailing. Margaret turned to watch the plane flying away from us.

'Strange, they normally come out of the south,' she said.

'Probably testing our inland defences,' I said. 'Final checks before the invasion.'

We watched the plane disappear over the horizon. I wondered why it wasn't being chased by our fighters. Presumably our men were all over France.

'What was the training?' I asked.

'Guns. Explosives. Evasion. Resisting interrogation,' she said, stepping away from me and looking down over the parapet. 'That was the worst. They put me in a box. Literally a box. When they let me out they asked me how long I thought I'd been in there and I said a couple of hours. They said it had been ten minutes. It was useful, though. They taught you how to listen out for ways they would try to trick you. Like they'd drop into conversation a fact about your unit, to see if you'd confirm it.'

'Did they teach you how to use that lot?' I asked, nodding towards the barn.

'I knew a bit about guns from Daddy. We were in India. Daddy was a diplomat. But really he was a spy. Mostly it was men behaving like boys, running around occasionally shooting each other. But I never got to do that hands-on stuff. They covered a lot in the training – although a lot of it was crawling about in the mud at night, trying to avoid detection while setting up explosives.'

'Why show me?' I asked.

'I've spent the last few months trying to work out what I'd do by myself, and I could do a lot. But I keep coming back to the idea that I'd be able to do more with some help. I've heard such a lot about you from Bill, I thought you might be a good candidate.'

'So you're the reason Bill's been so insistent on getting me down here for a drink?'

'He thinks you're God's gift, by the way,' she said. 'I was thinking you might want to join me. Maybe we could be a little team. Many hands and all that. Apart from anything, if we split up the weapons, if one of us gets killed during the invasion, there's still the other one left to carry on the work.'

'It explains why you let me walk you home.'

'Not entirely,' she said, turning back to me and stepping in close. 'Isfield's not exactly crawling with eligible bachelors.'

'Doesn't a man need a title to be eligible in your world?'

'We've been known to make exceptions,' she said.

'So, what do you say?' she asked, looking up at me with big eyes.

'I think we might need one or two more men,' I said. 'Do you have any other candidates in mind for a moonlit walk?'

'No,' she said, 'you're it I'm afraid. And don't be like that.'

'Like what?'

'You're acting like a bore because you think I led you up the garden path.'

'I might be able to come up with some others who'd be useful. Fill some gaps in our skills. I won't make contact until I've confirmed with you.'

'All right,' she said. 'Let's talk tomorrow. Meet me at the White Hart again.'

'Too public,' I said. 'Meet me at the old paper mill at eight.'

It was a test. Not many people even knew there was an old paper mill, let alone how to find it. She'd said she knew the land. People say a lot of things.

36

Frankie picked at his sausages, trying to cut out bits of fat and gristle. He didn't touch his tinned tomato and seemed distressed by the red juice covering his plate.

Mum stood at the sink, scraping the worst off some slices of burnt toast. I knew she was itching to ask where I'd been for half the night.

Nob drank his tea in silence, as always, his eyes flicking between the rest of us, like he was watching a tennis match.

There was a pounding at the door. Mum went.

'Oh my God,' I heard her say. 'John!' she called. 'Come here!'

Mum was standing at the door. A young lad stood in front of her. Doc's youngest, Harry.

'It's Jane,' Mum said.

'Mum's been hurt,' he said. 'Dad wants you to come straight away.'

I felt as if I'd been standing on the edge of a cliff and the ground had given way beneath my feet.

★

I took the delivery van. It wasn't elegant, but I didn't own a car, and this was the fastest way of getting over to Doc's house. Harry sat next to me, watching.

'What happened?' I asked.

'Mum took Shep for a walk. She came back crying.' He thought of something. 'Shep wasn't with her when she came back.'

Shep was their dog, a fiercely intelligent and loyal border collie. He'd die before he let anything happen to Jane.

37

Doc met us at the door and hurried me to the sitting room. Jane sat on the settee in front of the fireplace. She looked small and alone. Doc sat next to her and took her hand. She looked at me with a watery smile.

'What happened?' I said.

'I took Shep out for his morning walk,' she said. 'We walked around the field and, on my way back, I saw two men waiting by the gate.'

She took her hand back from Doc and held her head in her hands, covering her face like she was ashamed.

'I tried to get by, but they stood in my way,' she said. 'Shep was going crazy, and one of them kicked him in the head. He yelped, and then that was it. Like snuffing out a candle.'

'Did you recognise the men?' I asked.

She shook her head.

'No,' she said. 'They didn't look local. They were dressed funny, like they work in an office. Grey suits.'

'What did they say?' I asked.

She held her head, silent.

'They attacked her,' said Doc. 'Show John your wrists.'

'I'll tell it,' she said. She looked up at me. 'The one who kicked Shep grabbed me from behind. He wrapped his arms around me, tightly. I couldn't breathe.'

She dropped her gaze again.

'He put his hands inside my clothes,' she said, quietly. 'He was all over me. He put his fingers inside me. He said he was going to enjoy . . .' She petered out, then summoned an extra reserve of courage.

'He said he was going to enjoy fucking me, like he did with the other girl.'

The world reduced to me, Jane and Doc, and a feeling of pure rage.

'He said you're to forget about the girl. Or they'll come back and finish the job.'

'Finish the job?' asked Doc.

'With me,' she said.

She looked at me. It was probably the first time she'd truly looked into my eyes since I'd left her to go to war, twenty-five years ago. Funny how you don't notice a thing when it's absent.

'We've got to go to the police,' Doc said. 'You stay here,' he said to Jane. 'John and I will go.'

'No,' Jane said. 'No police.'

Doc was confused, but I wasn't. I looked at Jane for confirmation, and she nodded in reply.

38

I took the long way because I didn't want to be seen approaching The Grange. I didn't want anyone saying they'd seen me heading there. Everyone in town knew Doc and I were friends. They all knew Jane had been my fiancée, a lifetime ago.

I got to my viewpoint, back in the trees, overlooking the valley. The Grange was quiet. The farm was, too. Staying within the treeline, I made my way to the best place to watch the farm. It was still quiet.

I broke the cover of the trees and strode down the steep grassy slope towards the farm. I was completely exposed. If there'd been a sniper in any of the farm buildings, they would have had their pick of timing and angle. There wasn't even any wind. It would have been a perfect shot. But I didn't think there were any snipers, and if there were guards they wouldn't shoot. Not yet.

The slope levelled out as I approached the farm buildings. Now I wasn't an attacker sweeping down the hillside, I was a local man looking for someone.

I stepped into the yard and stopped, listening. Silence.

I walked over to the barn I'd seen during my reconnaissance. There was a padlock on the door. It was the only piece of metal in sight that wasn't covered by rust.

I heard a car approaching, the gears changing as it rounded a distant bend. I looked around for cover and ducked around the corner of the barn.

The car drew nearer, gears changing again as it slowed to turn in at the gate. The engine was running fast. The choke was still out, it must have been a short journey. Just a quick run from town.

The engine shut off and I heard the ratchet of the hand-brake and two clunks as the doors opened. Two voices as two men climbed out, shutting the doors behind them.

'Fucking idiot,' one man said.

'I told you,' said another. 'He's a fucking liability. The sooner we're shot of him the better.'

I stepped out from around the corner.

'Gents,' I said.

The two men were dressed in sharp grey suits. Spivs, Jack had called them. Incongruous in a farmyard. Incongruous anywhere.

They froze, flicking their eyes to each other, and to the padlocked door. They thought I'd been snooping. Their next thought was the logical one. Was I alone? They looked around the yard, and out across the grass slopes of the valley.

'Just me,' I said.

I took a moment to evaluate them close-up.

They were identical twins. Pinched grey faces with slicked-back hair, thick with Brylcreem. The one I'd seen the day before had a fussy moustache. The other was clean-shaven. Maybe it helped their mum tell them apart. They were in their twenties, and should have been called up. They must have paid off a doctor to give them an exemption.

'I've come to give you a warning,' I said.

The clean-shaven man smirked. He unbuttoned his suit jacket and brushed it back, revealing a pistol in a holster. It looked like a Colt, an American gun, useful if you were shooting coyotes on the range, not particularly practical for close-up work. Presumably it was effective at intimidating people who didn't know much about guns.

I wasn't intimidated. Their attack on Jane showed the level of their thinking. Rough up a woman and we'll scare them off. Probably a script that had worked for them before.

My script was different. I'd learnt it on the battlegrounds of France, and refined it in Afghanistan. It's a simple two-step script, designed for times when complex thinking will get you into trouble. Step one, find your enemy. Step two, kill your enemy.

'One of you put your hands on a lady this morning,' I said.

The spiv with the gun grinned.

Step one accomplished. Find your enemy.

His brother took a step to the side, putting some distance between them. It was a sensible move, trying to open up a triangle so I'd have to concentrate on two targets. This clearly wasn't their first fight.

But I wasn't there to fight.

Step two. Kill your enemy.

I didn't have a weapon. Not a problem in a farmyard, surrounded by rusting metal objects. Especially not a problem when your enemy stands in front of you and offers up a handgun like a shopkeeper displaying his wares.

I stepped forward and the spiv grabbed for his gun. He had a fraction of a second to finish things, but he fumbled the draw, and from then on it was a foregone conclusion. I punched him in the throat, my knuckles driving through to an imaginary stopping point a foot behind him. By the time he realised what had happened, he was already dying, his throat crushed. He fell to his knees and I kicked his head with the metal-capped toe of my boot. He went to the ground and I stooped down and grabbed his gun. It was unnecessary by this point, but there was a certain poetic justice in using it after he'd pointed it at me, so I checked it was loaded and shot him in the head.

The gunshot echoed around the valley, a familiar sound in the countryside. The smell of gunpowder filled the air.

I pivoted to his brother, who was backing away. I pointed the gun at his chest. He raised his hands. Now we could talk.

'What's in the barn?' I asked.

'Nothing,' he said.

'Who do you work for?' I asked.

He shook his head. Perhaps he thought that telling me would be worse than dying. He wasn't thinking straight, probably going into shock.

I wanted information, but to get it out of him I needed to give him the hope he might talk his way out of the situation.

'Your brother killed the girl and assaulted my friend?' I asked.

He paused. He looked confused. Probably hard to keep track. Probably trying to decide what to admit to and what to deny.

'Which girl?' he asked.

'Billy Baxter's girlfriend.'

He nodded, like I'd cleared something up for him.

'It was him,' he said, looking at his dead brother. Then he looked up at me with hope in his eyes. Probably figured I'd let him off. A basic human outlook, nobody ever truly believes they're going to die.

'Who do you work for?'

He kept his eyes locked on mine, and kept his mouth closed.

'Where are you from? Brighton?'

His raised his head slightly on Brighton. Just what I thought. Nothing good ever came out of Brighton.

'Last chance,' I said. 'Who do you work for?'

He paused, thinking. He was weighing up whether the truth would exonerate or convict him. His eyes flicked to the left. In my experience, that's the precursor to a lie. So I shot him.

He went to the ground like a slaughtered animal. I stepped to the side, far enough away to avoid the worst of the blood splatter, and shot him again, in the head.

The echoes from the gunshots subsided, and the valley was quiet once more.

I stood still, listening. If anyone else was around, they'd come out to take a look sooner or later. If they were scared, they'd start by waiting, listening. After a while they'd start an internal dialogue. 'They must have gone.' 'Nobody fires a gun three times and then stands completely still for a minute.'

So, I stood completely still for two minutes. Listening and watching. Nothing.

There was nobody around. Not even any sound from The Grange, quarter of a mile up the road. No shouts. No doors or windows opening.

I dropped the gun and turned my attention to the steel padlock on the barn door. I'd come here for justice, to kill the men who'd killed Mary and hurt Jane. Now justice was done, curiosity took over.

The lock was solid. It was fastened through an iron hasp that was firmly attached to a thick oak door. The door was hung on iron hinges that were about the size of my thigh, attached to oak doorposts thicker than railway sleepers. It was a solid construction.

I heard a distant noise. A lorry. It was far off but getting closer. I examined my options. There were two dead bodies on the ground. Nobody knew I was here. All things considered, that was a state worth maintaining. I had two options, run or hide.

I ran.

I ran past the farm buildings to the grassy slope beyond. The hill had felt steep on the way down, and now it felt like a wall. I ran as best I could, using my hands to grab clumps of grass, aware that I was sticking out against the grassy hillside like a sore thumb. The minute the vehicle turned into the farmyard they'd see me, fleeing the scene of the crime. My legs burned, and my heart pounded. The treeline at the top of the slope looked a mile away and to my imagination it was getting further away. I risked a look back. Nothing yet, although I could hear the engine getting closer.

'Give it all you've got for a count of ten,' I told myself, 'and see how that goes.' I tried, unsure whether it was having any effect. But when I looked up, the treeline was closer. I gave myself a count of five of normal running, then another ten of maximum effort. I burst into the trees and threw myself to the ground, now invisible to anyone down in the valley.

I lay where I'd landed, face down in the leaf litter, my hands pricked by generations of dry old holly leaves.

Down in the valley, I heard the engine noise change quality as the vehicle pulled into the farmyard and stopped abruptly as the driver saw the bodies. The engine shuddered, then shut off.

A man in brown overalls jumped down from the passenger side, took a quick look at the situation, and shouted back to the driver. I couldn't hear the words. He looked around, suddenly realising that whoever had killed the men might still be around.

The driver climbed down. He didn't seem so worried about the danger. He was a big man, and he stood in the yard as if he owned the place, looking around as if he was sniffing the air.

I recognised him instantly. He was as much a part of me as the fields and the woods. He'd contributed more to me becoming the man I was than any parent or sibling could, even more than Blakeney.

Lawrence and I had met in India. Like me, he'd found his place in the army and couldn't think of going back. It was the only thing big enough and strong enough to take all of his abuse and tolerate his existence, even put him to use.

I'd hated him at first, of course, as did most people who met him. He was a bully to those who were weaker than him. He spoke his mind to superior officers and ignored their orders if they didn't suit him. He took from the world like it could never repay the debt it owed him. I saved his life when he was pinned down by tribesmen. He told me later he'd been about to cut his own throat, rather than surrender and face the torture that the tribesmen meted out.

From that point on we'd been a unit. A two-man gang. Us against the tribesmen, the army and anyone else who crossed our paths. We hung around after the campaign and ended up in Hong Kong, which was everything a man with a grudge against the world and a desire for a short, violent life could wish for.

The last time I'd seen him, he was walking away from me, leaving me bleeding and almost certainly dying, in a dead-end alley in Hong Kong. I'd assumed he was still there, and I'd been happy with that situation.

Now, he stood in the farmyard, looking up at the treeline. He walked through the farmyard to the edge of the buildings, where I'd run into the long grass of the slope. He kept his focus on me, looking up the hill. I'd left a perfectly trodden trail in the grass. There was no way for him to know it was me. But I felt something shift. My quiet life as a gentleman farmer was on notice. Like opening the apple store and smelling rot, knowing that come spring the whole harvest would be ruined. Just a matter of time.

39

Doc was digging a grave for his dog in the shade of an azalea. Jane sat on a deck chair with a cup of tea, huddled under a blanket. Watching.

Doc took a break from digging, took off his pullover and rolled up his sleeves.

'Did you find them?' he asked.

Doc and I grew up together, we drink together, but we walk different paths. I wasn't sure how he'd react if I told him I'd killed two men with no more thought than you'd have killing a couple of rats in the cellar.

'We had a few words,' I said.

'What does that mean?' he asked.

'If the police ask, I was with you all morning,' I said.

I met Jane's eye. She tilted her head. I nodded. She returned the nod. Message received.

Doc sighed and walked over to his car, parked in the driveway in front of the garage. He gently lifted out a heavy hessian sack, stained with blood. He carried it back across the lawn, and knelt on the grass, next to the grave. He wiped his eyes with the backs of his gloves. I looked away.

'Tell me again what they said to you,' I said to Jane.

'They said to forget about the girl.'

'Which girl?' Doc asked. 'Mary?'

I thought about what he'd said. *Which girl?* It was the same thing the spiv had said, before I'd shot him. An odd choice of words on his part.

'I thought they were talking about Mary,' I said.

Doc took up his spade and started to fill in the hole.

Which girl?

'I was wrong. It's the missing evacuee. Elizabeth.'

Doc stopped shovelling and looked at me.

'Jane asked after her at the tennis court,' he said. 'You asked her to.'

'Yes,' I said. The thought had already occurred to me. I couldn't handle a crotchety old woman at the tennis club, so I'd sent Jane in to do the job herself.

Doc filled the hole to a level just below the grass. He picked up a rectangle of turf. He set it in the hole. It was slightly high, and he took it out again, and took off some of the soil. When he put the turf back, it fit perfectly. A neat piece of surgery.

He stood up and brushed soil from his trousers, treading down firmly on the implanted square of turf.

'So this is your fault,' he said.

'Mary died trying to help this evacuee. She came to me for help. She wanted to come to you for help, too. I told her you're a good man.'

'So where *is* this mysterious evacuee?' Doc asked.

'I don't know,' I said. 'She's probably gone home to London or wherever she came from. But there's a barn at The Grange with a big padlock on it. I was interrupted before I could get a closer look.'

'We have to tell Neesham,' Doc said.

I looked at Jane for support.

'He's right,' she said. 'If there's a girl in trouble, we should do everything we can to help her. That includes taking it to the police.'

40

I've killed a lot of men. Most of those killings were unavoidable – them or me. Most were soldiers who fate had put on the other side. In those situations, I took no pleasure from their deaths although I certainly took pleasure in my own survival.

The two spivs were different. They'd chosen crime, and their choice had put them directly in harm's way, me being the harm. They'd raped and killed a young woman and assaulted Jane. I was glad they were dead, and I didn't anticipate any sleepless nights on their behalf.

The crime was a problem, though. Kill someone in wartime and you get a promotion or a medal. Kill someone back in the real world, even someone who needs killing, and things get set in motion.

I'd been careful. I'd walked the long way. I was fairly sure I hadn't been observed at Baxter's farm. I'd left the gun with the bodies and wiped it clean of fingerprints, in case the police pulled out all the stops. But it's the things you don't know about that trip you up. Perhaps I *was* seen. Perhaps I'd left something behind that could identify me. Perhaps one of the men survived long enough to write my name in blood on the side of the barn, like something out of a Sherlock Holmes story.

I had things to do. First and foremost, I wanted to find Mary's evacuee, Elizabeth. The girl in trouble. Added to that, I had a lot more ideas to share with Bill Taylor about protecting the farm. I also wanted to see Margaret again. All of these things would be impossible if I were arrested.

I had a feeling the deaths of the spivs wouldn't be reported. If Lawrence was involved, I knew he'd steer clear of police involvement. I gave it eighty per cent I was in the clear. But that still left a measure of uncertainty that I wanted to clear up as soon as I could.

I walked into the police station and stood at the reception desk. The moment of truth. Nobody looked up. I wasn't their favourite customer, that was certain, but they weren't looking for me. Nobody grabbed a pair of handcuffs. Nobody picked up a telephone and made an urgent call. Nobody locked the door behind me.

The silent treatment wore on until it got tiresome.

'Tell Neesham I'm here to see him,' I said to the desk sergeant, who looked up as if he'd been unaware I'd been standing in front of him for five minutes.

'Detective Sergeant Neesham's not available at present,' the sergeant said. 'Can I take a message?'

'No message,' I said.

I'd done what I'd promised Doc and Jane. I'd tried to report the issue to Neesham. Not my fault he wasn't around to hear my report. I'd have to deal with things the way I'd been trained. If you want something done, do it yourself.

41

Mum met me in the lane, red-faced and flustered. My first thought was Nob, but it was the boy.

'He's gone,' she said. 'Taken his gas mask.'

'When?' I asked.

She looked up and down the lane as if the answer would be found there.

'When did you last see him?' I asked.

'He was looking at your maps,' she said. 'I sent him up to get ready for school about noon.'

They'd implemented a shift system at the school. Mornings for the local children. Afternoons for the evacuees. A good way of expanding the capacity. It also kept contact between the invaders and the locals to a minimum.

I looked at my watch. One o'clock. That meant he had less than an hour's head start. I looked back down the lane. It led north, to London. Was that what he was doing with the maps? It was over forty miles to London. A couple of days' walk.

*

I got to the station just as the London train was about to leave. I ran onto the platform, stumbling over a mess of suitcases someone had left and barking my shins. When I looked up, the train was already moving. I looked through the windows as best I could as the train passed me, picking up speed.

I didn't see Frankie, but he could have been in the corridor on the far side.

As the train pulled out, I stood on the platform, contemplating my next move. I'd have to talk to the schoolteachers who'd supervised the placement of the evacuees. Presumably they'd have Frankie's home address in London. I could get a later train, follow him up, and see if I could bring him back. Assuming his mum wanted me to, after the horror stories he'd doubtless tell her about his time with us.

An incoming southbound train caught my attention and I glanced across to the far platform. I saw Frankie dart behind an elderly couple, trying to hide from me. He was waiting for the Brighton train.

I ran up and over the footbridge, up the zig-zag stairs, through the plume of smoke from the incoming train, down the far stairs, and onto the platform. He was gone, but the train was still there. I pulled open the nearest carriage and saw him disappearing along the corridor.

'Frankie,' I called out.

His shoulders dropped as soon as he heard me. Knew he'd been rumbled.

★

We walked back up Belmont Lane, under the shade of the chestnut trees.

'I know it's hard being away from home,' I said. He ignored me. I was the prison guard as far as he was concerned.

'When I went off to war I hated being away,' I said. 'I used to think about the day I'd be able to walk back up this lane, fresh from the train, go home, and stay there forever.'

He gave me a sideways glance, then looked away when he saw I'd noticed.

'I couldn't work out why we all had to leave our homes and go and fight each other, when every man on every side just wanted to be left alone, or with his family, or at the pub with his mates, or working at his job.'

'It's stupid,' he said.

'You're not wrong,' I said. 'But it's the way things are. It's probably the way things will always be.'

42

'We're going to need some fresh timber,' I said. Frankie looked around at the cellar. He sniffed. The place smelt of mildew and damp.

When we'd declared war on Germany, everyone had expected the bombers to arrive that night. At the time I'd told Mum and Nob we'd use the coal cellar if it came to it, not really believing we'd need to. I'd half-heartedly thrown some blankets and candles down there. The skies had been mostly quiet since then, and I hadn't even opened the cellar door. Easier to ignore something you don't see.

The rickety staircase was usable but only just. The treads felt soft. We'd need to rip them out and put new steps in. Couldn't have Mum and Nob and Frankie going up and down rotten stairs in the middle of the night.

The rest of the cellar was even worse than I'd remembered. The box of blankets was chewed by mice. One of the blankets was usable if you weren't squeamish, but the rest were a chewed-up mess of wool and mouse droppings. I couldn't find the candles. A small window at ceiling height gave some light, filtered through decades of filth on the outside of the glass and cobwebs on the inside, but that only reminded me I needed to block it up for the blackout. I'd need to run an electric light down here. Did I have a spare light fitting? Did I have enough wire to run a new circuit from the batteries?

One wall of the cellar was lined with rough shelves I'd put in using cast-off planks. Every shelf was stacked with jars. Mum had been squirrelling. Jam. Chutney. Tinned potatoes. Tomatoes. Fruit salad. I was glad she'd been building up supplies. At least someone had been thinking straight.

The floor was dirt. It was damp and uneven. If we were going to spend nights down here, I'd need to cover it with a groundsheet. Then I could get some camp beds set up. I'd need to level the ground. Frankie could help with that. Boys like playing with dirt. Give him a bob for some pocket money. He could buy some carrots.

★

I had a bench in an outbuilding where I kept my carpentry tools. When I'd brought the farm back to life, I'd done all the work myself, saving money and proving to the world I could make it happen through the sheer force of my will.

'There are lots of things in war that are out of your hands,' I said to Frankie. 'If you worry about them, it makes you feel like giving up. If you ever feel like that, get busy doing something. There's always a job that needs to be done.'

I dug out the saw.

'Has your dad shown you how to use one of these?' I asked him.

He shook his head.

'Dad's gone,' he said.

'Gone?'

He shrugged. I looked at him to see if he wanted to say more, but his face was a mask, defences on ready.

'I'll show you,' I said. 'Then you can get started cutting up some new stairs.'

He held the saw and dragged it across the first board. It skittered all over the place.

'Put your left hand next to it,' I said, showing him, 'then pull the saw back carefully. You want to make a groove. But don't cut your hand.'

I let him try. It took a couple of attempts, but he got the idea.

'I'll measure the boards,' I said, 'and you cut them.' I pulled out a pencil from my pocket.

★

We worked in silence, me marking up the boards with cut lines, him sawing. I had less to do, so pretty soon he had a pile of boards ready to be cut.

'I wasn't running away,' he said.

'If you were, you were going in the wrong direction,' I said.

'There's a girl from our road, she went in the first evacuation last year.'

I nodded.

'Where was she sent?' I asked.

'They said Brighton,' he said. 'She never sent her postcard home.'

He focused on the sawing. He wanted to get it right.

'Girlfriend?' I asked.

'I'm too young for a girlfriend,' he said. 'She just lived on our road.'

'Brighton's a big town,' I said. 'What was your plan?'

He shrugged.

'Don't know,' he said.

'Post gets lost all the time,' I said.

43

At teatime, we all listened to the news. Holland had fallen. They'd surrendered to the Germans at ten fifteen in the morning, about the time the spivs were drawing their last breaths. The French were in disarray. Their commander-in-chief, General Gamelin, had told them all to fight to the last man, but the way the newscaster was telling it, they'd interpreted that to mean ditch your uniform and start practising your German. Perhaps they had the right idea.

Frankie ate his stew quietly. He had blisters on his hand from the saw, but he didn't complain. He'd done a passable job. Nothing fancy, and I'd have to redo some of his cuts, but he'd stuck to the work.

I thought about what he'd said. Another missing evacuee, this one not seen again after being sent to Brighton. I thought of the spivs. From Brighton. A coincidence, almost definitely, but I'd feel better once I'd had a look in that barn.

★

Eight o'clock at the paper mill meant I had to leave at seven. I hoped Margaret would know where to find me. It was a test, but I wanted her to pass. I wanted to see her again.

I stepped outside and suddenly it was obvious I'd have to change my plans. Neesham was standing in the farmyard, in almost exactly the same place Mary had been.

He was waiting for me.

'Figured you'd be heading for the pub at some point,' Neesham said. 'How many pints does it take to quieten down your conscience?'

'Glad I'm that predictable,' I replied. I looked to see if there were any constables waiting to drag me off to jail for the murder of the spivs. I couldn't see any. Perhaps they were waiting down the road.

'I was wrong,' I said. 'She did play tennis, just not in town.'

I'd seen it, from my look-out point in the trees, but I hadn't noticed.

'She was at The Grange. They've got a court. It's all set up, ready for play. The net was clean. You leave a net like that out through the winter and it goes green with moss. Go and ask them and they'll tell you she was there. I'd lay odds they had an evacuee there as well, until she ran away. Mary came to you and reported her missing.'

'When were *you* there?' he asked.

'I went to have a look a couple of days ago. It's called investigating. You should try it sometime.'

'What else did you see while you were investigating?'

'The Chief Constable showed up. I assume he was grilling Baxter the way you've been grilling me. The two of you should co-ordinate. He's probably got the case sewn up by now.'

I was expecting a pithy response, but he didn't answer. Instead, he looked up at the sky. There was a distant noise, like a giant swarm of bees. We both looked for the source. The noise grew louder, until I could feel the ground shaking. I put my hand on the side of the barn and felt the vibration deep in the old timbers. The noise grew until it was a roar, the sky filling with more bombers than I could count, all heading south-east.

'That'll put a dent in their advance,' Neesham said.

'Long-range bombers,' I said. 'Probably going to take out industrial sites in Germany. Poor sods.'

'You've got a better idea?' he asked.

'No,' I said. 'Just doesn't seem fair to kill a man because he works in a factory.'

We stood in silence for a while. Fine with me, but I've found it makes other people uncomfortable.

'Something's going on at The Grange,' Neesham said, eventually. 'Stuff's been coming and going. Large quantities. Noticeable. A lorry every day or so. Normally when something's going on people will talk but none of the farm hands have been saying anything. Either they don't know anything, or they're scared.

'The Chief Constable said he'd look into it,' he continued. 'He came back and said he'd had a word with Baxter. Said he'd sorted it out. Baxter's got money trouble. It's an open secret. Gambling debts with some heavy hitters from Brighton. He let them use one of his barns to store some things, no questions asked. The Chief Constable told him they'd have to pitch their tent in some other town. He told me that would be the end of it.'

'You don't know what they were storing there?' I asked.

Neesham shook his head.

'Never got close enough. I can't very well stop the lorries when they're driving through town. It's a free country, at least for a few more weeks, and if someone wants to drive a lorry from Brighton to Uckfield and back again there's no law against it. I never had enough evidence to justify barging in and kicking down doors.'

'You said you were told it had all been wrapped up.'

'Which puts me in an awkward position. I could go back to the Chief Constable and tell him I think Baxter's up to his tricks again.'

'But?' I asked.

He looked around, checking we weren't overheard.

'The Chief Constable and Baxter are old mates. Either Baxter's not listening to him because he doesn't feel like he has to, or the Chief Constable's a bit more involved than that, and I'm on a sticky wicket.'

'Anyone else in the station know?' I asked.

'This is a complicated situation,' Neesham said. 'I don't think there's anyone else in the station who'd understand the nuance.'

'So, what are you going to do?' I asked.

'Nothing,' he said. 'As far as I'm concerned, there was something going on and I did my job by reporting it to my boss. My boss told me it's all gone away, that means it's all gone away. If it's all gone away, there's no reason for me to do anything.'

'You'd need someone to go and take a look,' I said. 'Someone who wasn't intimidated by Baxter or any of his friends from Brighton.'

'I hadn't thought of that,' Neesham said.

I looked over at the toolshed where Frankie had been sawing, small piles of sawdust still fresh.

'What about Mary's friend Elizabeth? The evacuee?' I asked.

'What about her?'

'Mary said she was in trouble, and now she's missing.'

Neesham shrugged.

'Evacuees run away,' he said. 'Wouldn't you?'

44

Margaret was sitting on an ancient brick wall, overlooking the rushing weir. It was a precarious place to sit. The speed and volume of water surging over the weir would kill her if she slipped.

'The mill' was a misnomer. It was a dank hole in the ground, with traces of brickwork hundreds of years old. The weir was the only clue that this had once been a centre of industry.

'Is being late part of the test?' she asked. 'Like a loyalty thing?'

'Sorry,' I said, stepping out onto the wall overlooking the weir and sitting beside her, 'I got caught up with the police.'

'What's going on?' she asked.

I thought about brushing her question off, but it was useful to have someone to talk with. Doc was already involved and I didn't think he'd be able to keep a clear head after what happened with Jane. I needed an outsider who'd listen to my story and point out what I was missing.

So I told her what had happened, with Mary, with Jane. With the missing evacuee. I told her about the spivs. She sat quietly and listened and when I got to the end, with Neesham giving me tacit permission to look in the barn, she nodded silently. She was a good listener; I'd been more honest and open with her than I'd intended. Blakeney wouldn't have approved, but fuck Blakeney.

'You killed two men because they assaulted your old girl-friend?' she asked.

'That's not exactly how I'd put it.'

She thought about it, watching the water roaring over the weir.

'What are you going to do?' she asked.

'I'm going to go and have a look in the barn.'

'When?'

'Tonight.'

'Do you need any help?'

My instinct was to say no. Always. Do it yourself. Do it right. It had served me well, most of the time.

'Better if it's just me,' I said.

'And what happens once you've found out what's in the barn?'

It was a good question. I didn't have an answer for it. I wasn't thinking that far ahead.

'So, about my thing,' she said. 'What do you think?'

'Do I want to play soldier with you, killing Nazis until they eventually catch us, torture us and hang us in front of the town hall?'

'Exactly,' she said.

'If we're going to do it right, we'll need more people,' I said. 'We've got you in Isfield, me in Uckfield. We need people on our flanks.'

I was thinking about Cyril Butler, the radio expert in my first unit in France. We'd kept in touch after. Had a few pints every year or so. He kept himself to himself, lived miles from anyone out past Cross in Hand. He'd be up for it in a heartbeat.

'Anyone you trust?' she asked.

'As much as I trust anyone,' I said.

45

We took Margaret's car, a rusting open-top Alvis F-series that trailed clouds of burnt oil and sounded like a traction engine. She navigated the back lanes through Framfield and out to Cross in Hand with a joy I couldn't share. I spent every second of the journey looking out for oncoming cars or cyclists.

Cyril wasn't in his local. The landlord said he owed him half a crown and a new wireless set. He said we should pass on the message that Cyril would be welcomed back once those debts were settled in full.

We motored out to Cyril's place, down a lane that got so narrow the hedges pressed in on both sides of the car. It ended abruptly with a five-bar gate tied up with wire. There was no room to open the car doors, so we climbed out over the bonnet, and over the gate.

Cyril's house was a dingy cottage almost reclaimed by a tangle of brambles. We threaded our way through to the peeling front door and I banged on it, knowing I wouldn't get any response. The house was dark. It felt empty.

The trail through the brambles led around the side of the house. We followed it to the back garden, a graveyard of mossy statues almost buried in waist-high grass. I walked out through the grass to get a look back at the house. I imagined Cyril holed up inside, watching the visitors, waiting for them to leave. I wanted him to see it was me. But if he did see me, he didn't want to talk.

Margaret walked past me to the edge of the woods.

'What's that?' she asked.

She pointed at a wire running twenty feet up between the trees. Like a tripwire, but too high to be a defensive feature. She followed the wire into the trees. There were more wires, like a man-made spider's web. We followed them deeper into the woods until they converged on a rusty metal pole. At the base of the pole, hidden inside a thick holly bush, I could make out a window. I circled the holly bush, and at the far side found a wooden door.

The door opened suddenly and I was surprised to find a gun pointing at my chest. Cyril.

'Cook? What are you doing here?' he asked. He kept the gun up.

'Brought you a message from the pub. They said you broke their wireless,' I said. 'Going to make it difficult for us to get a pint.'

Cyril looked around nervously.

'This is Margaret. She's a friend. I brought her to meet you.'

Cyril eyed Margaret suspiciously. She returned the look. From her point of view Cyril wasn't a particularly impressive specimen. He'd been in his thirties when we'd served together in France, so that made him late fifties or sixties now. He looked like he'd gone feral. I tried to remember how long it had been since I'd last seen him.

He lowered the gun.

'Come in,' he said, and we followed him into his shed.

It was a small building, with a single window giving a view back towards the house, through the woods. He must have been watching us coming. Below the window was a bench, covered with radio equipment. A small speaker gave out the hiss of static. Cyril took a seat at the bench and tuned the radio, bringing Morse code through the speaker.

'Something's going on,' he said.

There weren't any other chairs, so Margaret and I stood behind him, squeezed into the small space.

I listened to the Morse code, translating automatically in my head, but the words didn't make sense.

'It's German,' Margaret said.

'Of course it's German,' Cyril said. 'Why would I waste time listening in to the English?'

'It's a code,' she said.

'Of course it's a fucking code,' Cyril said. 'But listen to the way they're talking.'

We listened. All I heard was dots and dashes. Random letters.

'This is Guderian's radio operator, calling from Abbeville,' Cyril said. 'He's angry. You can tell from the way he's rushing through his code. You can almost hear him slamming down the key.'

There was a pause, and then the Morse resumed. This time it was more measured.

'This is Wehrmacht High Command in Berlin,' Cyril said. 'They've been going back and forth all evening. They're arguing. Well, Guderian's man is arguing his point and Command is refusing him.'

'How do you know who they are if it's all encrypted?' I asked.

He sighed and looked at me as if I'd disappointed him.

'Let's say I'm Churchill's operator, and you're out in the field with the BEF. You call me. Before we get to business and switch on the encoder maybe you ask me what the weather's like, or if Betty liked the dress I bought her, or if my toothache cleared up yet. The sort of things you say to colleagues before you get down to business.'

'And they give their names?' I asked. It didn't fit with my image of the Germans being a professional outfit.

'Of course not,' he said. 'But if they mention the weather, I can look up the weather, and the time, and anything else they say, and compare it with the BBC's European weather report. You do that for a year, and you start to get enough information to work out who's who.

'You can also use their movements,' he continued. 'The people who keep moving are out in the field, obviously. They're the ones who ask how things are going back home. Then the one who's on the other side of all the different conversations, he's at the centre of the network. He's High Command. He also types more exactly, like he's got Keitel standing over his shoulder. You can tell he's got his uniform buttoned up and his brass polished and Hitler's boot up his arse.'

'So what's going on?' I asked.

Cyril held up a finger and listened. Then he shook his head and turned the volume lower.

'I think High Command's ordering Guderian to do something he doesn't want to do. I think they're ordering him to slow down.'

'Why would they do that?' I asked.

'You're the master tactician, Cookie. I'm just the radio man.'

'Does MI know?' Margaret asked.

Cyril looked at Margaret like she'd appeared out of thin air.

'Who the fuck are you?'

'Margaret,' she said.

'She's all right,' I said.

Cyril looked at her more closely.

'Well, if you're with Cookie, you can't be completely all right.'

'Cyril,' I said, 'we're putting together a small unit of people who'll be interested in making a nuisance of themselves once the Germans have invaded.'

'Sounds like a good way of getting killed,' he said.

'Probably is,' I said.

'They reckon resistance fighters will have a life expectancy of about three weeks,' Margaret said.

I didn't know where she got that from, but it cut the conversation dead. Cyril turned away from us and put on a headset, fiddling with his dials.

He started tapping on his own Morse code sender.

'What are you doing?' I asked him.

'Sending a message to a friend of mine at Bletchley,' he said. 'Just in case.'

'We'll count you in, then,' I said.

He stuck two fingers up, and kept up the Morse code signalling.

★

'Life expectancy of three weeks?' I shouted, as we reversed back down Cyril's lane. Margaret had one hand on the wheel, her other arm over the back of my chair, her head turned to face the back of the car. We were going too fast for the manoeuvre, but she was holding it pretty steady.

'That's what they told me during training. On average, they said.'

'Funny time to bring it up, when we're trying to recruit someone.'

'We don't want anyone who doesn't understand the risks.'

'Cyril signed up for the last war the day it started, and he fought until the day it ended. He understands the risks better than you or me,' I said.

'What if I don't think he's right?' she shouted. 'This is my show. I thought we were going to see him so *I* could decide if *I* wanted him.'

46

I timed my walk to get me back to the look-out point at two in the morning, by now a familiar route. A cloudy sky had settled in. It was going to be a dark night. A good opportunity to get a look inside Baxter's barn.

Of course, there was a chance the whole thing was a set-up, Neesham sent to goad me into action. I took it slowly, creeping quietly through the trees for the last hundred yards, not easy with all the dead leaves underfoot. I heard plenty of noise, but all of it the natural sounds of a Sussex woodland at night.

I reached the edge of the trees twenty yards from my regular spot. I crawled out into the long grass of the sloping valley and looked along the treeline. If there was a sentry, I'd expect him to be where my trail in the grass had disappeared into the trees. Nothing.

I trained my binoculars on the house, and then the barn. No lights thanks to the blackout. Complete darkness.

Stepping out of the relative protection of the treeline felt like going over the top from a trench. An exercise in overcoming my fear. Trust the darkness, I told myself. Easier said than done. I expected a shot to ring out any second.

I kept low, crouching and feeling my way with every step. I kept my eyes scanning from side to side, using my peripheral vision which was more light-sensitive, and allowing my unconscious mind to build up a feeling for what was out there, rather than trying to see with my eyes. It was a trick I'd learnt from Afghan tribesmen who made night manoeuvres seem like a walk in the park.

I made it to the looming blackness of the farmyard. I stood at the edge of the yard and quietened my breathing, listening and watching. Still nothing.

I took my rucksack from my back, slowly and silently pulling out my bolt-cutters. Two-foot-long handles made of ash, with Sheffield Steel blades. A half-inch thick padlock wouldn't slow them down too much.

I kept to the darkness at the edge of the yard and made my way around to the locked barn. The bolt-cutters slid on the new steel padlock, refusing to get purchase. Sheffield vs Sheffield. On the third attempt I got them to bite. I put everything into it, and they snicked shut. The padlock hit the ground with a thud.

I stepped into the dark barn, and pushed the door closed behind me. I'd have to use my torch, otherwise I was likely to blunder into a pile of farm equipment and either hurt myself or cause a racket, or both.

I held my hand over the lens of the torch, and turned it on, letting only the barest sliver of light escape.

The barn was full of crates, many of them stamped with names of familiar food companies. Chivers. Brooke Bond. Lever. They were stacked to about chest height, as high as a man could comfortably lift a heavy box. The layout of the crates created aisles, and I walked along the centre.

I stopped at a box with markings I didn't recognise, and looked inside. Medical supplies. Bandages. Syringes. Scissors.

At the end of the row was a tower of boxes all marked with the same number. The printing looked military. I opened a box. It was filled with gas masks.

Next to the gas masks, there was a crate with markings I recognised. Shipping labels from various places. New Jersey stamped on some of them. I didn't need to open the boxes to know what I'd find inside.

You heard stories about the black market, always told fondly, with the criminals cast as heroes. It was up there with apple scrumping, taking a few things here and there and passing them on to those in need, like Robin Hood and his merry men. When food was scarce, and everyone had to queue to get what little was available, what harm could there be in someone giving you an extra tin of salmon under the counter? The logic was backward. The reason for shortages was that things disappeared between the docks and the corner shop. Rations were set based on known availability of a resource. If the resource was stolen and stock-piled, it became scarce. When it was leaked out to the market, always done 'as a favour', at four times the price, people were so glad to be in on the secret they didn't complain.

I wondered how many millions of pounds the inventory stashed in the barn represented. This wasn't apple scrumping. If Mary had been asking questions, it would have made her a threat.

The weapons and army supplies were worrying. I wondered what route they'd taken to end up here. Was Baxter working with Bunny, or had he collected these weapons from another of Bunny's recipients? And where did Lawrence fit in?

There was an interior door at the back of the barn, the kind you'd have leading to an office in an adjoining lean-to. I looked through the cobwebbed glass window in the door. Nothing. I carefully opened the door and stepped in. Always better to check than to assume.

The office was about twelve by twenty feet. It had lower ceilings than the barn. Once upon a time it had had windows, but they'd been boarded over.

There was a bed frame, no mattress. A chest of drawers with a water jug sitting on top. Not much dust. Someone had been living here recently, or at least someone had tidied up. I wondered why the mattress had been taken away.

If Elizabeth had been hiding here, or kept captive, she wasn't here any longer.

There was one more room, filled with seldom-used tools and half sacks of seed and fertiliser. The sort of place you put something when you thought it might be useful again one day, and never returned to. Something caught my eye underneath a sack, a gleam of white. I pulled the sack away and found what had caught my eye – Mary's bike.

Her bag was still in the front basket, along with a bulging paper bag. I checked the bag. It was full of tennis balls.

I looked back in the room set up as a bedroom. Probably where she'd been killed. Would have soaked the mattress with blood. They'd have had to get rid of it.

I checked the floor around the bed frame and found what I expected. A patch beside the bed with no dust. The floor had been wiped, hurriedly. I knelt down and smelt the floor. Damp. Dirt. Mouse droppings. And something else. Blood. I panned the beam of the torch across the floor. Small drops, black in the torchlight.

She hadn't been cycling to my place. She hadn't been cycling anywhere. She'd been killed here and they'd dumped her body in my field. The other side of town. An easy but effective misdirection, nudged along with an anonymous phone call. The bike wouldn't have fit in their car, so they left it here. A problem for them if anyone had seriously investigated the killing, but Neesham had fallen for their misdirection hook, line and sinker.

I looked at the bike in the junk room. I thought of leaving it and tipping off Neesham, but that didn't feel right. It felt like a further betrayal. I thought of Mary, pedalling out of my farmyard. She wouldn't have wanted me to leave it.

I wheeled the bike out of the barn, and left the door open

behind me. Let them worry about who had seen inside. If anyone wanted to come after me, let them come.

As soon as I got out onto the lane, I got on the bike. It was too small for me, but it rolled, and it was slightly downhill towards the woods and back into town. Better to roll than to walk. It made a quiet clicking sound that took me back to my child-hood. At rolling speed, the air felt cooler, like diving into a lake. The moon had come up, lighting the lane almost like day.

As I got closer to the woods, my freewheeling slowed, and I heard rubber grinding on the road. A puncture.

I could push the bike the rest of the way, but I had it in my head to cycle.

A girl like Mary would have a puncture repair kit, proba-bly in a saddle bag. Her father would have put it in there and made sure she knew how to use it. There was a small, leather bag tucked up high under the saddle, caked in dirt from the road, but perfectly dry and clean inside. I found the rectangu-lar tin I knew would be there and opened it, checking I had all the right elements before I started.

There was an envelope, folded twice to fit into the rectan-gular tin.

The envelope was addressed to Mr Wm. Baxter, The Grange, Uckfield. There was a postmark, but I couldn't make it out in the moonlight.

I pulled out a single sheet of thin paper, wartime stock, made since ordinary paper was rationed. I unfolded it.

The top half of the sheet was a typed copy of a notice you'd find in a newsagent's window. 'MISSING. Elizabeth Potter. Evacuated from London on 1st September. 12 y/o, blond hair, fair skin. A good girl. Never been away from home before.'

Underneath this section, below the equator line of the central fold, was a different message, this one handwritten.

'Final payment due. End of the month.'

47

'I found what Mary's killers were looking for,' I said to Billy, standing over him as he sat in a deck chair by the runway, watching the sky. I waited for a response, but didn't get one.

Mary had died protecting a secret. It had been important enough to someone else that she had been killed to protect it.

I'd parked on the main road across the forest and climbed over the fence they'd strung up as a security perimeter. There hadn't been any security patrols. Every spare man we had was across the Channel, running backwards across a French field or digging in for the next stand against General Guderian and his Panzers.

Billy was in his flight suit, either ready to go or just back. He'd watched me walking from the outfield but didn't move. Even when I stood in front of him, he barely moved his head, just tracked me with his eyes as I stood in front of him, blocking the rising sun.

'I should have you thrown out,' he said, eventually. 'This is a tier-one military installation.'

'She was at The Grange the morning she was killed,' I said. 'Your father's men raped her and killed her, then dumped her body on my land.'

He looked away, watching a ground crew prepare a Hurricane, calm and efficient.

'She wanted me to join her there for a game of tennis,' he said. 'She was being a real pill about it. I told her I was on duty at nine but she kept nagging. I told her to go and practise her serve by herself if she was so desperate to play.'

'There's something else,' I said.

I handed him the letter. He unfolded it and read.

'I assume you opened it by mistake when it arrived,' I said. 'Or maybe she opened it for you. Sitting at breakfast. Going through the post while the servants pour your tea. Isn't that what you lot do?'

Billy watched a distant plane, no more than a speck in the sky.

'Elizabeth Potter's your evacuee?' I asked.

'She ran off a few weeks ago,' he said. 'They all run off. Back to the slums. Everyone says so.'

'Why would someone think she's missing if she went home?'

'I don't know. I didn't write the letter.'

'You don't think it's your responsibility to make sure she got home safely?'

He sighed. He didn't answer.

'I can't,' he said, 'I don't know her home address. When we got her, she wrote a letter home and we posted it. That's how their parents know where they end up. I didn't look at it. Other than that, it didn't come up in conversation.'

'You didn't talk about her home?'

'She's a kid. She was an annoying part of the furniture. I didn't engage her in conversation.'

'London? Birmingham? Manchester?'

'London,' he said. 'She talked about going up west.'

'Mary had this letter, and now she's dead,' I said. 'Doesn't that make you want to find out what it was about?'

'You make it sound like an Agatha Christie story. I've got other things to worry about. Forget about the girl.'

Everyone wanted me to forget about the girl.

48

Frankie's school started at one in the afternoon. We walked across the fields into town. It seemed like a lifetime since I'd promised the young schoolteacher I'd see about helping her dig a victory garden.

I thought of the way Billy Baxter had described their evacuee. An annoying part of the furniture.

'There's another girl who's missing,' I said to Frankie. 'Just like your friend.'

He looked at me like I was about to play a trick on him. I wondered what his life had been like before he'd been sent away.

'I'll see what I can find out,' I said.

We walked for a while.

'How are you going to find them?' he asked.

'I don't know,' I said. 'But it's better to do something than nothing.'

★

Miss Spencer walked me out to the cricket pitch behind the school. It was where I'd learnt to play, and I couldn't believe how small it looked. It didn't seem right talking about ploughing it up, like admitting that the war was the only thing we had to look forward to.

'You're sure you don't want smaller beds round the side?' I asked. 'More manageable for the children to work.'

'No,' she said, 'it's not right for us to be saving the land just for games when people are going to be starving. They say we've all got to do our bit.'

I wouldn't have liked to be a boy in her class who took it upon himself to test her patience.

'I'll have Bill Taylor bring the tractor tomorrow,' I said. I hoped the old Fordson would make it all the way into town, it had been playing up recently and we hadn't been able to get the parts to fix it.

'What are you going to plant?'

'Potatoes over there. Tomatoes and lettuces this summer if it's not too late. Cabbage and sprouts in the autumn. Rhubarb down the side.'

She had it all planned out, full credit to her.

'Here's where I want the slit trench,' she said, walking me around the side of the building. There was just enough room between the schoolhouse and an ancient laburnum hedge.

'They say six feet deep and three feet wide. The council are going to supply the boards. We just need to dig it out.'

The thought of putting children in a trench gave me chills.

'What about sanitary arrangements?' I asked.

'Buckets,' she said. 'The council said they'd supply them.'

So this was total war. We were digging trenches for children, in playing fields, in sleepy towns and villages across the country.

'Bill can have the men dig it after they plough the wicket,' I said.

I walked her back to her classroom. It was empty, the kids were still in the playground.

'Do you ever get any complaints from the evacuees, about their situations?' I asked.

'Sometimes,' she said. 'Is Frankie all right?'

'You'd have to ask him,' I said. 'Did you ever hear anything from the girl at The Grange, before she ran off?'

Miss Spencer frowned. 'They don't have an evacuee there. I asked them if they'd take one last year and they refused. Said they couldn't possibly. It's usually the ones with the big houses who say no.'

'Perhaps it was before you were involved?' I asked.

She shook her head. 'Oh no, I've been running the show since it started. And I keep meticulous records.'

'I assume they got her from another town then?' I asked.

'Impossible,' she said. 'It's all done very strictly. Town by town. We have to keep track of the children and we can't have them placed willy-nilly.'

'What if someone has a child and then moves house?'

'We'd rehouse the child, or we'd pass on paperwork to the new location. We haven't received any paperwork from anywhere else. And anyway, Mr Baxter's always lived in Uckfield.'

Miss Spencer flushed. 'I'm not meant to share details like this,' she said. 'But you did say it was connected with Mary.'

'I'll keep mum,' I said, tapping the side of my nose.

'I gave the same answers to Mary when she was asking.'

'Mary was asking you about an evacuee at The Grange?'

'Yes. She had a bee in her bonnet. No, that's not fair. She was very upset.'

'When was this?' I asked.

'Last week,' she said. 'Just before . . .'

She looked at me as she put it together. She put her hand to her mouth.

'I'm sure it's not connected,' I said.

'I don't think you think that,' she said. 'I don't think you think that at all.'

49

The farmyard was emptier than usual. There were piles of sawdust on the ground, where Frankie and I had been cutting the planks for the stairs, but the planks were gone.

I'd hurried home from my meeting with Miss Spencer determined to finish the cellar. With the Germans on the move, seemingly unstoppable, it was only a matter of time before the bombers arrived, that much was certain. The bomb shelter was no longer a luxury, but a necessity.

I'd have to redo some of the boards that Frankie had cut. He'd had his fun, playing with the saw, but now it was time to get the job done properly. If I could finish it before he got back from school he'd never know. I didn't want to discourage him.

But the missing planks made all that impossible, and there was only one person who would have taken them.

*

Eric was in his back garden, feeding his chickens. He had quite an operation. Sheds and runs for about fifty feet, with what must have been several hundred chickens. Farms were required to register their chickens so the eggs could be shared out. Keeping a few in the back garden was allowed, even encouraged. Eric's operation was a grey area.

He lived with his nan just outside Newick, not far from the western boundary of my land. He'd been kept out of the army because of his back. He was a painter and he'd fallen off the roof of the bus station. Fell thirty feet and landed flat on his back on the concrete floor. Broke his back and spent six months in the hospital. He'd tried to sign up the day Germany invaded Poland but the army said they didn't need men who couldn't carry a rucksack, so he made himself useful in other ways. He dropped a rabbit or two off with Mum every week, and I heard he kept a lot of Newick similarly supplied.

He saw me coming and pretended he wasn't bothered. Made quite a good job of it.

'Mr Cook,' he said. 'I've got some nice eggs for you.'

'You've got something else of mine,' I said.

He looked at me like butter wouldn't melt in his mouth.

'I borrowed some of this chicken wire from one of your barns. Thought you wouldn't mind, seeing as you got rid of your birds.'

'You can keep the chicken wire,' I said. 'Can't have the foxes wiping out your stock.'

'Your mum said I could take any scraps of wood I could find,' he said. Probably true. 'I was dropping off a chicken for your dinner.'

I nodded. Eric had been good to us. He'd been good to a lot of people. Useful to have a man like him in your corner.

'I do need the wood,' I said. 'Got to get the cellar ready.'

He watched as I opened up the back of his van. My planks were still there, along with a treasure trove of knick-knacks.

'You can drive me back,' I said. 'Then I've got something else I want to talk to you about. I'm looking for someone I can trust. Someone who knows the land. Who knows how to move around without being seen or heard. Ideally someone who knows his way around a rifle.'

'For what?'

'Fighting back, after the invasion.'

50

The meeting place was a small stand of trees in an otherwise open expanse of fields. Lewes was just visible on the horizon, nestled in the gap in the Downs. An almost imperceptible line in the field signified the ancient route of a Roman road, a slight shadow caused by ground that was a few inches higher than the surroundings.

We wouldn't be disturbed. The landowner was a drunk who was barely holding on to his farm. He probably came out here once a year, if that.

Cyril would come from the east, and Margaret from the west. They would bring dogs, or walking sticks, maybe shotguns, rendering themselves invisible. A man walking these fields would be entirely commonplace. A woman alone less so, but still not uncommon. I'd seen the writer walking these fields. Virginia something. Kept meaning to look up one of her books.

Down by the river, a dot. Cyril. The footpath took him around the edge of the field. He'd tidied himself up. Made an effort. I was glad.

'Cookie,' he said.

He looked around, stepping into the stand of trees to look up into the leafy branches. I let him conduct his reconnaissance, as I would have liked another man to let me do my own in the same situation. He walked around the perimeter of the trees and returned to me, looking out across the fields.

'Good position,' he said. 'Give a man a Bren and enough ammunition and he could hold this for hours.'

'I wouldn't want to be that man when the tanks came through the gap at Lewes,' I said.

He nodded, contemplating this.

'No,' he said.

Eric arrived from the west. He didn't speak, just waited. The junior man unsure of his standing. I nodded to him.

'Cyril, this is Eric. Knows the land around Uckfield like the back of his hand.'

Eric stepped forward eagerly, and they shook hands.

'How you doing for petrol?' Cyril asked him.

I left them talking about the new regulations for petrol rationing and sat on a grassy patch at the edge of the trees. A quiet afternoon. After several days of sun, the ground was warm, and the soil crumbled at my touch. A hare ran across the field, zigzagging to throw off an imagined pursuer.

Margaret was last. There wasn't any handshaking. Everyone nodded politely and kept their hands in their pockets. Three very capable men, and yet we were all a bit thrown by the presence of a woman.

'All right,' I said, bringing the meeting to order. 'We all know why we're here. The Germans are almost at the Channel and that means they could be here in a few weeks.'

We all looked south, to Lewes.

'Assuming the worst, they'll have all of our tanks and artillery,' I said, 'and by all accounts their air force outguns ours by a significant margin. So we have to assume they'll win. We'll be occupied, just like Czechoslovakia and Poland.

'Margaret's been asked to put together a team. I've already said I'd join her. The last line of defence. People who know what they're doing. People who can move about the countryside, disappear and then reappear where they're not expected.

People who want to do their bit and don't mind if things get a bit sticky.'

I looked at each of them in turn.

'They told us these units will have a life expectancy counted in weeks, rather than months,' Margaret said. 'The Germans will hunt down any signs of resistance, and they'll rely on local informants. It's working very well for them in their other occupied territories. A lot of people would love a few extra pounds in their pockets and a chance to get rid of a neighbour they've had a grievance with. Think about anyone you've ever rubbed up the wrong way, or who's jealous of something you've got. Think about how that might help them decide to turn you in if they find out you're in the resistance.'

'There's no shame if any one of us wants to walk away, carry on your afternoon walk and leave this conversation behind you,' I said. 'But we need to decide now, so we know who's in, and who's out. So, what do you think?'

Eric was the one who worried me most. He had responsibilities. But I needn't have worried.

'Sounds like you're trying to scare me off,' Eric said, 'but I'm the only one who goes out every night breaking the law just to keep food on the table.'

I looked at Cyril, expecting a sarcastic quip, but he just nodded. We all looked at Margaret. She nodded.

'How do we know we can trust each other?' Cyril said. 'Like she said, once Jerry's here, there'll be a lot of pressure.'

Everyone looked at each other.

'We can't be sure,' Margaret said. 'But even factoring in the risk, there are advantages to working together, rather than going it alone.'

'If anyone's uncomfortable with the risk,' I said, 'they're free to go. No hard feelings. What do you think, Cyril? You're the one with the concern?'

'I've got a bad feeling you cunts are going to get me killed,' he said. I took that as a yes.

'And if it turns out anyone's a rat,' said Margaret, 'we'll kill them.' I couldn't tell if she was trying to lighten the mood, or if she was serious. I suspected it was the latter.

For the first time since I'd met with Bunny, I felt some of the weight lift from my shoulders. I was part of a unit. Competent, smart people. People who didn't need to be told what to do. People who'd get things done. It had been a long time since I'd been part of such a team, half a world away in the foothills of the Himalayas.

'I can't think of a better group than we've got here,' I said. 'I'd be proud to serve with any of you, and it's my belief that if we put our heads together we can cause Jerry a lot of trouble before he catches us.'

51

Now we had the team assembled, I should have felt I was on top of things. But my thoughts kept returning to the note I'd found in Mary's saddlebag. I didn't like the idea of a young girl unaccounted for. Too many ways that could go wrong.

'Evacuees run off.' That was what Billy had said. Most likely Elizabeth had gone home. That shouldn't be too hard to check. I didn't have her address, but I had the letter. It was postmarked Brighton. A big town, but not infinitely big. Hemmed in by the sea and the Downs. There'd be a finite number of places where information about a missing girl might be found. Better to be doing something than nothing.

Twenty minutes by train. Isfield. Lewes. Preston Park. Brighton. Still no signs of defensive works anywhere *en route*. Seemed like our new Prime Minister was going for a head-in-the-sand approach.

Brighton station was as busy as ever. As well as being a key point on the coastal route, it was the southern terminus of the London to Brighton flyer, making it an outpost of the capital. People moved faster, shouted louder, and dressed more smartly than they would in any other southern railway station. Even the newspaper sellers stood a little taller, proud of giving privileged access to the latest words, hot off the London presses.

This was where thousands of evacuees had disembarked in various waves, starting last summer and continuing with further pulses every time the news suggested the German bombers might be on their way to London. I looked at the arrivals board to see when the next London train was due to arrive, curious to see if there would be a fresh crop today.

I found a tearoom, with tables and chairs spilling out onto the busy concourse, and sat with a cup of tea. I picked up a discarded newspaper and scanned it. Churchill had asked Roosevelt for the loan of forty warships. The article was scathing. At the rate we were losing ships in the Atlantic, those forty would last about a week. But it seemed like a good idea to me. If you want a big favour from someone, you start out by asking for a small favour, something that won't really cost them anything and will be almost rude to decline. Once they've done that, they've got used to the idea of helping you, and when you go back with a bigger favour, they'll want to be consistent. Churchill may have been ignoring the defence of the South-East, but he knew what he was doing with the Americans.

A London train pulled in, and before it even stopped the doors were swinging open and crowds pouring out. I watched for evacuees, curious to see how it worked here. I assumed there would be someone in charge of meeting them, some Brighton equivalent of our young Miss Spencer, processing the children's paperwork, and ensuring they got passed on to the correct host family.

But there were no evacuees. Maybe it had finally dawned on the brains in London that sending the nation's children directly to the likely invasion battleground wasn't the brightest idea.

I pulled out the paper I'd found in Mary's saddlebag. It was a notice of a missing child, the kind you'd post on a noticeboard, or in a shop window. I imagined Elizabeth's mother, travelling down on the train from London. The station would be the first place she'd enquire.

There was an information office signposted, so I followed the signs to platform one. Halfway down the platform was a closed door. A small, mean sign admitted that this was the information office. I knocked. No answer. I knocked again, louder and more insistent. Nothing. I waited. Perhaps the person behind the door was on a telephone call. Perhaps they were on the toilet. Perhaps they'd stepped out for a packet of cigarettes.

A porter hurried past me, caught my eye, thought about it, and stopped.

'Nobody there, mate,' he said. I looked back at the door to confirm we were on the same page.

'New rule. Shut the information office so it can't provide route information to German spies.'

It seemed a bit extreme, but the logic was sound.

'How long's it been shut?' I asked.

'About a week,' he said.

Suddenly I felt less confident about finding the source of the sign, but it was only the first hurdle.

My next stop was a newspaper kiosk near the station exit. It had a few notices on a board. Taxi companies. Cleaning services. No missing children. A bust at the second hurdle.

I imagined I was a parent, looking for a missing child. I wouldn't give up so easily.

52

Exiting Brighton station is a jarring experience. You've taken the train to one of England's great seaside towns, and you walk out of the station expecting the sea laid out before you. Instead, the eager visitor is presented with a mean-looking row of shops, with squawking seagulls the only sign of being near the coast.

One thing caught my eye. A newsagent's shop, directly across the road. I crossed the busy road, sizing the place up as I approached. It was an unremarkable newsagent's, like you'd find on every street in every town. Above the windows, a faded banner advertised the *Evening Argus* and Woodbines. If I were an anxious parent down on the train and looking for my child, I'd hurry over with the idea of putting a notice in the window.

As I suspected, the two windows were filled with notices. I started with the window to the left of the door. A yellowing index card advised the reader that rooms in the Old Steine were available, with use of a shared hotplate and outdoor privy. There was a section devoted to missing cats, and another offering articles of furniture for sale. I passed the door to look at the other window, and found what I was looking for, notices about lost people. I wondered how many runaways had left the capital and jumped on a train for Brighton, followed a few days later by a loved one. Most would never be found, and the loved one would end up at the shop opposite the station, their last-ditch effort paying a few pennies to post a sign with a description of the runaway and an address where the passer-by could apply for a reward. Almost definitely futile, but in that situation you'd do everything you could. I wondered if a sign had ever led to a reunion.

I pulled out the letter to remind myself of the details, then looked for its twin in the window, hoping the name would leap out at me. I scanned the window hurriedly, and stopped. Do it right, do it once. I started at the top left and methodically checked every advertisement from left to right, top to bottom. I didn't find anything about Elizabeth Potter, although there were other missing evacuees, all girls, more than I would have expected given all the propaganda we'd been fed about how much of a success the whole thing was.

I was about to move on to find another newsagent's when I noticed something curious. I checked the letter to be sure, comparing it to the notices in the window. Not the missing children or cats, but other signs. 'Ask us about newspaper delivery', a misspelled 'make you're phone call here!' and more. They were handwritten.

The writing was the same as on the letter. 'Final payment due. End of the month.'

53

The shop was tiny. Not much more than an alcove, two walls of shelves stacked with magazines and paperback books, and a central unit of shelves holding an array of knick-knacks and stationery. Opposite the door was a counter covered in newspapers. Behind the counter was a rotund, red-faced man with a wispy moustache and thinning hair combed carefully across his otherwise bald head. At the jangling of the bell, he hastily folded up a magazine and hid it beneath the counter. He stared at me openly and kept his gaze on me as I stepped into the small shop. It didn't seem like a very effective way of encouraging customers to stay and browse. That was all right with me. I wasn't a customer.

I looked back at the door. Slid a bolt closed and flipped the open sign to closed. Wouldn't do for us to be disturbed.

'Morning,' I said.

The shopkeeper didn't answer. Just stared. If he was put out by my locking the door, he did a good job hiding it.

'How do you know when to take the cards down from the window? For the missing people,' I asked.

He stared at me, and then pulled out a clipboard with printed instructions, and a single unused card. He handed them to me and I read the faded instructions on the clipboard. Notices could be put in the window for a prepaid period of either six months or a year. No responsibility was taken by the proprietor of the shop for the collecting or passing-on of information and no representation was made that the posting of a sign was a guaranteed rental of the space, which could indeed be taken back at any time without notice by said proprietor.

'Did you ever get anyone enquiring about Elizabeth Potter?' I asked.

The shopkeeper pointed with his ink-blackened finger at the relevant clause on the clipboard. No responsibility taken for collecting information. Or passing it on.

I wondered if he suffered from some kind of disability. Shell-shock, like Nob, perhaps. If so, manning a busy shop didn't seem like the best job he could have chosen.

I showed him the letter.

'A friend of mine received this letter,' I said. 'I'm here to pay.'

He glanced at the letter. It was clear he recognised it. His eyes flicked around the shop. Nobody else around. He shook his head.

'Show me the original notice. I want to make sure you didn't make the whole thing up,' I said.

One of his hands slipped below the counter. Logical, but not sensible. My own hand shot out and I grabbed him by the neck. He tried to back away but the wall was right behind him. Nowhere to run. I tightened my hand.

'I'm protected,' he said. 'You can't touch me.'

I squeezed. He had an erroneous understanding of his situation and I needed to remedy that mistake. I counted to nine. Eased off. He gasped.

'Hands where I can see them,' I said.

He raised his hand, and I heard a clunk as something metal hit the floor. Sounded like a knife. Not heavy enough for a gun.

'Hands on the counter,' I said, 'and then we can talk.'

He put his hands palms down on the newspapers on top of the counter. I let go of his neck.

'All right, let's start again,' I said. 'I'm looking for this girl. Elizabeth Potter.'

He shook his head.

'Perhaps I wasn't clear enough,' I said. 'I need the address for this girl. I promise you I won't leave here until I get it, unless of course you die in the process of not telling me. That leaves you with quite an important decision to make.'

'You're making a mistake,' he said.

It seemed like he didn't believe me. So I skipped ahead. No point in slowly escalating things if both parties weren't on the same page.

I slammed my hands on top of his, trapping them. With my right hand I picked out his index finger, keeping my palm pushing down on his. I wrenched his finger back quickly. The cartilage snapped first. I kept pulling, breaking bone. Not a very pleasant sound, if you were on the receiving end.

'Stop!' he shrieked.

I pulled out his little finger and bent it in on itself. I needed to be sure he was paying attention.

'I'll tell you,' he said. 'Don't!'

I wasn't sure he was on my wavelength, so I crushed the little finger. It was overkill, but better safe than sorry.

'You've got one chance,' I said. 'No funny business.'

He nodded furiously.

'Well?' I said. 'Time's running out.'

'I need my hands,' he said, between gritted teeth.

I lifted my hands up. Easy to grab him again if I needed to. His knife was on the floor and he was trapped behind the counter.

He felt below the counter with his intact hand and pulled out a cardboard folder. It was stuffed full of carbons. He leafed through them. A man on a mission.

There were hundreds, but he seemed to be working to a system, and he was sufficiently motivated, so I let him do it. Finally, he found it, offering it proudly.

MISSING. Elizabeth Potter. Evacuated from London on 1st September. 12 y/o, blond hair, fair skin. A good girl. Never been away from home before. Send information to Mrs J. Potter, 12 Sangdale Rd, South Norwood. November 1939.

'How did you know she was at Baxter's?' I asked.

He shook his head. I grabbed his left hand, the one with the broken fingers.

'Don't,' he begged.

'How did you know?' I asked. 'I won't ask a third time.'

'They'll hurt me worse than you will,' he said.

'Impossible,' I said.

'They're savages,' he said.

'I could kill you right here,' I said.

'They'll kill me,' he said, 'a lot more slowly.'

He'd made his mind up, like a stubborn animal. The harder you pull, the more they dig their heels in. When you get to that point, you have to let them think they've won.

There was a payphone on the back wall of the shop, surrounded by more notices.

'Can I use the phone?' I asked.

He looked at me like I was crazy. Probably not what he was expecting.

I dug in my pocket to see what change I had. The smallest I had was a shilling, and the call would be a penny.

'Change,' I said.

He fumbled with the till. Not easy. Dug out a handful of pennies and slammed them down on the newspapers.

I took the coins and went to the phone, keeping my eyes on him in case he got any ideas. I put one penny in the slot and dialled '0' for the operator.

'Person to person, please,' I said, when the operator came on. 'Isfield Park. Lady Margaret.'

The request got results, and I heard the tone of the operator's voice change.

I waited for Margaret to come to the phone. I pictured her walking through her massive house.

Eventually she picked up. 'Isfield Park, Lady Margaret speaking.'

'It's John Cook,' I said, 'from Uckfield. We met briefly at the White Hart.' I had to be careful. You never knew who was listening at the telephone exchange.

'Mr Cook, of course,' said Margaret, 'how lovely to hear from you. What can I do for you?'

'I took it upon myself to see if I could track down your missing serving girl, Elizabeth Potter. We were talking about her the other evening.' I hoped she would catch on, but I needn't have worried.

'Of course, we've been worried sick,' she said. 'How good of you to take an interest.'

'Here's the thing, I'm in Brighton, and I've got the address of her family in London. I was wondering if you'd like to join me on a trip into town.'

'Today?' she asked.

'No time like the present,' I said. 'Unless you have another engagement.'

'I'm tied up at the moment. How about later this afternoon? We could get dinner in town.'

'Perfect,' I replied, staying formal for the operator who I had no doubt was listening.

'Then it's a date,' she said. 'Where shall we meet?'

'I've got some more business in Brighton,' I said. 'I'll be having lunch at The Ship at noon, then heading up to town after that. Why don't you meet me at East Croydon at three?'

'Marvellous,' she replied. 'So glad you thought of me.'

54

It was a normal day at the seaside. You wouldn't have known there was a war on. Young mothers and nannies sat on blankets while children played amongst the pebbles, and on the rare patches of sand. Canadian servicemen were the only clue that something was up. They were everywhere you looked. A group were playing cricket on a patch of wet sand down by the water.

I stood at the railing and looked out over the sea. Across the Channel was the French port of Dieppe, which would be a major embarkation point for the invasion force. If Bunny was right, the Germans would be on the French coast in a matter of days. It was hard to reconcile that fact with the scenes on the beach.

Brighton beach would be a perfect landing zone. It should be mined. I'd want concrete and steel obstacles in the surf and all the way up the beach, and then I'd want thick concrete bunkers built along the front, where I could place machine-gunners.

I assumed it was a matter of manpower and resources. Perhaps Brighton was less of a priority. It was further west, and thus further from France, than Newhaven, Eastbourne, and Dover. I assumed we were getting those sorted first, before working along the coast.

I checked my watch. Twelve.

When I'd been in India, I'd seen the way villagers hunt a tiger. Tigers are reclusive animals, hunting territories of thousands of square miles. Pointless going after one. You knew they existed from the evidence – missing livestock, scratched trees, occasional sightings, but you'd never track one in such a massive area. So how did you hunt one? You lured it out. You got a goat, tied it to a stake in a clearing, and sat and waited.

It's an easy enough principle to adopt, as long as you've got a goat. For this tiger hunt I was using myself. I'd used the phone call to tell the operator and the newsagent I was looking for Elizabeth Potter. If anyone wanted to talk with me about that, I'd told them where they could find me. Now it was up to them. I had high hopes for the newsagent. He'd said he was protected. My money was on the protection and the person trafficking a young girl being the same person. I also had a feeling the telephone operator would be in on it as well, listening in on every call in and out of the exchange, passing on intelligence now and then. Nothing like two channels of communication passing on the same message to give it a sense of urgency.

I got to the corner of Ship Street at five past and waited. If anyone was going to meet me at the pub, I wanted to give them time to arrive. And if they were inside already, it wouldn't hurt to have them start to second-guess my intentions. There was a fish and chip shop just down the prom, so I ducked in there and bought a portion of chips, extra salt, extra vinegar. I stood on the prom and watched the waves glinting in the sun while I ate my chips.

At quarter past, I finished my chips, balled up the newspaper and stuffed it into an overflowing bin. I strode across the road and walked into The Ship, a large, busy pub, filled with smoke.

For a weekday, it was doing a roaring trade. More Canadians, boisterous and brassy in their immaculate uniforms, all of them as yet untroubled by combat. Day-trippers from London. Local drinkers. And a healthy crop of spivs.

The wireless behind the bar was tuned to a French station, and the barman was listening intently to the news as I tried to get his attention. He noticed me, and held up a finger. Clearly, the news was important. I nodded, to let him know I could wait, and grabbed a stool.

When he came over to me, I ordered a pint of best, and asked him what the news was from France.

'They've taken Amiens. Mostly tanks and those fucking dive bombers. They'll be at the Channel in a day or two.'

He looked out at the crowded pub, and I turned to follow his gaze.

'One of those Stukas would make short work of this place,' he said. 'Soon as my shift's over I'm off. My brother's got a place in the Lake District, said he could find me work up there.'

'I was hoping to meet some friends today. Anyone come in in the last fifteen minutes, looking for someone?' I asked.

'End of the bar,' the barman said in a low voice, 'although I'm not sure he's the kind of friend you want to meet.'

The barman moved away to pull my pint. I leant forward, to look down the length of the bar. At first I didn't see him. Then someone took a step back and I saw him, right at the other end. By himself, reading a paper. The only person not interacting with anyone else. Like an unaccountably calm patch of water in an otherwise busy stream.

Lawrence.

55

Lawrence had always been a big man. His neck was so dense with muscle it made you wonder how he'd turn his head, and his arms were the size of most people's thighs. He was in his shirt-sleeves, rolled up tight over his elbows, as if he had just walked in from the beach, and he wore a flat cap. A cigarette hung from his lip as he read the paper. He could have been a street-sweeper on his lunch break, or a day-tripper on his one-day holiday from London.

I took my pint from the barman, paid my shilling, and put another shilling in the Spitfire Fund, then pushed my way through the Canadians to the far end of the bar.

Lawrence read his newspaper, ignoring me, re-establishing the pecking order in case I was in any doubt. It was an effective technique. I stood next to him, openly studying him. His cheek still showed the scar from our last disagreement, as our time in Hong Kong had reached the bitter end.

Eventually he folded up his paper and looked past me, scanning the crowd.

'You're in trouble,' he said.

'With you?'

'No,' he said. He touched the scar on his cheek absent-mindedly. 'I'm not important enough. I heard your name and volunteered to be the messenger.'

He took a long drink from his pint then waved with his empty glass to the barman.

'Didn't know you were a Brighton man,' I said.

'You've upset the powers that be,' he said. 'I said I'd have a word. So this is me, having a word.'

'Should I be worried?'

He waggled his head, like a dial going back and forth. 'You've got yourself in the middle of some nasty stuff. Some important people would be in lots of trouble if you kept going. Very important people.'

'A girl's gone missing in my town. Another girl was killed. I'm not going to walk away from that.'

Lawrence nodded slowly, thinking. He was silent until the barman brought his pint and then withdrew to a respectful distance. He spoke without looking at me. 'If you don't leave it alone, there'll be a level of escalation you might find uncomfortable.'

'I'm quite comfortable with escalation,' I said. 'You know that.'

That got a smile from him. Like old times.

'Take the weekend off,' he said. 'Go up to London with your Lady Margaret. Show her a good time. Stay clear of The Grange until next week. Then nobody will care if you go in there and beat up some more farmers, maybe even take that prick Baxter off the pitch.'

'What's happening this weekend?' I asked.

He ignored me, and kept scanning the pub.

'Is what they're doing connected with the invasion?' I asked. 'If I leave them alone, am I on Hitler's side?'

Lawrence sighed. He talked without looking at me. 'Not everything's about the war, Cook.'

I pulled out the envelope and put it on the bar. He opened it and read the note. He kept his face impassive. It was a good performance, but I could tell he was angry.

'I don't know what this is,' he said.

'You might want to show your boss. He's got a leak. Might want to check the newsagent's by the station.'

He nodded.

'How did Baxter get his evacuee?' I asked.

He sighed. 'I'll look into this,' he said. 'Leave it with me, and I'll take care of it.'

'What would you do if you were me?' I asked.

Lawrence turned to me. His blank demeanour cracked and he smiled, not necessarily a nice smile.

'What happened to that fiancée of yours?' he said. 'Go and settle down with her. Raise a family. Leave the rough stuff to those of us who don't have a choice.'

56

I took the London train from Brighton and was glad to finally see the first sign of defensive works. A company of engineers was working in the valley beneath the Balcombe viaduct, setting demolition charges. Blowing the viaduct would take out the main line from the coast to London.

I met Margaret on the platform at East Croydon. She was dressed conservatively, like many of the women on the platform. She could have been on her way to a job at the Ministry or a factory.

We took a suburban line to South Norwood, one of the many towns and villages that had been swallowed up by London's spread along the train tracks. A suburb of neat villas near the station tapered off into street after street of terraces, each house a step up from the London slums that its inhabitants had escaped, but only just.

Sangdale Road was five minutes from the station, dominated at the far end by Selhurst Park, home of Crystal Palace football club. The site of its namesake, destroyed a few years earlier, was a few streets behind us, up on the hill. Mum had taken me there a lifetime ago. It had been the biggest, most marvellous thing I'd ever seen, and now it was a pile of rubble and twisted steel. Progress.

Margaret put her hand on my arm.

'We can't just knock on the door and say we're two concerned landowners from a town twenty miles from where her daughter went missing,' she said.

'What do you suggest?' I asked.

She reached into her bag and pulled out two Salvation Army armbands.

'Put this on,' she said. 'We're from the Salvation Army, and we're doing a follow-up of everyone who was reported missing in Brighton in the last few months, to see if there's anything we can do to help.'

She put her armband on, the black fabric with the Salvation Army insignia turning her into a trusted figure.

'I didn't have you pegged as a believer,' I said.

'These belong to my cook,' she said. 'She thinks she lost them.'

I put on my own armband. I had to hand it to her, it was a clever and effective disguise.

In a street of hundreds of near-identical houses, each home had its own character. Number twelve looked like it had been given up on. There was a terracotta plant pot by the front door with a dried-up stalk of a chrysanthemum. Cigarette butts littered the street in front of the step. The curtains were drawn and the house was dark.

Margaret knocked on the door, but there was only the hollow echo of her knock in response. The house felt empty. She knocked again.

The door of the house next door opened, and a woman peered out. She was dark-skinned, from the Indian subcontinent, dressed in brightly coloured fabrics. She looked scared.

'Are you looking for Mrs Potter?' she asked.

'We're enquiring about her daughter Elizabeth,' Margaret said, with a voice I hadn't heard from her before. Every inch the caring-but-competent public servant.

The neighbour shook her head.

'That's a terrible business,' she said.

'Has Mrs Potter gone out?' I asked.

'She had some other visitors just after dinner,' she said. 'About two o'clock, the Irish programme was on the wireless.'

She leant forward to us, reluctant to step out of her house, but wanting to get closer.

'There was some shouting and crashing,' she whispered. 'I tried not to listen, but the walls aren't very thick.'

I looked up at the house. A locked front door and two closed windows. Not much to work with if we wanted to get inside.

'Did you see the visitors leave?' I asked.

She shook her head.

'She's not answering the door,' I said. 'I'm worried she might need help.'

'I've got a spare key for the back door,' the neighbour said. 'Come through. You'll have to take your shoes off.'

Margaret went first, following the woman through her house. I followed. The house was immaculately kept. There was a strong smell of lentil dahl, the staple dish of the Himalayas, which hit me with a wave of memories.

The house was two rooms downstairs, a tiny sitting room which we entered from the street, and a tiny scullery behind it. From there, a door led out to the backyard, where we put our shoes back on. At the far end of the yard was the privy, and a gate to an alley.

The neighbour gave Margaret a key.

'There's no lock on her back gate,' she said. 'This is for the house.'

We stepped carefully into the Potters' backyard and paused, listening.

The back door was ajar.

Margaret looked at me.

'I think we're too late,' she said.

57

Mrs Potter lay on the kitchen floor, staring up at the ceiling, dead. Her throat had been slit from ear to ear and the kitchen wall was sprayed with blood, as was the floor. It looked like her attacker had held her from behind and sliced through her neck, then dropped her to the ground. A swarm of flies lifted off from the blood as we stepped into the kitchen.

I picked my way across the floor, avoiding the blood, into the sitting room. A staircase led upstairs, and I looked up. I didn't think the attackers were still in the house, but that was the kind of thinking that got people killed. Taking the stairs was the main risk. No way to do it without exposing myself to someone waiting upstairs.

I listened. The house sounded empty. I waited. Counted to ten. Then twenty. Still nothing.

I ran up the stairs, no attempt at quiet, prioritising speed. I reached the top and threw myself into the back bedroom. Nothing.

It was big enough for a small double bed, and a wardrobe, but not much else. Everything in its place.

I checked the front bedroom. Elizabeth's room. A thin single bed with a cheap chest of drawers.

Margaret joined me.

'We should go,' she said. 'If one of the neighbours sent for the police, we'd be in trouble.'

'I thought I was being clever,' I said, 'broadcasting my intentions in the newsagent's, but I got this woman killed.'

'We should go,' Margaret said.

We retraced our steps out through the backyard. The neighbour was standing by the back gate. I wanted to get her back into her house before we told her what we'd found. It would be better for her to be in a safe environment, and better for us if she didn't start screaming out in the open. I asked her for a cup of tea.

She made it in a saucepan, with milk and spices, the way I'd had it in so many Himalayan homes. When she passed out cups, Margaret bowed her head.

'*Namaste*,' she said.

The neighbour's face lit up.

'You know my country?' she said.

Margaret smiled.

'I travelled there with my father,' she said. 'From Calcutta to Kathmandu. The friendliest people I've ever met.'

I kept quiet. My own time in Nepal had been strictly off the books.

'My husband was a Gurkha,' said the neighbour. 'We came here when he fought for the Empire. When he died, I stayed with our children.'

I looked around at the mention of children.

'They were evacuated at the start of the war, the same as Elizabeth,' she said.

'How did it work?' I said. 'Were you told where they'd be going?'

The neighbour poured tea for me and handed me a cup.

'It was chaotic,' she said. 'Such a surprise in this country, where everything is so organised. We were told to take the children to the school with a suitcase each. But the schoolteachers didn't know what to do. We all went together to the station, and there were hundreds of children. They put them all on trains, but they couldn't even tell us where they were going. Nobody knew. When the trains left, I thought I'd never see them again. It was the hardest day of my life, harder than leaving my own family in Nepal, harder than the day I lost Sujan. Letting your children go when you don't have any trust that they'll be taken care of. And then, with what happened to Elizabeth. We were right to be worried.'

'What do you know about what happened?' Margaret asked.

'Two days after they left on the train, I got postcards from my children. They were safe, and together. They were in Brighton, with a nice family. They sent me the address so I could write back. I even visited at Christmas. But we never heard anything from Elizabeth.'

She shook her head and wiped a tear from her eye.

'I went with Jenny to the Ministry. They said they had no record of Elizabeth. They said she couldn't have been on the train, because it was impossible that they would make a mistake. They had a system. But I was there. There wasn't a system, just lots of frightened people desperate to save the children from the bombs we thought would come that same day.'

'We should check at the Ministry,' I said to Margaret.

'They won't tell you anything,' said the neighbour.

'We'll do our best,' Margaret said.

58

It was the end of the day, and we wouldn't get to the Ministry in time, so we decided to stay up in London for the night and try our luck first thing in the morning. A delicate matter, getting a hotel together.

We took a suburban train up to Victoria. From there, we jumped on a bus and rode the route up past Buckingham Palace and then back along Piccadilly, where we got off across from Simpsons.

'Any preferences?' I asked.

'I only ever stay with friends when I'm up in town,' she said. 'I've never had the money for a hotel.'

My own experience was limited to a few times when I'd needed to crash after a bender with army friends. None of those had been the kinds of place you'd take a lady to.

We crossed Piccadilly Circus, and found ourselves sucked into the hubbub of Leicester Square. The big cinemas were busy and there was a festival atmosphere, even though the outsides were muted without their usual lights. There was a hotel in the far corner that looked civilised.

The rates were ludicrous. I could have rebuilt a barn for what they wanted for two rooms. I got one, and muttered to Margaret that I'd take the floor. Signing the register as Mr and Mrs Cook, I felt like more of a fraud than when dressing up as a Salvation Army officer earlier. I told myself I wasn't the first unmarried man to check a woman into a London hotel.

We were shown to our room, and left alone. It was a large room overlooking Leicester Square.

Margaret put her bag on the bed, then went to check out the bathroom. I heard the splash of water in the bath.

'Indoor plumbing *and* hot water,' said Margaret from the bathroom.

I peered in. She was sitting on the edge of the bath, feeling the water as it gushed from the tap.

'I assumed you had hot water at your place,' I said.

'Are you joking?' she said. 'I can't imagine how much it would cost. I'll leave that headache to the next owners.'

I looked at the bath and she caught my eye.

She stood up and moved close to me.

'Seems a shame to waste all that water on one person,' she said.

She unbuttoned the top button on my shirt. I reached behind her and reciprocated, undoing the top clasp on her dress. She carried on, so did I. By the time she had my shirt half undone, her dress fell to the floor. I slid my fingers under the straps of her slip, and helped them over her shoulders. It, too, puddled to the floor. I unfastened her bra. She peeled off my shirt, and I wrapped her in my arms. We kissed.

The water took its time. It was a large bath. We took our own time, kissing and undressing.

The bath was perfect. She was slippery, and smooth, and my hands traced all of her curves, soaping and rinsing. We forgot about the war, and The Grange, and the missing evacuee.

★

Afterwards, we walked out into the dark city, across Leicester Square, into Soho. In Golden Square, buildings loomed high above us, dark silhouettes against the moonlit clouds. Above the buildings, barrage balloons formed the next layer of silhouettes.

After a year of austerity, I was surprised to see the restaurant trade in London was still booming. I remembered Mum reading us something from the paper about rationing not applying in restaurants, but at the time I'd assumed she was wrong. It wouldn't make sense to restrict the food supply of everyone who had to cook their own meals while leaving the wealthy free to eat as much as they wanted at a restaurant table. Didn't seem in the spirit of the whole exercise.

So I was shocked when we walked into a busy restaurant on Frith Street. They managed to fit us in, but only just, and as we squeezed past our fellow diners I saw plates piled high and champagne flowing like it was the roaring twenties. A waiter cleared a table, carrying more food back to the kitchen than an average person would have brought home from a shopping trip. This wasn't the country we'd been promised when the Great War ended.

'So tell me what you think has happened, from beginning to end,' Margaret said, as she browsed the menu.

'It starts with a girl from South Norwood, Elizabeth,' I said. 'Elizabeth Potter was evacuated last year, when war broke out and everyone thought the bombers would be arriving any minute, and then she disappeared.'

'How did she disappear?' asked Margaret.

'We know she was taken to the school,' I said, 'and then the station, just like the neighbour's children. The train took the children to Brighton, and the other children got to their evacuation destination, and were placed with families, but Elizabeth disappeared from the process at some point, between the station at South Norwood and the destination family.'

A waiter took our order. Lamb chops for her, toad-in-the-hole for me. Margaret ordered a bottle of wine. When I asked if they had beer I got a look that showed me I was in the wrong place.

'We can assume she got on the train,' I said, once the waiter had left us. 'Otherwise she would have been on the platform after it departed. So she was on a train full of evacuees heading for the south coast.'

'Then what?' Margaret asked.

'I don't know,' I said.

'Guess,' she said. 'Don't overthink it, just tell me what might have happened.'

'OK,' I said, trying to imagine the scene. 'She stayed on the train with all the other children for the journey to Brighton. There were intermediate stops, people getting on and off, but she had no reason to get off, and the children would have noticed if she did. Then they got to Brighton and everyone got off the train, and it was even more chaotic than earlier, because now there were no parents, just a trainload of scared children, in a strange town, and some young volunteers there who were doing their best to keep them together.'

'Where did all the children go?' she asked.

'You need to match them with host families,' I said, 'but you wouldn't do that at the station. Too noisy, no place to get organised. I'd use a church hall nearby. I'd walk the children there, a crocodile, holding hands two by two, holding their suitcase with their other hand. At the church hall I'd have someone write down the details from the evacuation labels, and then we'd match each child with a host family, until we ran out of children. Then we'd send a copy of the report, with the details of the evacuation labels, to the Ministry.'

'But the Ministry told her mother they don't have Elizabeth's details,' she said. 'How could that have happened?'

'It couldn't,' I said. 'It's a very organised process, run by people who like running organised processes.'

'Why lie to Elizabeth's mother?' she asked.

'Because they can. Because they're the Ministry, and because they can't admit they made a mistake. They've got to evacuate millions of children, with millions more to come if the bombing turns out to be as bad as they fear. If word got out that the system was imperfect there'd be chaos.'

'What would you do if you were at the Ministry?' she asked.

'Lie,' I said. 'Getting millions of children out of harm's way is the greater good.'

'There's another reason to lie,' she said. 'What if it wasn't a mistake? What if someone involved in the evacuation process took her, then altered the records to cover their tracks?'

59

Frith Street was teeming with people when we emerged from the restaurant. Most of the men were in uniform, a mix of the services with a generous amount of the ubiquitous Canadians. I felt out of place. An able-bodied man not in uniform. Not doing his bit.

The two spivs at the end of the road must have had the same thought, their distinctive look making them conspicuous at the best of times, now even more so. They ducked under the canopy of a Greek restaurant as my eye flicked past them. Both of them turned away from my gaze at the same time.

'We've got company,' I said to Margaret, reaching for her hand in the crowd. 'The end of the road, under the blue awning. Two men trying not to look at us.'

Margaret stood in the flow of people and reached into her handbag for a pack of cigarettes. She held the pack to her mouth, pulling one out with her lips. I held up my lighter and she leant in.

'I see them,' she said. 'What do you want to do?'

'Find out what Mrs Potter told them,' I said.

She kept watch on them over my shoulder.

'I don't think they asked her any questions,' she said. 'They were sent to stop her talking to us, not to extract information from her.'

I thought back to the scene in the kitchen. A clean kill. No other bruises on her body. No signs of the house being searched.

'They probably know where Elizabeth is,' she said.

'Agreed,' I said. 'We just need to make them realise they want to tell us what they know.'

★

We walked through Soho, looking for somewhere quiet, somewhere we could talk with the spivs without being disturbed. I was out of my element. If this had been the woods around my farm, or even the streets of Hong Kong, I'd have had the advantage.

By the time we crossed Jermyn Street we were running out of back streets. We stepped out onto Haymarket, just as a crowd emerged from the Odeon.

'The park,' I said, pulling Margaret through the cinema-goers. We walked hand in hand along the wide pavement, a tempting target for the spivs who hung back. I was curious to know what their orders were. Were they sent to kill us, or to find out what we knew? As I walked with Margaret, I felt the adrenaline build. My heart was pounding, and every sense was heightened.

We crossed The Mall, the spivs now closing on us, having given up on the pretence. I looked back at them and they quickened their pace.

'Run,' I said to Margaret. 'Head for the trees.'

Up to that point we could have been tourists, out for an evening stroll, getting a look at Buckingham Palace. Now we stood out, sprinting past Horse Guards, under the shadow of the War Office, darting into St James's Park. The two spivs ran after us, into the trees.

We made the cover of the trees at the eastern edge of the lake. On the streets we'd been in spiv territory, a world of flick knives and leather-soled shoes. Now we were in my kind of place.

It was pitch-black in the trees. No light from the blacked-out city. No searchlights. No moon.

I whispered to Margaret, she nodded, and we split up.

I crunched a path through the dead leaves, breathing heavily from the exertion of the run. If the spivs didn't follow me, they weren't worth half of what Lawrence was paying them. I paused, and heard them behind me.

'Shit,' I said, bending down to massage my shin, imagining a branch that might have caught me.

There was a click of a spring-loaded knife. I smiled to myself in the dark.

'Who's there?' I said, turning. Trying to sound like a confused Londoner. It was dark, but I could just about make out the shape of one man. The other must have followed Margaret. The plan was working.

He didn't answer. The first sign I was dealing with someone who knew what he was doing. No polite discussions before the action. No need.

The shape lunged towards me and I dodged to the side. I felt a splash of warm liquid on my cheek and wiped it with the back of my hand, confused. There was a rustle of leaves on that side and I felt a breeze as a hand moved past my face. A low branch blocked it, and instead of a blade, I felt a bunch of leaves pressed against my neck. I dropped to my knees as the man in front of me lunged again, his hand swishing over my head. My plan hadn't worked, they'd both tracked me and now I had two assailants, both of whom clearly knew what they were doing. Blood was pouring from my cheek and when I put my hand to it again I felt a flap of flesh.

A foot kicked me in the shoulder from the side. It wasn't very effective as an attack, but it helped the man who'd slashed my face locate me. The other man was still in front of me.

I wondered if this was it. I'd dodged fate in the trenches, and in the mountains of the Khyber Pass. I'd come out ahead in countless bars and alleys in Hong Kong. Mere statistics told me I wasn't invincible. One day things wouldn't go my way.

I heard both men breathing. No verbal co-ordination between the two, but both clearly comfortable. This wasn't their first time.

A gap in the clouds gave a moment of moonlight through the trees. I saw the man in front of me. He was holding the knife to his side at waist height. I was kneeling. I launched myself at him. If we were playing rugby I'd have put my head to the side of his thighs and wrapped my arms around his legs. But we weren't playing rugby, so I aimed my head at his crotch, driving into him with all of my weight, pushing off from my legs. I felt the knife hit my back, dropped by a man who suddenly had different priorities. He went down and I scrabbled for his head in the darkness. Grabbed it and twisted. I felt the snap of cartilage as his spine detached from his skull, and his body went limp under me.

I heard a rustle as his partner repositioned to get behind me. The best place for him to attack, and also the safest place for him to be, barring a sudden kick. He was still a dangerous adversary, but he'd just seen his odds of success halve.

I felt in the leaf litter and found the dead man's knife. My opponent's odds halved again. Not his night.

He ran. Always the best move. I heard him pushing through the undergrowth with no thought of stealth, only of survival, his goal to get back to the road, back to civilisation, to pints of beer and uniformed bobbies keeping order.

I chased him. He was nearing the edge of the trees. I wasn't going to catch him. Then he went down. One second he was running, the next he was sprawled on the ground in the dark. I saw another shadow emerge from behind a tree and sit on top of him. Margaret.

There was a grunt, and I saw her falling. He was trying to flip the situation, to get on top of her.

'Please!' she screamed. A neat trick. A woman's cry, appealing to the man. Perhaps it would make him pause for thought.

He raised his hand and I saw the glint of his knife. He wasn't swayed by Margaret's appeal. He'd already killed one woman that day. Another one wasn't going to make him break stride.

I hit him from the side, carrying him off Margaret. His hand was still outstretched, and he swung it towards me, looking to bury his knife in my back. It would have worked, if he was still alive, but my own knife was already buried in his brain, thrust upwards from under his chin, no resistance until it hit the top of his skull from the inside. I twisted the knife to speed things up.

*

We hurried through the trees and made sure to emerge far from where the bodies would be found. Nobody saw us. As soon as we got back into a semblance of moonlight, we stopped. I pulled my hand away from my cheek and Margaret looked at it, wincing. She pulled a handkerchief from her pocket.

'Hold it,' she said. 'I'll have to sew it up when we get back to the room.'

*

We walked back up Haymarket, pushing our way through the crowds. I was angry with myself. I'd started the day with a solid lead on finding Elizabeth. I'd tried to be clever, with my tiger hunt, and my telephone call. But my being clever had got Elizabeth's mother killed. Then I'd had a chance to redeem myself, to find out more about Elizabeth from the spivs. I'd been overconfident heading into the trees. I'd almost got Margaret killed, and in the end we walked away with no information.

'We're no worse off now than we were before we saw the spivs,' Margaret said. She'd been thinking the same thing. Telling herself the same story.

'Doesn't feel like it,' I said. 'Feels like we've been up here on a honeymoon while there's a missing evacuee out there, in trouble.'

Margaret held out her hand for me as we pushed our way through the crowds. I took it, but I didn't feel like I deserved it.

'We'll find her,' she said.

She was putting on a brave face, but I could tell she didn't believe it. I didn't believe it either.

60

The Ministry of Health was in an imposing stone building near St James's Park, its stone façade blackened by centuries of soot. A steady stream of civil servants hurried in, all bustle and busyness at the start of the day, and we joined them, walking unchecked into an austere reception area. It was typical of the government, I thought, to take a magnificent old building like this and make it dull and oppressive.

A commissionaire sat behind a desk, warming his hands with a mug of tea, and Margaret headed towards him. I caught her sleeve and pulled her back.

'Best to ask forgiveness, rather than permission, in my experience,' I said, wincing as the stitches in my face pulled when I talked. I must have looked a fright, but I wasn't the only wounded man in the city.

We continued up a sweeping staircase to the first floor, where a corridor stretched out in front of us for what seemed like a mile, full of bustling people.

'Do you have any paperwork in that magic bag of yours?' I asked. I talked without moving my jaw too much. It still hurt like hell, but it didn't feel like I was going to rip my face open.

Margaret rummaged in her bag and produced an opened brown envelope. I took the envelope and accosted the first person I came to.

'Excuse me, old chap, got a delivery for the evacuation department,' I said. 'Where do I find them?'

The man glanced at my face, then nodded down the corridor.

'Last door on the left,' he said, before hurrying on.

At the end of the corridor, we pushed open a scuffed oak door. It led to an antechamber about the size of the hotel room we'd just left, with a fireplace and a couple of armchairs, guarded by a matronly-looking woman sitting behind a desk piled high with manila files.

'Yes?' she said, barely looking up from a file she had open.

Margaret stepped forward, so that she was looming over the seated woman.

'Lady Margaret,' she said, 'I have an appointment to see the co-ordinator for the Sussex coast.'

The woman peered at her file.

'No, you don't,' she said. She returned to her work, doing a good job of ignoring me and Margaret.

'Is he in?' asked Margaret.

'Yes,' said the woman.

'Can I see him?' asked Margaret.

'No,' said the woman.

'Why?'

'You don't have an appointment.'

Margaret sighed, and looked at me.

'Can I make an appointment?' asked Margaret.

'You'll have to telephone his secretary,' said the woman.

'Are you his secretary?' asked Margaret.

'No,' said the woman.

You could argue with this type of gatekeeper until you were blue in the face, and they would feed on it. I could already imagine this woman telling her hen-pecked husband the story at the end of the day, triumphantly narrating her victory over an unprepared adversary who had the temerity to walk into her office, where the people she defended were doing important work.

I walked to the far corner of the antechamber and opened a door.

'You can't do that,' said the woman.

I ignored her. The less I talked, the better. I walked through into a larger room. I could hear the scrape of the woman's chair behind me.

The room was about the size of a tennis court, with high windows along one wall. Rows of desks faced the front, like a schoolroom, except the people working at the desks weren't schoolchildren but civil servants. A good number of them were smoking, the room thick with a haze of smoke.

At the front of the room, adding to the classroom feel, was a portable blackboard on a wheeled frame. The blackboard displayed a set of handwritten dates, the first of which was next Friday. I presumed the dates represented upcoming waves of evacuations. There was a hum of activity in the room, and nobody seemed disturbed by my entry.

I walked to the front of the room and knocked on the blackboard. Most of the people in the room looked up at me curiously, although some ignored me and carried on with their work.

'Who covers Brighton?' I asked.

A young woman in the front row looked at her neighbour, a grey-haired man in a dapper knitted-wool pullover. He shook his head at her.

'Come on,' I said. 'Must be one of you.'

The woman looked at me. She looked like she wanted to help.

'Nobody covers Brighton,' she said. 'It's in a sending area, not receiving.'

'Who covered it last year?' Margaret asked.

'Nobody here,' she said. 'Brighton left ages ago. Most of us are new since then.'

'We're looking for a girl who was put on a train at South Norwood, but didn't make it to a host family,' Margaret said.

'What's going on here?' said a stern voice from behind me. I looked around to see an elderly man in a tweed suit, his oiled hair perfectly combed and his moustache just as immaculate. The boss, I assumed.

'We need to talk to someone about operations to Brighton last year,' Margaret said.

'I told them they'd need to make an appointment,' said the gatekeeper woman, bustling in from her end of the room.

'Damn the appointment,' said the boss. 'Get out of here or I'll call the constable. This is a restricted area and everyone's busy. We don't have time to stop work for every Tom, Dick or Harry who wants to second-guess our operations.'

I looked at the young woman, who had seemed like she wanted to tell me something.

'Where's good for a cup of tea around here?' I asked.

'There's a Lyons on the corner,' she said. 'It's not very fancy, but it's fast and the tea's hot and strong.'

61

We sat in the teashop and waited for one of the waitresses to take our order. I ordered tea and toast. We hadn't had time for breakfast at the hotel.

'Question,' Margaret said, fixing me with a stern look. 'That night you came down to Isfield and we met in the pub.'

'Yes?'

'You let me think I was recruiting you.'

She looked at me, a challenge in her eyes.

'But you were there looking to recruit someone, weren't you?'

I looked around at the other patrons, almost all of whom looked like they worked in the surrounding government buildings. Our waitress was bustling between tables, our tea not quite ready.

'You seemed so enthusiastic about it,' I said. 'Didn't want to spoil your fun.'

I kept an eye on the front door. I was betting the young woman in the office would find an excuse to slip out. It looked like she had something she wanted to share. I imagined the office settling down after my disturbance, perhaps some whispered discussions, speculating and gossiping. She wouldn't be able to leave straight away, but equally she wouldn't want to miss us. She'd be calculating how long we would sit with a cup of tea. Twenty minutes felt about right. If I were her, I'd try to make an excuse after fifteen minutes, and hurry out to find us.

'When were you going to tell me?' Margaret asked.

'Does this count as telling you?'

She glared at me. Thankfully I was rescued by the arrival of our tea.

★

Fifteen minutes came and went. Margaret and I both finished our tea, and I asked for some hot water to refill our teapot. The waitress brought it grudgingly. We were taking up valuable space.

At twenty-five minutes, I was surprised. It wasn't the young woman, it was the older man with the knitted pullover. He stepped into the tearoom and scanned the tables. He caught my eye and made his way to us, carefully looking around as he did so.

He borrowed a chair from a nearby table, and sat with us. He was nervous, and I signalled to the waitress for a fresh pot for one. It arrived almost instantly. They must have had them ready and waiting.

'Thanks,' he said, as I poured his tea. He took a sip, more of a slurp, to calm his nerves. He looked around again, anxiously.

'Thanks for meeting with us,' Margaret said.

'We're not meeting,' he said. 'I don't want to know your name and you don't know mine. I just popped out for my morning stroll, everyone knows I walk around the block twice in the morning and twice in the afternoon. Everyone knows.'

I nodded.

'You wanted to talk about the Sussex evacuation from wave one last year?' he asked.

'We wanted to ask how it worked. How did the children get their labels, and what information was captured,' Margaret said. 'We're also looking specifically for information about a girl who went missing between getting on the train at South Norwood and her destination in Brighton.'

'Elizabeth Potter?' said the man. 'Her mother's been raising quite a lot of trouble for us. She won't take no for an answer.'

'Her mother was murdered yesterday,' said Margaret, 'which makes us think Elizabeth is in trouble too.'

'Christ Almighty,' he said.

'What can you tell us?' I asked him.

'The way the process is meant to work, we give each child a label at the station and write their name on a form,' he said.

'So you'd have a record of who got on the train that you could then match with the record from the receiving end,' Margaret said.

'Exactly,' he said, pleased to have found a receptive audience. 'If you didn't do that, the labels would be meaningless.'

'Do you have a record of Elizabeth Potter getting on the train?' I asked.

He shook his head. 'It was one of the first days of the evacuation. It was a mess. Thousands of children, crying parents, untrained volunteers. We had to get them out. We thought the bombers were on their way. It was a matter of minutes. We just passed out the labels in bunches. Take one and pass it on, you know the drill.'

He gulped more of his tea. 'We got the list from the receiving station and filed it, and thought nothing more about it. We improved our process at the sending end, and now we do it properly. A lot of people got moved out of the Ministry after the first wave, so the people up there now don't even know how much of a mess it was at the beginning.'

'You said Mrs Potter has been bothering you?' I said.

The man shook his head. 'It's not just her,' he said.

He reached into his pullover, and rummaged in the top pocket of his shirt. He pulled out a folded piece of paper and laid it on the table, keeping hold of it. I looked across the table and read it. It was a list of names, with Elizabeth Potter at the top of the list.

'We've had complaints from fifteen families,' he said. 'Fifteen missing daughters, aged between ten and sixteen. All described by their parents as pretty, all missing between getting on a train and getting to the receiving station.'

The sounds of the busy tearoom faded away as I looked at the list. This wasn't an accident. It wasn't someone in the Ministry losing a label, or one girl deciding to run away to the bright lights of a seaside town.

'What do the police say?' asked Margaret.

The man shook his head. 'Nobody knows,' he said, almost under his breath.

'Nobody?' asked Margaret.

'Do you have any idea what this would do to the evacuation programme if the news got out?' said the man. 'Every parent in England would call back their child if they've already gone, and they certainly wouldn't send their child the next time we need to get them out.'

He leant in closer. 'The Germans are coming,' he whispered, 'forget the bombers. The tanks will be here in weeks. We need to get the children out to the countryside, even to the dominions if we can.'

He slid the paper across the table. I nodded, took it from him, folded it up, and put it in my pocket.

'This can never become public knowledge,' he said. 'We've got four hundred thousand children ready to go in the next wave. We got a briefing from the War Office this morning. Top secret. The Germans are close to the French coast and they're not slowing down.'

62

'How do you hide fifteen kidnapped children?' Margaret asked.

'You don't,' I said. 'You don't hide any of them. Every rural house in England's got evacuees. No need for hiding. No need for stories.'

'But fifteen?' she asked.

We sat on the train. Thinking. Looking out of the window at the passing scenery and letting our thoughts percolate. We had a compartment to ourselves. I'd let her have the direction of travel. It felt like the sort of thing a couple would do. I wondered if that's what we were, after our night at the hotel.

'Split them up,' I said. 'One or two in each house. Baxter got one. Probably his friends got others. Nothing to see. Besides, you'd be charging for them. I bet there are men out there who'd pay hundreds of pounds for a young girl, no questions asked. I doubt anyone could afford more than one.'

'Baxter hasn't got any money, everyone knows that. He's in more debt than I am,' Margaret said. She tried to pass it off as a joke, but I heard the bitterness in her voice. I wondered how pressing her money problems were.

We stopped at Upper Warlingham, and waited for doors to slam shut, the conductor to blow his whistle, and new passengers to get situated. That moment of concern that your space might get invaded, only dissipating as the train pulls out of the station and you sense everyone settling down. We were lucky. No newcomers with their grimaces of apology, settling of baggage and rustling of newspapers.

'I think Baxter's doing a quid pro quo. They use his barn as a forward operating base, like a distribution centre in the middle of the county. He gets a girl as payment. Maybe they forget some of his other debts as well.'

'What about the note? It was a demand for payment?'

'That was from the newsagent,' I said. 'He was running his own scam – blackmailing Baxter.'

There was a roar as we passed into a tunnel, under the North Downs. Too loud to talk, so we sat in companionable silence. From having a view of the countryside, I was now looking at Margaret's reflection. I didn't know her well enough to know all of her expressions, but she looked worried.

'So where did Elizabeth go, if she didn't go home?' she asked, when we had emerged from the tunnel.

'She didn't go anywhere,' I said. 'She's still at The Grange. I saw the housekeeper hanging out a girl's laundry and I didn't put it together at the time. Maybe she started acting up, maybe she did try to run and they caught her and brought her back.

'Maybe,' Margaret said.

'She's there,' I said. 'Hidden away. While we've been playing detective, she's been kept prisoner. Baxter's secret girl.'

'So what do we do?' Margaret asked.

'I'm going to get her out,' I said.

'What about Baxter?' she asked.

I thought about it. I still couldn't believe what we were talking about. Keeping a girl captive.

'We'll have words,' I said, 'but frankly I don't see this ending well for him.'

63

From my lookout point, all was quiet down at The Grange. A couple of rooms downstairs showed lights on, glimmers escaping around the edges of blackout curtains. The moon was already up, and the scene was bright enough for me to see well through my binoculars.

I looked up to see if the clouds were planning on co-operating. They'd looked like they would draw in, obscuring the moon, but that was now reversing and they were thinning out. I couldn't walk down the hill if the whole valley was lit by moonlight. In my black clothes and balaclava I'd stand out like an ant on a tablecloth. Better to wait.

I used the time to think about the result of my tiger hunt. When Lawrence had met me at The Ship, he'd told me he was only the messenger. But that didn't sit with what I knew about him. Lawrence was nobody's messenger. If Elizabeth Potter had disappeared from an evacuation train in Brighton and ended up at The Grange, in the same place Lawrence was hiding black-market goods, that was no coincidence.

And if it was a business that had any profit, he would do it again, and again, until he was stopped. I was certain he was behind all fifteen of the missing children to date, and I was equally certain he had bigger plans for the future.

I waited an hour, but the passing of time didn't help. The clouds thinned, then disappeared. An empty sky, with a searchlight of a moon, almost as bright as day. Go or don't go. If in doubt, err on the side of action.

I lay on my stomach in the leaves, and inched forward, out of the cover of the trees. I froze for ten seconds, forcing myself to count, then crawled forwards another foot and froze again. I pictured Baxter standing at an upstairs window, looking out at the moonlit hillside. The eye is drawn to movement. If he saw something move, he'd look at it to see what it was. If there was no subsequent movement, he'd write it off. Perhaps the shadow of a clump of grass. Perhaps a boulder, or even just a trick of the light. Every time I moved and then froze I imagined his eyes on me.

Progress was slow, and the hardest thing was not lifting up my head to look at the house. The human brain is wired to recognise other human faces, and I didn't want to risk Baxter seeing anything that might trigger his stone-age sense of being approached by an enemy, even if I was quarter of a mile away. Half an hour of this got me a few hundred yards.

A third of the way down the hill I encountered a section of deeper grass where I could hide between clumps. It made progress faster, and I risked a look up, through the leaves. The back side of the house was dark.

I was about to move again when I heard a car engine, and the darkness was pierced by thin shafts of light. I hugged the ground, trying in vain to disappear. The lights swept over me, across the hillside, and when they didn't return, I risked a look up. The car swept around in Baxter's gravel driveway, then disappeared from my sight, blocked by the house. I pictured it pulling up in front of the house, and listened for the sound of a door. Sure enough, I heard a car door thumping closed and even thought I could hear the crunch of feet on gravel.

I heard a bell ringing in the house, rude and insistent. The visitor was angry or upset, normal rules of civility cast aside.

The ringing stopped, followed shortly afterwards by muffled thumps – likely the sound of someone hammering on the door with their fist.

Any plan has to be flexible enough to take advantage of surprises. Baxter would have his attention on the front of the house. I imagined him getting out of bed, looking through the curtains, debating whether or not to attend to the front door. Or sitting in an armchair, setting aside a book, marking the place. It was a valuable distraction, and it wouldn't last forever.

I was two hundred yards from the house. Open grassland shone brightly in the white moonlight.

The only thing I could do was to run, and hope, so I did both.

64

I ran over the open ground, my feet pounding and my rucksack clinking, expecting a cry of alarm, a light to go on in the
house, or worse, a shot to ring out from a sentry.

Thirty yards from the house I reached the crumbling brick
wall of the kitchen garden and threw myself against it. There
was a gate leading to the house. I opened it and it screeched.
Too late for stealth now, I hurried through.

I made it to the back door of the house just as the hammering on the front door subsided. I heard the front door open,
then close, and through the window in the back door I saw
lights come on as the visitor was admitted.

I listened carefully, but all I could hear were the quiet sounds
of the countryside. It was a big house, with thick walls, and as
long as I was outside I wouldn't hear anything useful.

I tried the handle on the back door, hoping that perhaps the
housekeeper kept it unlocked. It would have been nice, but no.
I'd brought a selection of tools in my rucksack for the eventu-
ality. A knife to cut the putty out from around the window in
the door. An old chisel in case I could find a gap around the
door. But first I checked the vicinity. A small window, shoulder height, was ajar. I thanked the housekeeper and used the
knife to push up the latch, easing it up off the brass catch on
the window-frame. I pulled the window open.

I left the rucksack hidden in the flower-bed at the base of
the wall, and pulled myself up, crawling through the window.

There was a wooden counter inside, with a deep sink set into it. I pulled myself through the window, hands planted on either side of the sink. It wasn't pretty, and I'd be a sitting duck if anyone found me, but it did the trick. I pulled my legs through.

I was in a laundry room, smelling of soap and damp wood. The preserve of a housekeeper who took pride in her work.

I heard distant voices. I left the laundry and crept silently along a utility corridor. At the far end, a door showed a glint of light from the other side. I pushed the door ajar an inch and looked through. I was looking out into the entrance hall. Directly opposite me, about thirty feet away, was the front door. On my left, a sweeping staircase rose up and around to a galleried landing, and on my right was an open door, from beyond which I heard voices, now clearer and more distinct.

'. . . shouldn't have come.'

'I heard from our man in London. Cook was there, asking questions.'

I recognised the voice but couldn't place it. Someone I'd heard recently.

'For Christ's sake,' barked Baxter, 'you've got one job here, to keep the thing secure. You've made a right royal mess of it.'

There was the clink of glass as drinks were poured, then a crunch of gravel from the front of the house. Another car arriving.

'Are you expecting anyone?'

'No,' said Baxter, 'unless some idiot got the date mixed up.'

I listened to a repeat of the sequence of noises from earlier. Engine cutting out. Clunk of car door. Footsteps on gravel. Then pounding on the door.

Baxter walked wearily to the door, holding his glass of whisky like a man disturbed from a pleasant evening with his books. The other man stayed in the room, just out of my sight.

I shrank back a few inches, into the shadows, not wanting to show even a sliver of my face through the crack in the door.

Baxter opened the front door. It was Doc.

'Doctor Graham,' said Baxter. 'What can I do for you at this time of night?'

Doc stood at the door, like an actor who's forgotten his lines. He'd been drinking.

'Some kind of medical emergency somewhere?' asked Baxter. 'Should I telephone for an ambulance?'

'Your men attacked my wife,' Doc said.

'Don't follow you, old man,' said Baxter. 'Look, I think you've had a few too many.'

Baxter put his hand on Doc's chest.

'Why don't you toddle off home and sleep it off?'

He pushed Doc, who compliantly stepped back, off the step and onto the gravel.

'Good night, Doctor Graham,' said Baxter.

'If you so much as look at her again, I'll cut you open from your balls to your throat,' said Doc.

I was taken aback. I didn't know Doc had it in him.

Baxter considered this. He glanced back into the library. Then he took a step towards Doc, invading his space and forcing him to back away.

'No,' said Baxter, his voice suddenly firm, losing all pretence of civility. 'You won't. If I want to send my man to rough up your wife, I'll do that. If I want to have her dragged back here so I can tie her up and fuck her while she begs me to stop, I'll do that.'

Doc stumbled backwards.

'You're insane,' he said.

'You're the one with the vulnerable wife and children making threats against me,' said Baxter. 'So which one of us is thinking straight right now?'

Doc was silent.

'Good night, Doctor Graham,' said Baxter. 'Drive safely.'

He shut the door, and waited, listening.

The other man stayed back behind the library door. 'Wait,' he said. More of a command than a suggestion.

After what seemed like an age, Doc's car started with a roar, then pulled away in a shower of gravel.

'This is a bloody mess,' Baxter said. 'Half the town knows.'

The other man stepped out into the hallway. It was the Chief Constable.

'No,' said the Chief Constable, 'it's Cook. He's the organ grinder. Doc Graham's just the monkey.'

'So what are you going to do about it?' asked Baxter. 'And don't give me any guff about using the Brighton boys to frighten people. They've done enough damage. I want you to sort this out personally.'

'I'll take care of Cook,' he said.

'I've heard that before. You never should have let him go.'

'He was talking about your son. If we'd held him, he would have made too much trouble. Letting him go was the best way to make the whole thing quiet down.'

Baxter looked at the front door.

'It doesn't feel like it's quietened down.'

'If the good doctor causes any more trouble, he can have an accident on the way home from the pub. End of story.'

'That's what you said last time, but the story keeps going, doesn't it?' said Baxter. 'This whole thing's a fucking shambles.'

Baxter strode back into the library. The Chief Constable stayed in the hallway, watching out through the window next to the front door. He was about to follow Baxter, but paused and looked around. He looked towards my door.

I readied myself to hurry back along the service corridor. There was about ten yards before I'd come to a corner.

Perhaps I'd get there before the Chief Constable saw me. Perhaps not. I took a step back, ready to go.

The Chief Constable listened, then turned and walked into the library, shutting the door behind him.

65

I didn't know how long they'd be in the library. I had to make the most of the opportunity. I'd come here looking for Elizabeth, and I had to press on. If Baxter was keeping anyone captive, they'd be kept in the far extremities of the house. The attic or the cellar. The cellar felt more likely to me. Someone in the attic might be able to cry for help. There might be a window they could smash, or even a way out through the ceiling and then the roof. But I didn't want to assume. I'd start at the top of the house and work my way down.

The grand staircase loomed in front of me, but it was too exposed. Walking boldly up the wide stairs right in front of the library door felt like asking for trouble. There would be at least one other staircase used by the servants, probably a number of them, so I turned back into the servants' quarters, the working heart of the house.

I retraced my steps to the laundry room. The corridor I'd been using continued on, so I took it. There'd be a back way from the bedrooms to the laundry. You wouldn't want your staff carrying dirty bedsheets down the grand staircase and through the main hall. At the end of the corridor I found a narrow staircase, giving me the option of going up or down. I went up, treading carefully at the edges of the stairs, where they would be least likely to creak.

I paused at the first floor and looked along a carpeted hallway. These would be the family bedrooms. Central to the house, with windows giving out onto the front or the back. Least likely to be holding captives. I kept going up. The staircase from the first to the second floor was steeper and narrower, designed for occasional access rather than every-day use. The walls looked like they hadn't been painted for decades, perhaps centuries. At the top of the stairs was a door.

I heard a voice below and froze, listening for more. Per-haps a strange acoustic feature of the house, transmitting the sound from the library to the attic, or perhaps Baxter was on the move. Most likely in the hallway, saying good night to the Chief Constable.

I opened the attic door and stepped into a narrow corri-dor with peeling wallpaper. There were numerous doors, all closed. The first one I came to had a brass label holder nailed to the doorframe, and in it a yellowing piece of card lettered in a painstakingly careful script. 'Master James Robb, Under-Butler.' I opened the door and looked in. The room was empty. Master Robb was long gone.

The rest of the rooms were similar. Names of former servants, detritus, dust. One room was stuffed with crates. I wondered if I'd found stolen goods, but the contents were worthless bric-à-brac.

The attic was a bust, but now I knew.

I stopped on the way down and quickly padded along the car-peted corridor, peering into the family bedrooms. All were made up for guests, the beds made, flowers in vases, clean surfaces freshly dusted. I'd been warned to keep away over the week-end, and Baxter had mentioned an invitation. Something was planned, and people were going to be staying the night. It would be Empire Day. It seemed like the kind of thing this lot would celebrate. Croquet on the lawn. Champagne on the terrace.

I hurried on, wanting to get to the cellar. As I got to the ground floor, I heard laughter, Baxter and the Chief Constable.

He hadn't gone. It sounded like they were settled in for the evening.

The servants' staircase continued down, into the darkness. I flicked on my torch, keeping my hand over the light to stop it spilling out too broadly.

I crept down the dark stairs, feeling the air grow cooler as I descended. At the bottom of the stairs I found a wine cellar, depleted. Empty shelves led off a central aisle, like a reference library. At the end of the aisle, about thirty feet in front of me, was a heavy wooden door.

The door was locked, but there was a key in the keyhole. There's no reason to lock an interior door. You're not stopping intruders. The only reason is to lock someone in. Looking at the key in the lock, I knew, and I felt a pang of dread. Nothing good would be on the other side.

I quickly stepped back to the bottom of the stairs and listened to see if I could hear any movement from Baxter. Nothing.

I returned to the door, turned the key silently, opened the door.

It was a set-up similar to the attic. A long corridor receding into pitch-darkness, with evenly spaced doors along both sides, probably staff offices or storage rooms. It had the sour smell of damp. I walked silently along the corridor, keeping my torch low.

The first door was ajar, and I pushed it open and stepped into a small room. It had a desk stacked with old papers, but nothing amiss.

The next door was ajar, and the next. The last door was locked. Another key in the lock, on the outside.

I unlocked the door as quietly as I could. If there was someone inside, I didn't want to alarm them. I also didn't want them to call out. I was at the end of a subterranean tunnel with only one way out, and if Baxter and the Chief Constable suddenly appeared, they'd have me trapped. If one of them had a gun, it would be like a shooting gallery, and I wouldn't have a chance.

I pushed the door open gently and shone my torch into the dark room.

66

The only furniture was a small bed. On the bed was a girl, partially covered by a thin blanket. She was asleep, or dead. Even in the yellow light of my torch she looked deathly pale.

I stepped into the room and knelt by the bed. I didn't want her to wake up to see a strange man towering over her.

Up close I could see a bump above her hips. She was pregnant. I wasn't an expert, but she looked quite far gone.

I put my hand on the blanket covering her shoulder and whispered.

'Elizabeth.'

She didn't stir.

I shook her shoulder gently, expecting to feel her flinch away from me. But she didn't wake up.

I touched her face.

'Elizabeth,' I said, louder.

Her eyelids flickered open. Her face was slack and her expression didn't change. I couldn't tell if she was seeing me, or if she was still unconscious.

It didn't matter either way. I could carry her out whether she was conscious or not.

I stood and smoothed the blanket over her, wrapping her up, ready to carry. But as soon as I lifted her I heard a metallic chink, and her arm was pulled out from under the blanket.

She was chained to the wall, like a dog.

The chain was thick steel, with a cuff tightly fastened on her wrist, the other end running through a steel loop set into the wall. Fastened with a heavy padlock.

I looked around the room. It would have been too good to be true for there to be a set of keys, dangling from a hook. I had to check. Nothing.

'Leave me alone,' she said.

I knelt again.

'Elizabeth,' I said, 'I've come to get you out of here.'

She looked at me, trying to wake up.

'Don't touch me,' she said, pulling the blanket over her shoulders, trying to protect herself.

I thought of the list of names of missing children.

'Where are the other girls?' I asked.

She shook her head almost imperceptibly.

'Just me,' she said. 'Just me and him.'

If I was going to get her out of the house, I was going to have to deal with the shackle on her wrist. I allowed myself a second of recrimination for not bringing bolt-cutters, but that kind of thinking wasn't going to get me anywhere, so I focused on the situation in hand.

I examined the cuff on her wrist. It was iron, with a coat of black paint. There was a sturdy hinge that allowed the cuff to open and close like an oyster, and on the opposite side was a thick loop that was fastened with a padlock. The padlock was quite small, but was steel. It wasn't going anywhere. I ran my hands along the chain, feeling for the proverbial weak link, but it didn't exist. I reached the wall, where the chain had been fed through a large steel loop set into the wall and then refastened to itself with a second lock.

I examined the loop on the wall. It was welded to a steel plate that in turn was fastened to the wall by four bolts, probably carriage bolts fastening directly into the stone wall.

The wall would be the weakest link. Centuries-old stone, painted multiple times to keep the damp sealed in. I thought of the carriage bolts being driven into the stone. A thick screw thread would burrow in, but with any luck the damp sandstone would have crumbled slightly instead of holding tight to the screw threads.

I felt the wall plate, and got the edge of my finger behind it in the top left corner. There was about an eighth of an inch of movement. Movement was good. Movement could be turned into more movement, given the right encouragement.

If I had a crowbar, I could have got the plate off the wall. I looked around for inspiration, but the room was bare. Unsurprisingly, Baxter hadn't decided to store his crowbar collection along with his kidnapped evacuee.

I ran out into the corridor and looked along it. The rooms I'd already checked hadn't had anything I could use. There was one more room to my left.

'Where are you going?' asked Elizabeth, with a tinge of panic in her voice.

'I need to find something to cut that chain or pull it off the wall,' I said.

'Don't leave me!' she begged.

I wondered how far the sound of her voice carried. Would Baxter wonder what was going on, or was he used to his prisoner crying for help.

I tried the last room. It was incongruously set up as a dressing room, with a rack of dresses and a table with a mirror for make-up.

I almost left when something caught my eye. Set high in the far wall was a bricked-up window. On the sill was a familiar shape, a bulbous wooden handle. I reached up and grabbed it, brushing off a thick layer of dust and cobwebs. A screwdriver, about eight inches long. I thanked the carpenter who'd left it there, probably around the time of Victoria's coronation going by the dust.

I hurried back to Elizabeth's cell and tried the blade of the screwdriver between the steel wall plate and the stone wall. I pulled, slowly, adding pressure. I didn't want to snap the blade.

I felt the wall plate move, then stop.

'SShhh!' said Elizabeth, with a panicked look in her eyes.

I stopped and we listened. We heard distant footsteps above us. They got louder, then faded, as somebody presumably passed over our position. A faint shower of dust fell from the ceiling.

'He'll be coming soon,' said Elizabeth.

I pushed the wall plate back onto the wall, feeling the bolts grinding against their channels. Grinding was good. I pictured tiny grains of stone being shaved off by the serrated screws on the bolts, making the channels smoother.

I gave the screwdriver another pull. The plate gave up about an inch on the side I was pulling. Then it stopped. It was at an angle that was putting a new stress on the bolts, pushing them against the side of the channels. I'd have to move the screwdriver and repeat the process near each of the bolts.

'Were there ever any other girls here?' I asked.

'No,' she said, 'just me.'

I wondered what had happened to the other girls on the list. Had Baxter been involved in trafficking all of them, or was he just a customer?

'They're coming tomorrow,' she said.

'What do you mean?' I asked.

'There's going to be a big party for Empire Day. All of his friends, they're all bringing their girls.'

I worked on the wall plate, grunting with effort as I got it to move half an inch in the second corner. It was going to take a bit of work, but it was going to come out.

'Last time we went to another big house. All the men had dinner and drinks. I got to stay in a big room with a fireplace and a four-poster bed. He kept going on about how nice it was. Wasn't I lucky to be in such a nice place?'

'How many girls?' I asked.

She thought about it.

'More than ten, from what he's said. I had to stay in my room, but I heard some of them.'

'And you've been here the whole time?' I asked.

She shook her head.

'They got me when I got off the train in Brighton. The platform was full of children and people were coming up to them and taking them. A man said I was to go with him so I did. I lived upstairs for most of the year, but he wouldn't let me leave. When I told him I was having a baby he brought me down here.'

The wall plate wasn't playing ball. The bottom corner was jammed tight. I was scared I was going to snap the screwdriver blade if I pulled too hard. I tried gradually increasing the pressure on it.

'You can come back again tomorrow to get the other girls,' she said, 'after you've taken me home to Mum. She'll be worried sick about me.'

I stopped pulling, and looked at her.

You can come back again tomorrow to get the other girls.

If I took her now, they'd know. They'd cancel the event. The other girls wouldn't be brought here.

I returned to my work, but my mind was working on the problem. Save the girl in front of you and condemn ten or fifteen more to an unknown hell. Or turn your back on the girl in front of you, to save them all.

I stopped trying to get the wall plate off.

'What are you doing?' she asked, panic in her voice.

The correct answer was clear. Not easy, but clear.

'I can't take you now,' I said. 'I've got to leave you here one more night.'

She shook her head.

'No,' she said. 'Don't leave me here.'

I pushed the plate back into the wall, and pushed the screwdriver into the darkness under the bed. I stood up.

Elizabeth watched every movement, her eyes wide with panic.

'Don't leave me!' she begged.

I turned my back on her.

67

I hurried back up the hill towards the safety of the trees. I couldn't shake the certainty that I'd done something very wrong. I kept running through the logic. My decision was sound in terms of risk versus reward. Leave one girl for one more night to save fifteen the next day. But it didn't feel like the right decision.

I could have killed Baxter and stayed in the house, waiting for the other men to show up with the girls. But there would be others. Staff. Catering. Arrangements. Baxter would be missed. The alarm would be sounded. The girls would be spirited away, never heard from again.

I thought of Elizabeth watching me. Watching as I pushed the plate back onto the wall. Watching as I abandoned her.

The sky had clouded over, and now I had darkness to hide me. Looking back at the house and the valley, I saw a distant light in the woods. A light where there shouldn't have been one. Down in the trees. A gamekeeper's cottage perhaps.

I had a vision. Doc, driving away from The Grange. Angry. Drunk. A dark lane, trees on either side. Probably just my imagination. Probably a gamekeeper's cottage. But once the picture was in my mind it was hard to shake.

Better to check. Better to feel foolish finding a cottage than to leave Doc if he needed me, even if it was his own fault. Maybe it was just the guilt about leaving Elizabeth, wanting to do something useful to cover up that feeling.

I hurried back down the dark hillside, across the lawns around the side of the house, emerging on the lane between the house and the farm.

I walked along the lane, sensing more than seeing the hedgerows that formed high walls to each side. Beyond the farm, the lane descended towards the looming darkness of a wood. I heard a fox bark, but otherwise all was silence.

The lane took me into the darkness of the wood, and suddenly it was pitch-black. The light I'd seen from the hillside was gone. The gamekeeper had gone to bed, presumably. I couldn't see my hand in front of my face. I considered trying to walk in the darkness, but concluded I was far enough away from the house to risk using the torch. I rummaged in my rucksack, and flicked the switch.

A distant glint of red light flashed as I swept my torch through the darkness. It died away as I moved on. A reflection, not a light. I panned the torch back and got it again, aware of a metallic ticking sound. Perhaps a hundred yards further down the lane. Difficult to judge. I hurried towards it, keeping my torch zeroed in on the red spark. As I got closer I saw it. The reflective element in Doc's rear light. His car was buried in the trees by the side of the lane, like a dog trying to get into a rabbit hole.

I ran to the car. It was worse than I'd thought. Doc had driven into an oak tree at speed. The bonnet was crumpled, and there was a starry web of cracks in the windshield. Doc was hunched forward over the steering-wheel, blood on his head and on the glass.

I pulled on the door handle. No movement. The door or the frame must have buckled. Not surprising considering the damage. I tried the passenger-side door but it didn't want to give. I raised my hand to hit the passenger window with my torch, but thought better of it. The glass would be stronger

than the flimsy torch, and the last thing I wanted was to lose
my light.

I tried the boot, and it opened. There was a spare tyre and
a bag of tools, wrapped neatly in a tartan blanket. I pulled out
an L-shaped wrench.

I used the wrench to punch out the glass in the passenger
window, and leant in. I felt Doc's neck for a pulse and found
one.

'Cook?' he said.

'Stay still,' I said.

'Swerved to miss a fox. Think I missed it.'

I shone the torch on his face. His forehead was a mess of
blood and hair and glass, from where it had smacked against
the windscreen.

'Must have dozed off,' he said.

'How are your legs? I asked.

He concentrated, then spoke.

'Toes wiggling all right,' he said. 'No spinal damage indi-
cated.'

'Can you move?' I asked.

'Think so,' he said.

'Let's get you out,' I said. 'You'll have to climb over here
and through the window.'

I backed out, to give him room.

Awkwardly, he climbed over to the passenger seat and then
came out through the window, headfirst, planting his hands
on the road.

'I went to see him, Cook, gave him what for. He'll think
twice next time.'

'Good for you,' I replied.

'Cook,' he said, 'I can't see.'

'It's dark,' I replied.

'No,' he said, 'eyes aren't working.'

I grabbed him under the arms and supported him while he got his legs out. His foot got caught and he struggled with it, eventually coming free and sending us both sprawling on the road.

He pulled himself up and sat on the ground, holding his hands over his eyes.

'Shit,' he said.

He lay back down on the road, one arm over his eyes as if shading them from the sun.

'Bumped my head,' he said. 'Just need to rest for a while.'

I looked at the car, blocking the road. The Chief Constable was still at The Grange. He wouldn't be able to get past. He'd go back to the house. Call it in. Drawing attention to the place. Would it be enough to spook Baxter into cancelling the party? It wasn't a chance I was willing to take.

The front of the car was tight up against the tree, but most of the damage was to the sheet metal and the bumper. I got down on my knees and looked under the engine, looking for dripping fluid that would signify real damage. I couldn't see anything. Of course, all the fluids could have already drained, but I couldn't smell petrol, or oil, or anything that wasn't the smell of the woods. That was a good sign.

The front left wheel was suspended in the air, above a drainage ditch. That wouldn't help. I checked its partner, and found that one above solid ground, but several inches up in the air. The car was tilted down into the ditch.

Of course, getting traction with the wheels would be a moot point if the engine wouldn't start.

I climbed back into the car, through the passenger window, and slid into the driver's seat. I turned the keys and the starter motor turned over. I felt the engine trying to spark, but instead of the expected roar got silence and the smell of petrol. The carburettor was flooded. I felt for the choke and found it full out. I pushed it in to halfway and tried again, this time feathering the accelerator carefully to see if the engine would bite. Nothing.

Waiting was the only thing for it. At least a minute, for the excess fuel to drain from the carburettor. Hard to do nothing when the adrenaline is screaming at you to get moving, even when doing nothing is exactly what you're meant to do.

I counted to sixty, slowly, then tried again. Got a gravelly cough from the engine, let up with my foot, then gently pumped it again. The engine caught, and roared.

'You might want to move out of the road,' I shouted.

I heard Doc shuffling across the road, then a rustle of leaves as he settled himself out of the way.

I put the car into reverse, gunned the engine, and let out the clutch. The engine ran far too easily, confirming my fears, the front wheels were spinning.

I needed to get the wheels into contact with the ground. The left wheel was hopeless, suspended over the ditch, but I remembered the right wheel being a lot closer to the ground. If I could get purchase even for a second I'd get some backward movement.

'What were you doing at Baxter's, by the way?' I shouted to Doc.

I bounced in the car seat, revving the engine and holding the clutch at the biting point. I felt stupid, bouncing in the chair like a toddler, and got no result.

'I saw the way Jane looked at you,' he said, 'when you came back from dealing with the men.'

I kept trying. With my weight, and the weight of the car, I got a rhythm going, and I felt the vertical distance of each bounce increasing. I felt the car grab the ground, and it moved back, only an inch at first, but enough to give me hope.

'I'm fed up with being the man she chose while she was waiting for you to come home,' Doc said.

I carried on with my bouncing, and talked to keep Doc engaged.

'If you think Jane's still got feelings for me after all these years, you really have hurt your head,' I said.

Funny how it was easier to speak with him when he was lying blinded in the darkness and I was running the conversation with only half my attention. We should have tried it ages ago, I thought. Could have saved a fortune on beer.

'You're not the consolation prize,' I said, feeling the car start to get purchase.

Each time the car grounded I inched it back onto firmer ground. The last bounce got both wheels back into play, the left wheel back out of the ditch. The car levelled, back to rights. I turned to look over my shoulder, instinctively, before reversing properly, and saw two thin pencils of pale light throwing up eerie moving shadows on the wall of trees. The lights got closer, then stopped.

I pushed the clutch back in and let go of the accelerator. There wasn't enough space for me to reverse into, with a car blocking the lane behind me. I now had the ability to manoeuvre the car, but not the space.

I watched in the rear-view mirror as the door of the car opened. I could only see a shape against the headlights, but then I heard a voice.

'Having a spot of bother?' asked the Chief Constable.

68

The Chief Constable stood in front of his hooded headlights, casting a shadow across my car.

Not the most useful development from my point of view. Supremely useful from his. This would be the perfect chance for him to take us out of the game, as he'd promised Baxter. Almost prophetic, with Doc wrapping his car around a tree. But men say a lot of things in the presence of other men. It's only when it's time for action that you see where they really stand. I knew the Chief Constable was comfortable ordering others to do his dirty work. Perhaps he'd flinch when it came to doing it himself.

'No problem here,' I said loudly, wanting to project strength and confidence above the combined noises of our two car engines. 'Swerved to miss a fox and found a tree instead. I'll walk home and send someone for it in the morning.'

Only fair to give him a chance to walk away. Not that I wanted him to take that option. This wasn't a good man who'd made a bad choice. This was a man who'd abused his position of authority in the worst possible way, by enabling the kidnapping of children and the murder of Mary Staunton to cover it up.

The next sound I heard made it all so much easier.

A sequence of metallic clicks. Unmistakable. A highly tensioned hammer being pulled back. The firing trigger safety being disarmed. A Webley most likely, kept from the last war, regularly maintained. The prized possession of a man who evidently took care of his tools and kept them ready for use.

No more decisions to be made. Identify your enemy. Kill your enemy.

He'd made his choice, and he had one chance. I was a sitting duck in the car, lit up in front of him. If he fired quickly, and if his shot was true, I'd be dead. If I was still alive in five seconds' time, it would be a different matter.

Not a time to sit around and find out.

I floored the accelerator and raised the clutch. The wheels grabbed the ground and the car shot backwards.

I was pushed forwards against the wheel as the car shot back, and then jerked back into the seat as I hit the police car, destroying its lights, plunging us all into darkness.

Had I hit him? No shot had come. Hopefully he'd be sandwiched between the two cars, legs broken at the very least.

Even if he'd ducked out of the way, he'd missed his chance for the clear shot. His loss.

I grabbed for my torch on the passenger seat, but it wasn't there. It must have been thrown forward into the footwell by the sudden reverse acceleration. I felt for it, fumbling in the pitch-darkness. I couldn't find it. Every nerve in my body hummed with adrenaline and I told myself to slow down. In the coming fight, the ability to dictate who could see, and when, would be the winning edge. I methodically swept my hand across the carpeted floor, from left to right, front to back. I found the torch wedged under the front of the seat and pulled it loose.

I straightened up and a shot rang out. He wasn't dead, and he'd finally found his nerve. I felt the windscreen blow out. I ducked back down. Another shot. The woods lit up with the explosion from the shot, showing his position somewhere on the passenger side of the cars.

'Cook? You all right?' cried Doc from the dark of the woods.

'Doctor Graham,' shouted the Chief Constable. 'Please step out onto the road and surrender yourself.'

'Stay where you are, Doc,' I shouted.

I had to get out of the car, but going headfirst out of the passenger window directly towards the enemy didn't appeal. The newly shattered windscreen presented my best chance.

I wanted one more shot from the Chief Constable. I imagined him holding the gun out in front of him, peering into the darkness. Every shot created a bright light, which would take out his night vision for twenty or thirty seconds. I wanted to reset that clock.

With the torch in my right hand, I reached as far as I could behind the driver's seat, into the rear of the car, and flicked on the torch.

A shot blew out the rear passenger-side window, thankfully missing my hand and the torch.

I launched myself forward, headfirst through the shattered windscreen. I hit the bonnet of the car and rolled to the left. He had a gun but couldn't see. I had a torch. It was a fair fight.

He would be expecting me to come around the back of the car. The road was that way, with everything that meant to a human mind in the dark woods – the right of way, the cleared path, civilisation. Added to that, he was right-handed. Like lining up to hit a cricket ball – a lot easier to swing to your left. That's where he'd expect me.

So I took the long way, around the front of the car, into the woods. I trod carefully, feeling for sticks that might snap and reveal my presence. I didn't need absolute silence. Firing a handgun only a couple of feet from your ears is deafening, and his ears would still be ringing from the shots, but still it wouldn't do to give him any help.

I needed to get some light on the situation, but the torch would provide an easy target. I found a tree with a low crook in the trunk that allowed me to wedge in the torch, pointed approximately at the Chief Constable's position. I set it in place, switched it on, then dropped to the ground and rolled to my left, avoiding the inevitable shot that zinged past me into the woods. I hoped there weren't any poachers in that direction.

I could see him, lit by the torch, crouching to the side of his car, aiming across the bonnet and into the trees at my torch. Rolling to my left had put me at about one o'clock, if the torch was twelve o'clock for him. I hurried around the back of a thick holly bush to his three o'clock.

I was on his wrong side, side-on, with the benefit of sight and hearing. I allowed myself a second's pause, to see if I felt any kind of remorse for what I was about to do. Quite the opposite, I discovered.

I ran at him, keeping low. At the last minute he turned and fired, his bullet at chest height, whizzing over me. I hit him in a rugby tackle, shoulder to thigh, arms wrapped around his legs, immobilising him. He came down like a felled tree, and his head hit the tarmac with a crack. I heard a clatter of metal on stone as his gun slipped out of his hand and slid across the road. He wouldn't be needing it. Neither would I.

I grabbed his hair, slick with Brylcreem, and lifted his head. I didn't pause for a pithy last statement. Jimmy Cagney wouldn't have approved. I just slammed his head against the tarmac and felt his skull crack. I did it again, and this time it wasn't a crack, but a wet crunch. I did it once more, for luck.

I sat back on my heels and listened for other cars, or any sign that another human was aware of what had been going on. All I heard was the quiet of the woods and my own breathing.

'Are you all right?' I asked Doc.

'I've been better,' he said. 'How about the Chief Constable?'

'Dead,' I said. I wondered how Doc would react. He saw a lot of death, but he'd taken an oath to do no harm. He knew I'd killed men in war, but this was different.

'Why was he trying to kill you?' he asked.

'Long story,' I said. 'I'll brief you on the way home.'

I walked back to the tree where my torch was resting, and cast the light around. It was a mess. We had two damaged cars and a body, and Doc sitting in the woods out of action.

We needed to clear things up so that nobody would know what had happened. Number one priority was for Baxter to go ahead with his party the next evening.

The police car looked serviceable. My assault on it with Doc's car hadn't caused much damage apart from the lights and the bumper. I checked inside. The keys were still in the ignition. It started smoothly. I reversed it back up the lane twenty feet, then drove it forward again. All good.

Doc's car was another matter. There wasn't a window left intact. The bonnet was a concertina, and the rear bumper was hanging off. But it didn't need to win a car show. I knew it ran from my activity a minute earlier. It would have to do.

'How's your vision?' I asked.

'Terrible,' Doc said. 'My car looks like a disaster and you look like shit. I preferred it when everything was black.'

'You all right to drive?' I asked.

'Not sure there's much choice,' he said.

Now, to get rid of the Chief Constable's body.

I opened the police car's boot. It was full of equipment. I wouldn't be fitting a large man's body in there any time soon. I opened the rear door.

'Help me get him in,' I said.

Doc pulled himself to his feet and joined me on the road. He stood by me, looking down at the Chief Constable's body.

'Fractured cranium?' he asked.

'Fractured the first time,' I said, 'destroyed the second time. I thought that would do the job.'

'I think you're right,' he said, and bent down to grab the body under the shoulders.

Not easy to get a dead body into the back seat of a car. Doc went in first, backwards, then dragged the body in on top of him.

'Reminds me of medical school,' Doc said. I was glad he'd kept his sense of humour. You can never be sure how men will handle the stress of combat when it arrives.

I pushed the legs in, kicking them sideways so I could shut the door. Doc backed out his side, and slammed the door just as the dead man's head lolled sideways, causing a final sickening wet crunch. Still, it wasn't like he was getting any more dead.

'You sure you'll be all right?' I asked Doc.

'Not really,' he said.

'Tough,' I said.

69

There was a glimmer of light in the sky, catching the sea on the broad horizon. I looked down from the crumbling cliff edge. Hundreds of feet below me, waves crashed against the shore. I took a step back. The cliffs were famous for crumbling at the slightest provocation. Every year people went over by accident, while backing up to take a photo of their girlfriend or trying to rescue an over-enthusiastic dog. Many more went over deliberately. Beachy Head was the suicide spot of choice for many in the region. They said it even drew people from all around the country. Looking down at the pounding waves I could understand the attraction. Once you took that last step, you were fully committed. No changing your mind. No second chances.

Doc and I reversed the sequence from earlier, manhandling the Chief Constable's body out of the car. We carried it to the cliff edge and unceremoniously threw it off. Like throwing a sack of feed. We stood and watched it fall. It was too far down for us to hear any kind of splash.

We drove home, and I stood in the farmyard watching Doc drive back down the lane. I put the police car in my barn. It was a risk, keeping it, but the sky was getting light. Better to wait for another night before dumping it.

I was so intent on locking the barn door I didn't see the man stepping out of the shadows by the house.

'Sergeant Major Cook,' he said, stepping forward, his uniform crisp as if it wasn't the early hours of the morning.

'General Blakeney wants a word,' he said. 'I've been sent to bring you to Chartwell.' He gestured to the animal sheds. The nose of a motorcycle sidecar protruded from the darkness.

He threw me a helmet.

'I don't think he's going to be pleased we're so late,' he said.

★

It was my first time in a sidecar. It was small and womblike. An odd sensation, being cocooned while the world rocketed past, thrown about at every corner and every bump. The rider must have been waiting a long time. Must have been getting very worried about Blakeney's reaction. He took it out on me and the bike. The journey only took fifteen minutes at the speed he was achieving, but it felt like an eternity.

He showed me through a servants' entrance to the kitchens. Blakeney was sitting at the table, mug of tea in hand.

'Looks like you've been busy,' he said. I looked down at myself. I was covered in blood.

I washed my hands and face in the kitchen sink. The water was red with the Chief Constable's blood. I dried my face on a tea towel. Churchill's staff would have something to say about that, no doubt, but I'd be long gone.

'I got a call from a friend at Bletchley,' Blakeney said, pouring me a cup of tea. 'They intercepted a radio transmission from this neck of the woods. Can't be sure where, only caught it on one receiver so they couldn't triangulate.'

I sat down and took the tea. It was hot. He hadn't been sitting here long. Or maybe this was his second pot.

'Care to guess what was in the message?' he asked.

'I have a feeling you're dying to tell me.'

'Four names,' he said. 'Yours was one of them. A woman. Two other men. There was a reply but the Bletchley people couldn't decrypt it.'

I sipped the tea. Thinking. Someone knew.

'I imagine it'll give you an extra incentive not to get caught by the Germans,' he said, 'knowing that they've got your name on a list. You'll be wanting to watch out for the ones with SS on their shoulders. They're the ones without a sense of humour about these kinds of things.'

'Thanks for the warning,' I said.

He got up. Threw his tea in the sink, same as last time.

'You seem to be making a bit of a cock-up of the whole thing, if you don't mind me saying,' he said.

I tried to think of a witty response, but the truth was I agreed with him.

'One thing,' I said.

He paused on his way out.

'Last time we met, you told me to forget about the girl,' I said. 'Not your usual area of concern, therefore a message you were given, to pass on.'

He stood, silent.

'You were here,' I said. 'Came all the way in the middle of the night to warn me off.'

I looked him in the eye.

'You might want to reconsider your relationship with whoever gave you that message. Whoever it was, he's not the kind of person you want on your Christmas card list.'

Blakeney turned and left.

70

I checked on the car in the barn. Just superstition, the need to have eyes on something that you don't want to lose. In daylight, it looked a lot more exposed than I'd like. I threw a tarp over it and moved some crates and bales of hay to break up the car-shaped lump. It was a camouflage that wouldn't survive anything more than a cursory glance. I debated the optics of putting a padlock on the door, and chose security over optics, even if a new lock caused someone to wonder what I was hiding. Let them wonder.

I sat with Mum, Nob and Frankie and we all listened to the radio while we ate breakfast. The news was grim, but that was becoming the norm. The Germans had captured Brussels. To their south, General Guderian had reached the coast, chewing up French villages without breaking stride. The roads were clogged with French and Belgian civilians abandoning their homes, trudging south and west with as many of their belongings as they could throw on a cart. I thought of our troops, retreating across fields, leaving their heavy equipment, carrying what they could, listening out for the shot that would signify the end.

I set off across the fields to Isfield. I had to tell Margaret I'd found Elizabeth. I wanted her to tell me I'd made the right decision leaving her, but the chances of that were diminishingly small, and rightfully so. In the cold light of day, my leaving Elizabeth shackled in the cellar was looking more and more like the act of a coward seeking the easy path.

Billy Baxter was sitting on the grass in the meadow, staring at the Messerschmitt. He'd pulled off the covers and it glistened with dew. It had a presence. A machine designed for killing, lying in wait.

'This is where it all went to shit,' he said. 'I wish I could go back in time and take it back.'

'Keep your eyes looking forward,' I said. 'Start second-guessing yourself and the next bullet will have your name on it.'

He was surprised. Probably imagined I'd pile in on him with some sermonising. I'd felt the same when I came back, assumed everyone was judging me for the things I'd done.

'I found Elizabeth,' I said. 'She's still at your father's place. She's been there all along.'

He didn't argue with me. I wondered how much he knew, and how much he'd suspected. No young man wants to think evil of his father.

'He's been keeping her captive in the cellar,' I said. 'Chained up like a dog.'

'I didn't know,' he said. 'You probably find that hard to believe. I thought something might be up, but I didn't know. If I'd known, I would have done something.'

He was talking to himself more than to me. It was a bitter pill to swallow. We all take the easier path at times, and it's never pleasant to have that weakness brought to light.

'Mary was right,' he said. 'She wanted me to stand up to him but I told her she was imagining things. Even when she found that letter, I didn't want to believe it.'

'It's not too late,' I said, 'to do something.'

He turned to me, almost desperate. 'What do you have in mind?' he asked.

I had an idea. It wouldn't be easy. In fact, it would be highly dangerous for him. I talked him through it, and as soon as he understood, he agreed, in spite of the danger. Probably agreed *because* of the danger. Made him feel like he was doing penance.

'Midnight,' he said, confirming the plan.

'Midnight,' I said. 'Look for the lights. That'll be the go signal. No lights, turn around and forget the whole thing.'

He held out his hand and we shook. As he walked away his posture changed before my eyes. He'd arrived a beaten man, weighed down by his own demons. A victim. Now he was a determined soldier. A writer of his own story. A man with a mission and a way out of the darkness. I envied him. He still thought life was a series of pluses and minuses you could tally up and hope to come out ahead.

71

Margaret came running out of the barn as soon as I walked into her stable yard. Something was wrong.

'They're gone,' she said.

I followed her into the barn. A block and tackle hung over the trapdoor to the cellar. The dusty barn floor showed tracks – multiple people and a vehicle. There'd been a lot of activity here.

I followed her down into the cellar and looked around at the empty space. All the crates were gone.

'When?' I asked.

She shook her head. 'I don't know. It must have been while we were in town.'

'What about your farm manager? What did you tell him was down here?'

'There isn't a farm manager,' she said. 'There's hardly any-one here. They're all in France.'

'What about the gamekeeper?'

'He doesn't come in here.'

'Doesn't usually, or doesn't ever?'

She shook her head and looked at me.

'Did you tell anyone I was coming to London with you?' she asked. It sounded like that was the idea she'd fixed on.

'No,' I said. 'I didn't plan it. I called you from Brighton when I had the idea.'

'Maybe someone at the telephone exchange?' she said.

It could have been Lawrence and his gang of spivs. They'd known Margaret was out of town for the night. But they wouldn't have known she'd been hiding a barnful of weapons. It would have been an extremely lucky guess for them to come up to Isfield and then find the only valuable thing she possessed.

'This is the end of it all,' she said. She was panicking.

'No,' I said. 'It's just logistics. If we need more guns, we can get more guns.'

I tried to project a confidence I didn't feel.

She nodded. She wanted to believe.

'Did you find Elizabeth?' she asked.

I paused. I didn't know how to tell the story in a way that would make her realise I'd done the right thing.

★

She drove. Much too quickly. We were heading for Newick to check on Eric, on the off chance we'd catch him red-handed with twenty cases of weapons. I didn't think we would. I knew who'd taken them and sent the radio message. We both did.

'You were in the cellar with a defenceless girl who was chained to a wall,' Margaret shouted over the noise of the engine and the wind. 'You're a trained killer. Just you and two old men in the house.'

She swerved to avoid a squirrel that had chosen the wrong moment to dash across the road. It stopped halfway across, frozen by fear.

'She begged you to rescue her. You had her unchained and ready to go. And you decided the best thing to do was to chain her back up and leave her there in the cellar.'

I didn't respond. She wouldn't have heard me. She didn't want a discussion. And she was right.

'And as far we know she's pregnant with Baxter's child,' she said, dropping into second as an upslope threatened to slow us down.

Dying in a car accident wasn't going to rescue Elizabeth, nor would it bring back our guns. These were things I thought but didn't say as we hurtled along the lane from Isfield to Eric's place. Probably cathartic for her to drive fast, I told myself.

*

Eric met us round the back of his nan's place, alerted to our arrival by the noise of the car. Half the village must have heard it.

Margaret was out of the car before the engine had died. She pushed past Eric and threw open the door to his storage shed.

'Where are they?' Margaret asked.

Eric looked at me.

'The guns,' I said. 'They're gone.'

'All of them?' he asked.

It was an odd thing to say. Sounded like if we'd said some of them were gone, he wouldn't have been surprised.

'Eric,' I said.

Margaret turned from the shed to look at him.

He raised his hands as if she was pointing a gun at him.

'I just took a few crates,' he said. 'Didn't seem safe keeping them all in the same place.'

Funny being taught doctrine by a young lad. But he wasn't wrong.

'Under the chicken coop,' he said.

*

I slid a crate out from underneath a raised coop. I saw another two in the darkness, covered with chicken shit and feathers. It was a good hiding place. I wouldn't have voluntarily gone crawling around in there.

'Is this it?' I asked.

Eric nodded. 'Promise,' he said. 'Like I said, I was trying to be useful. I thought if the Germans do come, they'll probably set up shop in her mansion and then we won't be able to get close to any of the weapons.' He didn't look at Margaret when he spoke. He was afraid of her, I realised. I didn't blame him. She was still fuming.

72

The lane to Cyril's place was littered with leaves and broken twigs. It looked like a hurricane had passed through. Or a big lorry, brushing against the overgrowth on both sides, snapping branches and leaving a trail of debris in its wake. His gate was open.

I rushed past the house to the shed in the woods. The wires in the trees were still there, but the equipment in the shed was gone. I heard a shout from the house. Margaret.

The back door was open, and I stepped into a dank, damp house. Barely inhabitable. Margaret and Eric stood in the kitchen. A half-eaten pan of congealed baked beans sat on the cooker. A note on the table. One word.

'Sorry.'

*

We searched the house but didn't find anything else. We regrouped in the long grass of the back garden. Better air out there. Easier to think.

'What do you think happened?' Margaret asked.

I thought of Blakeney's warning. A coded radio message. Shortwave. Strong enough to reach Germany. Four names. I wondered what the reply had been.

'He was told to sabotage our unit,' I said. 'Take the weapons. Eliminate the threat.' I didn't want to believe it but when you put two and two together you don't waste time wondering whether the answer is something other than four.

'He's not a German spy,' Eric said. 'I don't believe that.'

'You can believe what you want,' Margaret said, 'but four of us knew where the weapons were hidden. Three of us are standing here and one's disappeared, along with all our kit.'

I looked around at the untidy back garden. The gloomy house, almost derelict. Not much of a life, after serving your country in its greatest war. Maybe he'd been offered something better. Or maybe he thought he was helping prevent another war. Get it over with. Get the new leaders installed as quickly as possible so we could minimise the fighting.

'What's done is done,' I said. 'No use crying over spilt milk.' I put an extra dash of energy in my voice. An extra level of certainty. Time to be a leader. Eric responded. He raised his face to me. He wanted to move on, wanted to believe this wasn't the end of it all.

'We've got the weapons Eric put aside, and if we need more we can get more. All right?' I didn't mention the fact that now someone in Germany had our names on a list. Probably best to keep that to myself for now.

'We've got work to do,' I said. 'Eric, I've got a mission for tonight. It's not the Germans we'll be fighting, but it's just as worthwhile. Maybe more. What do you think?'

'What is it?' he asked.

I told him. Gave him the two-minute version that ended with me finding Elizabeth chained to the wall in a dungeon. He didn't wait for me to finish.

'When do we go?'

'I'm not going in without doing some reconnaissance,' Margaret said.

'I've done it,' I said. 'Exterior and interior. Besides, we can't just walk up in broad daylight.'

'Actually, we can,' Margaret said. She reached into her pocket and pulled out an envelope. She pulled a cream-coloured card out of the envelope and handed it to me.

It was an invitation. Lady Margaret and guest were invited to a garden party. Empire Day. The Grange.

73

The gardens had been pulled into serviceable condition. The lawn was rough around the edges and the flower-beds were a shadow of their former glory, but in the sunshine it all looked grand enough against the backdrop of the large house. A good enough show to give townsfolk the feeling they were lucky to attend, and to show Baxter's peers he was still in the game. There must have been a hundred people, all dressed in their Sunday best, sweating in the sun. A large marquee had been set up to provide shade, but inside it was stuffy and humid.

We'd parked in front of the house and followed the sound of a brass band playing a decent rendition of 'Sussex by the Sea'. I'd dragged out the smartest shirt I could find in my wardrobe, but I still felt like a tramp next to Margaret. She was dressed in a clinging ivory dress, and looked every bit the young heiress back from the colonies. I wondered what the other attendees made of us. We got a couple of knowing glances but nobody was rude. I tried to see myself as others would. A man of wealth who could perhaps help restore Margaret's own financial position. A long tradition in the English aristocracy. When you run out of cash, go out and marry some.

Margaret handed me a glass of wine as I scanned the crowd, looking for Baxter. I was also looking out for young girls. Were they here already? I'd got the impression the event was going to be a dinner, with the girls provided as evening entertainment. This garden party wasn't what I had in mind at all.

There were young children running about, I could hear their screams and shouts and see a couple of them emerging from the tent with a balloon. But I couldn't see any of Elizabeth's age. Were they already holed up in the house, or were they arriving later?

I looked at the house, trying to work out where Elizabeth's cell was, in relation to the building. The stairs to the cellar had been in the middle of the house, and I'd taken a right turn at the bottom. That would put her at the far end of the house.

'Let's walk the gardens,' I said to Margaret. She took my arm and we strolled across the lawn, pausing occasionally to admire the roses growing in ornamental beds near the house.

We neared the part of the house where I calculated Elizabeth was being held, albeit one floor below. I looked at the plantings at the base of the wall. Were there any low windows? I couldn't see any. The cellar was fully underground. Could Elizabeth hear anything of the party?

I heard the chinking of metal on glass. It was Baxter, standing in the middle of a circle of admiring guests, close to the tent. He was wearing his dress uniform, a chest full of gleaming medals, sweat beading on his pink forehead. Every inch the munificent host.

'Ladies and gentlemen,' he said. 'We've been celebrating Empire Day at The Grange for as long as there's been an Empire Day.'

This brought some applause and even some cheers from the tent. It sounded like some of the guests had already drunk enough to make the bother of getting dressed up worthwhile.

'Indeed, we've been holding celebrations like this since before there was an Empire,' he said. This got a few polite laughs.

Baxter looked at the sky, expectantly. He checked his watch.

'I'd like to toast all of the men in service today. So many of our family, friends and neighbours have already answered the call and our thoughts are with them as the scourge of Nazi oppression sweeps across the continent.'

His eyes were on the horizon, and I turned to follow his gaze. Three specks were growing larger. Baxter raised his glass and looked around at his audience.

'To our boys,' he called.

'Our boys,' the crowd murmured.

Everyone answered his toast, and then all looked to the sky, as the roar of three supercharged Merlin engines filled the air. Three Spitfires, flying in tight Vic formation, roared over the garden. The lead plane did a slow roll as it passed overhead. Men and children cheered, and women shrieked in mock terror.

I watched the aircraft. I wondered if Billy was flying one of them. The lead plane peeled off from the formation, rising almost vertically into the sky, as if its pilot was aiming for the stars. The sound of the engine faded as it flew higher and higher. Everyone watched, fascinated, as it seemed to disappear into the sun.

The distant engine sound cut out. There was absolute silence. Even the birds seemed to sense the moment and stopped their singing. The distant plane grew larger as it dropped out of the sky, falling like stone.

A hundred people watched, united in curiosity, then in fear, as the plane fell towards us. I looked around, planning an exit route in case we had to run.

The Spitfire was growing larger in the sky. It was aiming directly at the party.

A woman screamed. This time she meant it. Others joined her. People edged towards the trees at the edges of the lawn.

I looked at Baxter. He didn't move. He kept his eyes locked on the plane.

What started as a few people walking turned into a panic. People dropped their glasses and ran. A child was left abandoned on the lawn, and his mother ran back for him. She grabbed his arm and pulled like she was pulling a starter cord on a motor, yanking him off his feet. She dragged him as he screamed in pain and shock. Soon it was just me, Margaret and Baxter, standing in the middle of the cleared lawn, watching the sky.

The Spitfire seemed past the point of recovery. It was huge in the sky. I could see the pilot. I fancied I could see his eyes, locked on us.

The engine started with a roar. The plane accelerated towards us. This is it, I thought. Too late to run. I took Margaret's hand.

The plane pulled out of its dive and roared over us with feet to spare. Margaret and I ducked, instinct taking over. Only Baxter stayed standing.

The plane skimmed the tops of the trees in the nearby wood, where the night before I'd fought for my life against the Chief Constable. It stayed low, and almost immediately disappeared from our sight.

74

I took advantage of the chaos to lead Margaret around to the back of the house. Everyone was talking about the falling plane, all sharing their newly forming stories of their near-death experience, trying them out, seeing which elements got the best reactions, stealing details from each other. We left them to it, walking slowly, pointing at plantings as we went. If anyone watched us, they'd assume we were taking a horticultural tour of the gardens.

Once we were out of sight, I nodded to the back door I'd been using, and we hurried across the grass. Nobody was around. I looked up the hill on the far side of the walled garden.

'That's where I've been coming in from.' I pointed to the ridgeline. 'If we get the girls out, we can use this garden as a staging point, then up the hill to the woods.'

'If we've neutralised everyone in the house, we can just wait down here,' she said. 'Seems like an unnecessary level of precaution getting that far away.'

'Let's review that tonight,' I said, thinking to myself that any level of precaution was going to be worth taking if we were shepherding fifteen kidnapped children away from their abductors.

I tried the back door. It was locked. I eyed the window I'd used the previous night. It was still ajar. I looked around. It felt like too much of a risk in the daylight.

The door opened, and the housekeeper glared at us.

'House is closed,' she said.

'I'm sorry,' Margaret said. 'I was looking for the ladies' room.'

'House is closed,' the housekeeper repeated.

'Of course,' Margaret said. 'Did I just see Elizabeth coming in? I wanted to give her a gift.'

The housekeeper glared, but didn't take the bait.

'Your evacuee?' Margaret prompted, like butter wouldn't melt in her mouth.

'Gone,' the housekeeper said. 'And good riddance. Filthy city brats. Don't know how good they've got it.'

*

'She knows,' Margaret said. 'There's no way Baxter could keep a girl prisoner in the house without the staff knowing.' She was striding back to the party, livid. I grabbed her arm.

'Calm down,' I said. 'If you give the game away, they'll cancel the whole thing. They'll move Elizabeth, and we'll be worse off than before.'

She pulled her arm away from me.

'I'm not stupid,' she said.

She was angry. I was glad. When it had been me telling her a story about a girl in a house, perhaps it had felt remote. Perhaps she hadn't believed me. But now she'd seen for herself. She'd seen the way the housekeeper reacted.

I wasn't any more angry than I'd been before we arrived. My anger had long ago turned into something else. Determination. I had a problem in front of me and by the end of the night I was going to solve it.

75

Eric crawled through the bluebells and dead holly leaves. His face was blacked with burnt cork, and he had a black woollen hat pulled down over his forehead. It was late evening and the last of the day's guests had long gone.

'Cars coming up the lane,' he said. 'They're getting hung up about halfway from the woods to the house. I think they've put a checkpoint there.'

Margaret and I had left the party and rendezvoused with Eric. We'd all changed into operational gear – everything black. Eric had brought everything we'd need. Knives, handguns, even sandwiches and flasks of tea. He was evidently very used to lying low in the woods for long hours, staying invisible.

I took the binoculars from him and crawled out to the viewpoint. There was still a faint glow of light in the sky, and The Grange was a dark silhouette down in the valley. I could see thin beams from the cars' hooded headlights. As Eric had said, several cars were backed up in the lane. It looked like two men running a loose checkpoint. A waste of time and effort of course, blocking off a narrow lane, but leaving the rest of the valley undefended. It spoke of urban criminals, men who could only think of the world in terms of buildings and roads.

Eric confirmed my hypothesis when I told him what I thought. 'I've walked the outer perimeter, up on the ridge line,' he said. 'All clear. As far as I can see, the only sentries they've got are two on the road, checking cars going in.'

'Good work,' I said. I hadn't asked him to tour the perimeter. He'd known it would be useful, and he'd done it. My kind of soldier.

'I'll take the road and take out those sentries,' I said. 'Eric, you skirt round the valley and come down from the far side. One last check to make sure we're not going to be surprised from the flank.'

Eric nodded.

'Margaret, you stay up here until there haven't been any cars for ten minutes. Then make your way down and meet me by the back door.'

I checked my watch.

'Assuming there won't be many more cars, that should put us at the back door at twenty-three thirty.'

Margaret and Eric checked their watches and nodded. It would give us about half an hour to get in position down at the house. I was anxious to get going. I wanted all of the men in the house, but I didn't want to leave them too long. If they were truly meeting to abuse children, something I still couldn't quite believe, I didn't want to give them enough time to get started.

'Rules of engagement in case we do find someone?' Margaret asked.

'Up to you,' I said. I wanted to make sure we were all singing from the same hymn sheet.

'Fifteen girls kidnapped and probably much worse,' she said. 'If anyone wants to surrender, I'll consider it. Otherwise I'm shooting to kill.'

'Let's try to do it without shooting,' I said, 'until we've got the girls out safely.'

Margaret pulled a knife out of a scabbard she'd strapped to her leg.

'Fine with me,' she said.

'All right,' I said, 'let's get this done. See you at half eleven.'

★

I hurried through the woods up on the ridgeline, then down into the valley. I stopped my descent before I got to the road. I heard a car approaching. It drew closer then swept past. I waited. Where there's one car, there's often another shortly behind it, a pattern set many miles back by a traffic light or another bottleneck. As I predicted, another car rumbled past, followed closely by a third. Eric had counted ten so far. Add these and we were probably almost up to our full complement.

I tracked the path of the road, staying in the woods until I emerged from the trees into a field, sloping back up to my left. A hedge separated me and the field from the road on my right, so I stayed on my side, hurrying onward. Now I was out in the grassy field, it was easier going.

Up ahead, there was a flash of red light through a gap in the hedge. A brake light. I slowed as I neared the place I'd seen it, treading carefully to minimise the noise of my feet against the long grass. I heard the rumbling of an idling car. I peered through the hedge, but it was too dense to see what was going on. I got down on the ground and pushed aside the long grass at the base of the hedge. It gave me a better view, down where there were more stalks than leaves.

The road was lower than the field, so I was looking out at head height for someone in the road. And there was someone in the road. A spiv. Regulation grey suit and trilby, a heavy

machine-gun in his hands. A Bren. Too unwieldy for successful use at close quarters by one man, but it looked the part. He
was standing back while another sentry leant down on the far
side of the car, talking to the driver.

The spiv on the far side stepped back and spoke to his
partner. After some discussion, they stepped back to their
respective sides of the road, and waved the car through.
Another car pulled up, and the far sentry stopped it and
approached the driver's window.

On my side of the hedge, I was in no danger of being spot-
ted. It was sloppy security. Its purpose was to impress the men
in the cars, rather than keep out unanticipated visitors.

I moved on, intending to leave the men to their make-
believe security duty, then thought better of it, and stopped.
Leaving an enemy position in my rear wasn't good doctrine.
I knew what Blakeney would have had to say on the subject.

There was a gate, allowing farm vehicles or livestock access
to the field from the road. I carefully climbed the end near
the hinge, where it was least likely to creak or move. I waited,
perched on the gate in the darkness of the night, as a car swept
past me, the covers on the headlights helping me by ensuring
there was no spilled light on the side of the road. The passenger must have been only a few feet from me as they passed by,
but I was invisible.

I waited a minute after the car passed, to see if there would be
another one behind it. My night vision returned as I waited. When
it was fully restored, I jumped down from the gate, landing quietly
in the road, about thirty feet from the sentries. Behind them.

The two men stood together in the middle of the road, their
backs to me, watching out for arriving cars. I could smell their
cigarette smoke, another tactical error.

I closed the distance, silently. The men were talking, oblivi-
ous to my approach.

A simple problem. How to disarm two enemies from behind. One is easy. Any number of options are available. A kick to the back of the knee to drop your man, then a boot to the temple to make him go quiet. If you have a knife, of course, the choice is to go for the throat. Without a knife, the windpipe is still the best target, as is breaking the neck using sheer force, grabbing the head and twisting viciously. In all these scenarios, the key is to focus on the man, not the weapon. The man is your enemy, the weapon just a tool. If you take out the man, the weapon won't hurt you.

But a second man complicates things, especially when he has his gun at the ready. A second man will see you take out his partner and will have time to counter-attack, or to run. I didn't want either scenario. In particular, I didn't want any shots fired. There might be other sentries on the outer perimeter, or someone in the house might hear.

The Bren gun worked in my favour. It was too big for one man. The man holding it would be slow to pivot, and then he'd struggle to get the gun lined up on a surprise attacker.

The men stood close together, presenting an opportunity.

I walked up to them briskly and silently, grabbed both their heads, and slammed them together, pivoting each head slightly to achieve an impact of temple to temple, the weakest point of the otherwise well-designed human skull. All my upper body strength was tested, particularly my upper arms, chest, and shoulders. The exact muscles used when picking up and throwing a hay bale. Muscles I'd spent the past fifteen years developing every day.

One man went down properly, out for the count, his legs instant jelly. The man with the Bren kept his legs, disorientated by the blow and by the suddenness of the attack. He could have turned it into a fight, if he'd got his priorities right. He should have focused on me, going for my head, or my throat, or perhaps sweeping my legs to get me on the ground. Instead, he tried to bring the gun into the fight. But the gun was a distraction to him and a false hope. Bad choice for him, lucky for me.

I kicked him in the stomach, with every ounce of force I could muster, aiming for the space about a foot behind him. He doubled over, out of the game entirely. The big gun dragged him down, the strap around his neck. I grabbed his head and helped the downward motion, bringing my knee up into his face, crunching his nose. He went to the ground. I grabbed the gun and pulled it out of his hands, gripped it by the long barrel and drove the heavy stock into his temple. The momentum of the gun kept it going through his skull with little resistance.

I used the gun in the same way, a second time, on his partner, then stood quietly in the road, listening out for any sign that we'd been heard.

Nothing. Just the quiet of the night.

Probably ten seconds total from beginning to end. Two dead sentries and a machine-gun in my hands. My team sweeping down from the ridgeline in a double flanking manoeuvre. Fifteen men inside the house, some or all with military experience that was probably limited to standing about, shouting and blowing a whistle.

It wasn't going to be a fair fight. Blakeney would have approved.

76

The road ended at the gate to The Grange, and beyond the gate I could see red brake lights as the cars parked. I heard the slam of doors and the crunch of shoes on gravel.

The hedge separated the road and the gravel driveway. From the house it would have presented a wall of darkness. I climbed over the gate, stayed next to the hedge and worked my way around to a side-on view of the arriving guests. In normal times, I'd have been lit up by the lights of the house, but in the blackout, I was a dark shape against a dark shape. As long as I moved slowly, I was invisible.

Light spilled from the house as the front door opened. An elderly man hobbled up the steps, dressed in formal evening wear, his white tie correct for an event that would include the presence of ladies. The lady in question was a lot shorter than he was, and I strained to look closely. She was a girl. From my vantage point she looked about ten, dressed up grotesquely in a woman's cocktail dress. The man gripped her wrist tightly, and she resisted. He muttered something inaudible, and she flinched. He pulled her sharply by the wrist, as you might pull the choke chain on a reluctant dog, and she followed him inside.

I'd known what to expect, but seeing it was a shock.

I waited in the dark by the hedge, to see if there were any more arrivals. They would have all been given the same arrival time, and there would be the usual distribution around that time, with one or two early arrivals, some on time, some late. I wanted to make sure I had all the girls in one place before I raised the alarm. More than that, I wanted all the men in one place.

These men had chosen their paths. They'd kidnapped children, no doubt to abuse them. I hadn't yet fully decided, but I had a feeling none of them would be walking away. I previewed how I'd feel if I killed them all, and found I liked that feeling. It was the same feeling you get when you step back and admire the successful completion of a job that needs to be done. Like clearing a blocked drain.

I waited in the dark, but no more cars arrived.

The first step was to scout the house from outside. I wasn't expecting to see inside, the blackout curtains would see to that, but it wouldn't do to storm a house without first checking the perimeter.

I kept to the shadows and circled the house. As I'd thought, the house itself was buttoned up properly, all blackout regulations in effect. The only exception was a faint glimmer of light from a series of windows on the ground floor, so I crept up to the wall to see if I could see in. I chose a crack of light at the edge of a window and risked putting my eye to the light. But the gap in the curtains wasn't enough to reveal anything. I heard murmuring voices but nothing distinct. I'd have to get inside the house to see what was going on.

I completed my circuit of the house and satisfied myself that there were no sentries lurking in the garden.

I made for the back door. It was locked, but the window was still slightly ajar, as I'd left it.

I checked my watch. I was early. I could wait for the others, or go in and have a look.

77

I pulled open the window and climbed in, listening as I did so for signs of movement in the house. I pulled myself through, crouching on the wooden counter next to the laundry sink, and listened again. Nothing.

I quickly padded to the door that allowed me to look out into the main entrance hall. As with the night before, the door to the library was open, and I could hear voices. This time, though, the voices were numerous, and jovial. Quite the party. Raucous laughter and the clinking of bottle on glass.

I drew back into the shadows as a man emerged from the library, accompanied by cheers from within. He hurried to the stairs and bounded up them, like a conquering hero. From the library the cheers turned into chants. 'Boris . . . Boris . . . Boris . . .' rang out, egging on the man as he disappeared from view.

I hurried back along the service corridor to the servants' stairs, and quietly climbed up to the first floor. I peered out of the door along the bedroom corridor. The man was gone.

Another cheer rang out from downstairs, and the main stairs thumped as another man ran up, accompanied by chants. He emerged at the top of the stairs and looked left and right, deciding. He chose left, and prowled along the corridor towards me. At the first bedroom door he stopped, opened the door and peered in. He thought for a while, then moved on and tried the second door. It was evidently locked, and there was a good-natured male shout from inside the room. He moved on to the next door. There were still three more doors to go before he got to my stairway, but I readied myself for action. I'd either need to slip back into the stairwell, or burst through the door and take out the man.

He stopped after looking in the third door, looked back at the first door as if making a choice, then committed. He walked into the third room, closing the door behind him. I heard the sounds of his voice, but not the words. He sounded jovial and friendly.

I assumed the men in the library were going through some kind of process to choose the next one who'd get to come upstairs. Perhaps they had names on scraps of paper in a jar, perhaps they were pulling billiard balls out of a velvet bag. Whatever they were doing, I reckoned I had about thirty seconds before the next one would be coming up the central stairs.

Getting the girls out quietly was going to be complicated if there was a man with each girl. Even more complicated if they were locking themselves in. If the doors were unlocked I could slip into each room and overcome each man one by one. But if I had to kick down the doors then people would hear. If the men got wind that they were under attack, or at risk of being caught, they'd flee like rats leaving a sinking ship. Even with Margaret and Eric, we couldn't cover every door and window. I didn't like the idea of any of these men slipping away into the woods.

I stood and thought, allowing myself the pause to let my mind work, and another round of cheering rang out, followed by the creak of stairs, slower this time. An old man, easily into his seventies, reached the top of the stairs and walked slowly along the bedroom corridor. He looked familiar, and I tried to remember where I'd seen him. In his formal evening wear he looked like a politician. Someone I'd seen on the front page of the newspaper.

He opened the first door he came to, with the attitude of a man who didn't want to be walking along corridors any further than he had to. He looked into the room.

'Hello, beautiful,' he said, and my skin crawled. He stepped into the room, and my paralysis broke. I ran silently along the corridor, cursing him for choosing the furthest door from my viewpoint. I reached the door just as I heard him fumbling with the key on the other side. I grabbed the handle, turned it, and put all my weight into pushing the door open.

The door pushed open with only marginal resistance, but didn't swing open all the way, its travel curtailed by the man now caught behind it. I heard the loud snap of a bone breaking, and a cry of pain.

I stepped into the room and closed the door behind me. The man looked up at me in shock, cradling his right arm with his left.

'Get out!' he commanded. His shocked expression didn't change as he looked me up and down. 'Who the hell are you?'

I ignored him and looked into the room. It was a nicely decorated bedroom, made up for a visitor. Flowers in a vase on the chest of drawers, a bottle of wine and two glasses on a silver tray. A young girl of about ten in a frilly nightdress.

Her eyes were on me, but she looked dazed, like she wasn't really there. I could see her processing the events in slow motion. Puzzlement turned to fear, and she recoiled from me.

I put my finger to my lips and did my best to talk soothingly.

'It's all right,' I said, 'I'm here to rescue you.'

'Like hell,' said the old man. 'Just who do you think you are?'

I didn't have the time or the inclination to argue with him. Here was a man who'd spent his life with people bowing and scraping to him. He could have used that position to better the world, but he'd chosen the path that had led to this night, in a bedroom with a ten-year-old girl. Yet his sense of superiority was inviolate.

I grabbed the wine bottle from the dressing table. A full wine bottle is an almost perfectly designed weapon for close-quarters fighting. A nice thin shaft for the hand to grip, widening to a full, heavy bulb of thick glass. I swung it backhand, turning with it to add a little more momentum and to line up my shot. It caught the man just above the nose, and his skull caved in like an easter egg. He dropped to the floor.

The girl's eyes widened. In her confused state, it took her a while to process what had happened, and I watched it take place as she looked at me, then the body on the floor. She screamed. It was a loud, piercing scream.

I ran to the bed.

'I'm here to help,' I said, trying to sound calm and soothing, although I'm sure all she saw was a large man who'd burst into her room and killed someone, so I didn't hold it against her that she shrank away from me as much as she could.

The girl was tied to the bedpost with some kind of rope I hadn't seen before. It was slippery, and lightweight, and had been tied in very tight knots around her wrists.

My knife sliced through the rope like it wasn't there, and the girl pulled her hand away from me, shrinking towards the far side of the bed as much as she could.

On the far bedside table I found the reason for the girl's befuddled state – a bottle of laudanum. Ten per cent opium. Ninety per cent alcohol. Illegal, of course, but then so was kidnapping and molesting children. The girl looked anxiously at the body near the door as she swung her legs off the bed.

'He's dead,' I said. 'He can't hurt you any more, none of them can.'

'Are you a policeman?' she asked.

'No,' I said. 'I'm a soldier. And I'm here to look after you.'

I found a dressing gown in the dusty wardrobe, and the girl shrugged it on as she followed me down the hall to the service stairs. We slipped in and locked the door behind us, just as another man thumped up the main stairs.

'We're safe here. They won't use this way,' I said, keeping my voice low. 'But we need to be quiet. Do you understand?'

She nodded, looking back at the door to the bedroom hall-way as if it might open any second.

'Let's go,' I said. 'I'm going to get you out of here, then when you're safe I'll come back and get the rest of the girls.'

I led her down the stairs, going slowly and listening out for any sounds of alarm. At the bottom of the stairs, I peered out into the service corridor. It was quiet and dark, as I'd expected. Baxter and his friends would no more travel this way than they'd cook their own meals or launder their own clothes. I wondered about the whereabouts of the house-keeper. I assumed she'd been given the evening off. Even if she was in on the secret, which I doubted, many of the visitors wouldn't want to be observed.

I led the girl to the back door, and out into the garden. We hurried across the open lawn behind the house and made it to the safety of the walled garden. We hurried past the flower-beds to the greenhouse. Inside, it was warm and humid, and smelt of fertiliser. Shelves were set into the brick wall on one side, and underneath the shelf were sacks of fertiliser and seeds.

I pulled out a sack to make a space.

'Hide in here,' I said. 'You'll be safe from the men.'

She looked dubiously at the dusty space.

'I can't stay with you right now,' I said. 'I've got to go back and get more of the girls.'

She crawled into the space.

'What if you don't come back?' she said.

'I'll come back,' I said. 'I promise.'

78

Margaret and Eric converged on me at the back door.

'Any trouble?' I asked.

'Nothing,' Eric said. 'We've got the place to ourselves.'

'What's the situation?' Margaret asked.

'I've been inside for a quick recce,' I said. 'Some of the men are in the library on the ground floor, to the left of the main entrance. They're drawing lots, and then each man goes upstairs. The girls are in the bedrooms on the first floor. One girl per room. When a man chooses a girl he locks the door behind him. The girls are tied to the beds. I've got one girl out and put her in the greenhouse in the walled garden.'

'Any weapons?' asked Margaret.

'I haven't seen any,' I said. 'The men are dressed for dinner, nowhere to hide a gun. And these aren't the kind of men that carry their own weapons.'

'Guards inside?' asked Margaret.

'I haven't seen any yet,' I said. 'I think the big boys want the playground to themselves, no witnesses. I dealt with the two sentries on the road, haven't seen any more.'

'So how do we do this?' asked Margaret.

'I think it's time to show our hand,' I said, 'we can't rely on tiptoeing around and doing it quietly. At least two men are already locked into rooms and we won't get those girls out without knocking down doors.'

'You take the men in the library,' she said. 'Let them all know the party's over. Eric and I can take the first floor and get the girls out.'

'Start with the unlocked doors,' I said. 'Get the girls out as quietly as you can. When you've done that, start kicking down locked doors. Make sure the man behind each locked door stays where he is. I don't want any escapes. I'll make sure you don't get any more visitors coming up the stairs. Get the girls out to the walled garden, and then when we're all clear we'll withdraw up the hill to the woods. We need to get clear of the house.'

I looked Margaret and Eric in the eyes. They were determined. Ready. They knew what needed to be done.

'Remember,' I said. 'We're catching these men red-handed committing a capital crime. Even if you take them alive, it's a death sentence for them from the judge. None of them will go quietly.'

79

I went first, opening the back door and leading the others through the laundry room to the service corridor. I pointed to the two staircases at either end of the corridor. Margaret took the right-hand staircase, and Eric hurried off in the opposite direction.

The main hallway was empty, the door to the library ajar, and I heard low voices. The jocularity of earlier seemed to have subsided as the number of men in the room ticked down.

I stood to the side of the library door, leaning against an ancient sideboard topped with dusty vases. I was out of sight of the men in the library, and if someone stepped out through the door I'd be behind him as he walked towards the staircase. I decided to wait. Once I announced my presence, the chances of things going sideways increased massively.

I stood quietly, listening for sounds from upstairs. I could hear quiet footsteps and doors opening. Then more scurrying footsteps and then creaking from the servants' staircase. And all the while, the low voices of men from the library. The men were talking about the war, about the Germans' fast advance across France, about Churchill. Opinions were divided over whether the Germans would cross the Channel before advancing on Paris, and on the extent to which we should fight to the last man. I heard one man stridently asserting that we should let the Germans take London without putting up a fight. As he put it, it would just mean sending taxes to Berlin instead of to the Inland Revenue.

None of them talked about the girls upstairs. Why should they? Put a group of men in a room, would they talk about their wives and mistresses? Maybe. Probably not. Would they talk about their servants? Definitely not. Talk nowadays would be about the war, of course. Failing that, horses or the price of land. Things that men talk about. The girls upstairs didn't need to be talked about. They were a given.

One voice was distinct. Baxter. He was running the show.

'Drink up, Soames, your number's up.'

'Rather slim pickings, I'd say,' said another man, presumably Soames. I heard the creak of a leather armchair as he got up. 'About time we talk about getting a fresh crop. Sell these ones on. Might even make a profit if we find the right buyers.'

I heard footsteps, the clack of expensively soled shoes on the polished wood floor.

'If anyone looks at my cards I'll have his guts for garters,' said Soames, as he walked out of the library and headed for the stairs.

As he passed me, I gave the library door a shove, and it swung shut with a solid thump, as if Soames had thrown it shut behind him. Soames turned, confused, and I stepped out into the centre of the hall, putting myself about four feet from him.

He looked at the front door, wondering where I'd come from, then back at the library door, now shut.

I put my finger to my lips in a shushing gesture. It works more often than not. This time not.

'Baxter? One of your hoodlums has got himself inside the house!' shouted Soames. 'Be a love and get rid of him, he's not dressed for dinner.'

And with that, the creeping about was over. Time to move to our next operational posture. Kill or capture. I'd already decided about Soames. Unlucky for him.

I shot him in the chest. A single shot. Loud on the battle-field, deafening in the hallway. A cloud of red mist filled the air behind him. He turned to look at it, trying to work out where it had come from. He turned back to me to ask what had happened, and I shot him again. A headshot. Point-blank range. His head disappeared, his body slumping to the floor. I stepped back quickly to avoid the worst of the mess, and pivoted to cover the library door.

The gunshots had echoed through the house. From upstairs, I heard shouts. I heard someone running fast along the car-peted hallway, and then another shot. The footsteps stopped and a body hit the floor like a sack of grain thrown off a cart.

The library door crashed open. A short, overweight man with a red puffy face looked out at the scene in the hall.

'Bloody hell,' he said.

I stepped towards him, pointing the gun at him.

'Back inside,' I said, full command voice.

The fat man tripped backwards and grabbed a shelf, keep-ing himself on his feet. I followed him into the library and closed the door behind me.

80

There were three men sitting in wing-backed chairs around a fireplace, plus the fat man, plus Baxter. Baxter stood at a sideboard that had been set up as a bar.

'Get the hell out of here, Cook. This has got nothing to do with you.' He snapped this off as if he was giving his dinner order to the cook. A lack of clarity on his part, the result of generations of his ancestors giving orders to generations of my ancestors. A pattern of behaviour hard to break out of.

I thought about Mary, who'd come to see me hours before being killed by his hired men. I thought about Jane, who'd been violated in order to intimidate me and Doc. I thought about Elizabeth in the cellar, chained to a wall. But the time for thinking was over, and I was never very good at talking.

I raised the gun and fired. If your man is close enough you don't need to aim, just fire first. There'll always be the second shot to finish things off.

There was no chance for him to draw his own gun. One second he was standing in his library, king of his domain. The next second he was dying, his destroyed body going into shock as it tried to pull blood towards the core. I'd hit him in the chest, destroying his vital organs. Instant heart failure. He collapsed as gravity pulled the blood out of his head. The crystal decanter he'd been holding shattered on the floor. His legs buckled and he collapsed on the broken glass, his face hitting the floor with a wet crunch. No need for a second shot.

I turned to the fat man. He was too close to me for my liking.

'Sit down,' I ordered. He backed up to a settee opposite the fire and sat meekly. The three others froze in their chairs, like patrons of a club trying their best to ignore unseemly behaviour by a visitor.

'I'm going to pretend you're all decent chaps who've got caught up in something you shouldn't have,' I said. 'Let's say it was all Baxter's fault, he was the ringleader. He was the one who twisted your arms.'

I had their interest. They could see an escape route.

'One of you is going to give me the name of the criminal behind all of this and the details of how I can find him. The man that does that will walk out of here alive. The rest of you are dead. Who's up first?'

The men eyed each other. They'd just seen their leader go down, and the room stank of gunpowder and blood.

'One minute,' I said. I'd given them hope. Now I was giving them a deadline.

They looked at each other urgently. Nobody wanted to be the one who gave in, but nobody wanted to die. One of those desires was based on a social code, the other was absolute. It was just a matter of time.

'None of us is going to say anything to you,' said the man sitting closest to the fire. He was the oldest in the room. About sixty. Perhaps that gave him some kind of authority over the others. He'd probably been a general in the last war, manning a desk in Whitehall and sending millions of boys to their deaths. He sat stiffly, and looked at me with a level of distaste that only the English upper class can muster.

I checked my watch. 'You're all wasting your minute,' I said.

'Baxter was the one with the details,' said another man. He was in his forties. Pale blond hair and pale skin. White jacket instead of the usual black. Someone who liked to think for himself. 'You said it yourself,' he said. 'We're all just decent chaps who got dragged into something by Baxter. He's the one with the contacts in Brighton.'

I made a show of considering this. I wanted to give him hope. Hope makes men work hard. I needed one of these men to work hard to save his skin. If they all gave up, I'd leave the room with nothing more than I came in with.

'Tell me more about Brighton,' I said.

'I don't know any more,' he said.

'Bad luck for you, in that case,' I said. 'I bet someone in this room knows the slightest bit more than you do. That person's going to walk out of here a free man.'

They were starting to think. Thinking was good. It meant they were deciding to play my game.

The fat man spoke. 'I don't know much more than Tommy,' he said, 'I never met the man, but Baxter was afraid of him. He told me once the man tortured a rival and took over his territory. The story was he held the other chap's head over a fire until his face started cooking.'

'I told Baxter this would come to a bad end,' said the old man by the fire. 'You can't associate with these people without it coming back to bite you.'

'Thank you,' I said to the fat man. 'What's your name?'

He looked around nervously, as if for permission. 'Everyone calls me Tubs,' he said.

'Fuck everyone,' I said. 'What do you call yourself?

'Malcolm,' he said.

'All right, Malcolm,' I said. 'Looks like you're the winner. Grab your things and let's get out of here.'

Malcolm made to get up but was interrupted.

'Wait a minute,' said the pale man. 'I've got more.'

'Better than Malcolm's contribution?' I asked. 'Don't get my hopes up if you can't deliver.'

'Yes, yes, better than that bullshit. That story about the face, everyone knows that. I know where he is. I went to Brighton once with Baxter, and Baxter said he had to see a man about a dog. He left me in a pub, but I watched through the window and saw him go into a place just up the road. One of those tall black warehouses, built for hanging fishing nets.'

'Which pub?' I asked.

'I don't know,' he said. 'A pub. Just off the seafront, near a chip shop.'

I nodded to him. I wanted to keep him onside, in case he had any more useful titbits of information.

The door opened behind me.

'We've got them all,' Eric said. Margaret was beside him.

I checked my watch. Ten minutes to midnight. 'Open all the curtains,' I said. 'Upstairs as well.'

Margaret disappeared. I heard her taking the stairs two at a time.

'What do you want to do with this lot?' Eric asked.

'Tie them up and leave them in here,' I said. 'The police can come and get them tomorrow.'

'You said I could go,' said the pale man with the information.

'One more question,' I said. 'What's the name of the girl you've been keeping prisoner and raping?'

The pale man opened his mouth. Then he closed it. A tricky situation. Not something you'd want to admit to.

'I lied,' I said. 'You're staying here with the others. You can spend the night thinking about what to tell the police.'

Eric pulled open the wooden shutters. They folded back on themselves, into a space in the walls next to the windows. Intricate workmanship. Hundreds of years old. Opening them, letting the light spill out, felt wrong after a year of blackout regulations. Like a dream where you find yourself in public without your clothes on.

With the blinds open, he jammed his knife in the track to the side of one of the windows, cutting the sash cord. He pulled it out, through the pulley at the top of the window track. It was useful rope, dense, designed not to stretch, and rough, so that tight knots were hard to slip out of.

He took his freshly acquired sash cord and cut it into sections, then went to work tying up the men. He threw me two sections.

The men complained, but only enough to save face. They were relieved. They'd faced death and survived. They'd cheated me by holding back useful information, and they'd be able to face themselves in the morning. They probably had all manner of stories running through their minds whereby their friends in high places would help them get their revenge on me for humiliating them. It was the story that their lives had taught them to believe.

Eric nodded to me once we'd finished tying them up.

'Lock the doors,' I said. 'I don't want any of them getting out.'

Eric found a connecting door at the far end of the library, and locked it, bringing the key back with him. We locked the main door behind us on our way out.

'You sure about that?' he asked. 'I can go back in there and keep watch on them until the police get here if you want.'

'The police aren't coming,' I said.

81

We left via the back door and walked out into the bright, moonlit night. Eric led the way to the walled garden. The smell of flowers hit me as we walked into its protected space. The girls huddled together by the far wall, just outside the greenhouse, Margaret stood protectively over them.

'We've got to go,' I said loudly as I strode over to them.

I nodded up the hill behind the wall, to my lookout point in the treeline.

'We're not out of danger yet,' I said. 'We've got to get up there quickly.'

'Why?' asked Margaret. 'We can stay here. You can take a car into town and raise the alarm.'

A siren wailed in the distance, the air-raid warning from Uckfield, as if conjured by Margaret's words. Everyone looked at each other.

'Probably a drill,' said Margaret. She looked up at the bright moon. A bomber's moon.

Behind her, every window blazed with light.

'It's not a drill,' I said.

Margaret picked up on the certainty in my voice.

'What is it?' she said.

'A bomber,' I said.

'How do you know?' asked Eric.

'I know,' I said.

Margaret looked me in the eye. I nodded.

'All right,' she said, 'let's go.'

She called to the girls, rounding them up for the final push up the hill.

I scanned the girls, looking for Elizabeth. I didn't expect she'd be happy to see my face after I'd left her the day before. I needed to apologise. I needed her to tell me it had all worked out in the end.

But I couldn't find her.

'Where's Elizabeth?' I asked.

'Who?' asked Eric, as he picked up one of the younger girls.

'Elizabeth,' I said to Margaret, urgently.

She flicked her eyes over the girls, desperate to be wrong.

'Isn't she one of these?' she said.

'No,' I said.

I looked at them all again, slowing down. Looking closely. Perhaps I'd been wrong. Perhaps I'd skipped over her in the darkness. Perhaps I'd forgotten her face. But I hadn't forgotten, and I hadn't skipped over her. She wasn't there.

'Did you check the cellar?' I asked.

'No,' said Eric.

'I thought you were getting her,' said Margaret.

I looked at the house, looming against the bright sky, every window blazing brightly. I checked my watch. Three minutes to midnight.

As if on cue, a closer air-raid siren wailed into life, this one with the signal for approaching danger. And underneath the siren, another sound. More of a feeling than a sound. A deep rumble, felt in the stomach. A Messerschmitt 109 fighter-bomber, weighed down by a 250kg high-explosive bomb, invisible in the dark sky.

'Go,' said Margaret. 'We'll get these up the hill.'

She had to shout. I was already running back towards the house.

82

As I ran, I thought through the timings. One minute to the cellar. One minute to free Elizabeth, assuming she was still chained to the wall. One minute to get her back out. It was a fantasy of course, a best-case scenario that relied on everything falling my way.

The back door was the first hurdle. I grabbed the handle and pulled, but it didn't move. Eric must have locked it on his way out. I stepped back and pistoned my foot into the door, next to the lock. It burst open. Five seconds wasted. I ran along the service corridor, which was longer than in my memory. I took the stairs down to the cellar three at a time, ran through the wine cellar, yanked open the far door, and ran along the last corridor to her room.

I opened the door and fumbled for the electric light switch. After what felt like forever, but was probably a second, I found it.

The light came on. It was a weak bulb, dimmed further by wartime voltage. It gave the illusion of light, rather than the useful reality.

Elizabeth lay on the bed. For a second I thought there was a cat nestled on the bed next to her, but it wasn't a cat. It was a black shape – a thick, dark stain that spread beyond the bed and onto the floor. I hurried to her side and touched the blackness. My hand came back sticky. Blood. On the bed. Pooled on the floor.

Her left hand, still shackled, was cradled by her chest. I gently pulled it away from the blood. The wrist was torn and bloodied.

Her right hand had flopped off the side of the bed, and below it, on the floor, was the screwdriver I'd left the previous night. She must have used the screwdriver blade, dragging it across her skin repeatedly until it did enough damage to get to the artery.

I felt her neck for a pulse, half listening for the approaching plane, half praying. The plane would arrive in its own time. The prayer was going nowhere.

I couldn't feel a pulse. That left me with a decision. Leave her here or take her with me. But it wasn't a decision. Not really. She was coming with me. I'd left her once. I wouldn't leave her again. If nothing else, she would get a decent burial, in a pretty graveyard, where the sun would warm the grass, not here in her dungeon, the place of her torture and death.

I took the screwdriver from the puddle of blood. It was slick and I wiped it on my shirt. The blood was still warm.

I shoved the blade behind the metal wall plate, and yanked. The same routine as the night before. Each corner gave, and then stopped, and I had to move on.

As I worked, the noise of the plane grew louder, like approaching thunder. It built until I heard it roar over the house at what must have been rooftop height. I braced myself for the impact of the bomb. Nothing.

Perhaps the bomb had dropped but not detonated. Or perhaps it was a reconnaissance run. I pictured Billy getting his bearings, roaring up the valley where he'd spent his boyhood. Had it been him that afternoon, doing a practice run? Did it look different from above? I imagined him pulling up out of the valley, heading into the open sky before starting a wide circle, ready to come back on his bombing run.

The plate was clear of the wall by about an inch, and the thick bolts were loose. I grabbed the plate and pulled. I felt some give, but then the friction increased until it was jammed. The more I pulled, the more it jammed. I gave it a thump, to free it up, then went to work again with the screwdriver, corner by corner.

I kept working until the clearance from the plate to the wall was closer to two inches, and I could feel it getting looser. I grabbed the plate with both hands and pulled. I felt it give. I gave it more pressure, pulling with my arms and my back, leaning with it. It wasn't going to work.

Suddenly, it all gave way at once. I flew backwards, thumping my head against the old stone wall.

A bolt of pure anger surged through me. Anger at the world, anger at the war, anger at the men who would imprison a young girl, but most of all anger at myself.

There was a murmur from the bed. Or perhaps it was my imagination.

I hurried over and knelt once again by Elizabeth's side. I told myself not to get my hopes up. The noise had probably been an echo of my own shout, or it was my imagination. I touched her face with my blood and brick-dust-caked fingers. Her eyes flickered. She was alive.

But it was too late.

For the second time, the roar of the attacking plane had grown deafening. I felt the house vibrate as the plane passed directly overhead, and I knew we had seconds left.

I pulled Elizabeth off the bed, and rolled her under the metal bed frame, doing everything I could to cover her with my body, holding her for dear life. That was my last clear memory.

83

There was no sound. The earth moved sideways while we stayed still. Or perhaps we moved and the earth stayed still. The cellar wall that Elizabeth had been shackled to only a minute earlier was suddenly liquid, and we were in the air. But that was impossible, because there was no air, only dust. I tried to gulp mouthfuls of it, to refill my empty lungs, but that didn't work. I was drowning in dust. All I could do was to hold on to Elizabeth and hope they found our bodies when they dug through the debris.

I felt the house falling. I felt every brick grinding and sliding against its neighbour. I felt it pattering like raindrops, like standing under a waterfall. The air was forced out of my body, and out of the space, until there was no space, just the inch of dust-filled air in front of my mouth, and the inch where I could flex my fingers.

There was no pain. No feeling at all. I wondered if I was close to dying, or if I had already died. Elizabeth was cradled in my arms. I had an overwhelming desire to sleep, so I held Elizabeth, and breathed, and slept.

84

I heard voices, muffled by layers and layers of dust and bricks. People were talking with clear, measured instructions. They were calm, doing a job. A movement triggered a shower of dust onto me.

I held Elizabeth. Her back was to me, my arms around her. There wasn't much room to move, so we stayed as we were.

'They're coming for us,' I said. 'We were hit by a bomb, but I think we're going to be all right.'

There was a scraping sound as something large was moved above us. I hoped they knew what they were doing. It was like a game I'd played as a boy where you pulled sticks one by one out of a pile and hoped you weren't the one who brought the whole pile crashing down.

A chink of light burst through a gap in the rubble. I was shocked at how bright it was. I thought it was the middle of the night.

'Over here!' I heard a woman shout. Then the voice was clearer.

'Stay still,' she said, 'we're coming for you.'

85

We were in the midst of a well-rehearsed production. A calm woman, all business, asked us how many were trapped. I told her there were two of us. She asked if we could smell gas, and I said no. She asked if there was any water. I said no. She said they were bringing in heavy equipment to lift the larger pieces of masonry and concrete resting precariously above us.

I drifted in and out of consciousness, dreaming vivid dreams that all involved the physical sensation of being shaken like a rag doll.

I dreamt that Elizabeth was my daughter, and she was a baby. I was holding her, telling her I'd look after her every day of her life. In my dream I turned around to show her to my wife, but there was nobody there, and I woke up instead, with tears silently running down my face.

They cleared a way through the debris. A matronly-looking ARP warden, the owner of the all-business voice, crouched beside me.

'What's your name?' she asked.

It was hard to think. I was in a fog and I couldn't access my thoughts. My name came to me from somewhere.

'John,' I said, feeling like a child talking to his mother.

Two men joined her, standing behind at a respectful distance.

'Looks like you've got someone else with you, John,' said the warden. 'What's her name?'

'Elizabeth,' I said.

The ARP warden reached out her hands and brushed the hair from Elizabeth's face. She held her hand to Elizabeth's neck, and waited. She turned back to the men and shook her head.

'We're going to need you to let go of Elizabeth, John,' the warden said. 'We need to get you both out of here. You can lean on me as we climb out, and these men can carry Elizabeth out.'

'Be careful with her,' I said, 'she's pregnant.'

'We'll take good care of her, John,' said the warden. She was using my name whenever she could. It was very effective.

As gently as I could, I unwrapped my arms from around Elizabeth, and stood up. The world was swimming, and I sat down.

'No time for that now, John,' said the warden, 'we've got to get you out of here.' She looked back at the men, and they advanced on Elizabeth.

'No,' I said, 'I'll carry her.'

The men looked at the warden, and she nodded. They stepped back, respectfully.

I knelt down, and scooped up Elizabeth, holding her under her knees and shoulders. People talk about dead weight, but there's no such thing. She weighed exactly the same dead as she would have done alive.

I carried her up, out of the wreckage. As soon as we were out, the warden gave the all-clear, and a tractor that had been holding up a wall backed away, letting the wall collapse back into the cellar.

The site was lit up by two searchlights, powered by throbbing generators. A fire engine idled in the lane, and smoke rose from the far side of the rubble. I thought of what would have happened if fire had got to us while we'd been trapped.

He must have been coming down the valley from north to south. The bomb had hit just before the house. There was a crater about fifty feet across and almost as deep. The house was entirely gone. The shockwave had reduced the building materials to their base matter – sand, clay, wood, all mingled together in a fine dust that hung in the air and coated the trees and the people. At the far side of the driveway, in the shadows by the hedge, there was a row of bodies, covered respectfully with blankets.

I carried Elizabeth to a quiet spot, where the grass was soft, and lay her down. I felt a hand on my shoulder. It was Margaret. Behind her, in the shadows, the girls we had saved watched sombrely. Doc was checking them, one by one.

Someone handed me a mug of tea.

'They didn't think anyone would come out alive,' Margaret said. Her voice sounded distant, like I was underwater.

Doc hurried over, carrying his bag. He pulled out a stethoscope and put it on Elizabeth's chest, listening intently.

I saw Neesham in the shadows, checking on the line of corpses. He had his notebook out. He looked over and saw me.

I needed air. I needed to get away from the bodies. I felt Margaret reach out for me but her hand fell away as I started walking.

My legs complained as I headed uphill, the dark woods beckoning.

Behind me, I heard Neesham calling my name.

But I was already gone.

86

The Chief Constable's car drove smoothly enough, considering the amount of damage I'd inflicted the previous night. I took the A26 to Lewes, through the winding streets of the old market town, past the silhouette of the ruined castle. From there it was just a short run to Brighton, to the fairy-tale architecture of the Pavilion, spoken for by Hitler as his summer home, or so they said.

I stopped at a makeshift barrier on the seafront – a metal pole across half the road, counterweighted at one end so a sentry could raise it. Beyond the barrier, petrol tankers were queued up outside the aquarium, at the entrance to the pier. An elderly sentry reluctantly put down his book.

'What's going on, soldier?' I asked.

The police car worked its spell on him. 'Filling up the aquarium tanks with petrol, sir. Going to flood the sea and set it alight when Jerry tries to land.'

The insanity of the idea fit the night perfectly.

'Good man,' I said. 'Carry on.'

'Sir,' he said, saluting me as I drove the car around the barricade.

The seafront was deserted. Black waves pounded the beach. They'd strung up rolls of barbed wire. Better than nothing, but only just.

I turned in at Ship Street, past the pub, past a bend in the road that opened up a view of the next row of buildings – tall, wood-clad warehouses, black with tar.

A man stepped out of a doorway. A big man, tall, barrel-chested, arms like a gorilla.

He stepped into the moonlight, in the middle of the pavement. Beware. I'm here, and you shouldn't be. Be on your way unless you want to come to harm.

It probably worked on the punters kicked out of The Ship. Probably even worked on the occasional bobby who took a turn up here by mistake. But it didn't work on me. I wasn't looking to stay out of harm's way. I was the living embodiment of harm's way, as far as this man was concerned.

I drove past slowly and we eyeballed each other. He watched me to the end of the road, where I turned left, circling back down to the seafront.

I killed the engine and got out, smelling the sea air, my throat still thick with dust.

The pencil detonator was a small copper tube. A green stripe showed it gave a ten-minute delay, give or take.

I crushed the end with my heel and pulled out the brass safety strip. I shook the tube, just to make sure, and heard the tinkle of broken glass – the acid would be doing its work, eating through the wire that held back the spring-loaded detonator pin. When the pin was unleashed it would shoot along the tube, smashing into the percussion cap.

The detonator was designed to go with a combustible material, TNT being the preferred choice. I didn't have any TNT with me, but I had something almost as good.

I unscrewed the car's petrol cap, dropped in the detonator, and screwed the cap back on. Ten minutes, give or take.

87

I drove back up Ship Street, trying to ignore the crawling sensation going up my back. I watched the sentry as I rounded the bend. I didn't see any signs he had a gun. No sag in the suit jacket. No bulge under the arm.

I pulled up on the right-hand kerb. He leant down, arms folded on my open window, blocking my exit.

'Mr Cook,' he said, politely.

'I'm here to see Lawrence,' I said.

'Mr Lawrence isn't available to visitors at the moment,' he said, with a smirk. I assumed it meant Lawrence had a woman with him.

'That's a problem,' I said. I turned the engine off and pulled the key out of the ignition. Ten minutes. Give or take.

'Maybe for you,' he said, 'not for me.'

I put my hands back on the steering-wheel, a good excuse to keep them high, close to his face.

I pictured the acid, eating its way through the thin wire.

'They've put barbed wire on the beach,' I said.

He turned his head, slightly, towards the beach. An unconscious reaction. For a short second his eyes weren't on me, and the side of his face was exposed.

I launched my right elbow, already steering-wheel height. I caught him just under the ear, where the jawbone meets the skull. A weak point. He should have gone down, but he stepped back, groggy and reeling. I hoped it was enough for me to get the door moving. I grabbed the handle and put my shoulder into it. The door opened about a foot before it slammed into his chest. I kept pushing through. I've come close to death in a lot of places. I wasn't going to go out finally in a car that I'd bombed myself.

He pushed back, locking his leg on the pavement. I thought of the acid doing its work, and gave it everything I had. My survival instinct was stronger than his desire to win. I tumbled out of the car, rolling away from him as he kicked at me, his boot scraping my face. I pushed myself upright and we faced off against each other.

Now I had freedom of movement, the result was a foregone conclusion. He'd demonstrated a certain level of physical fortitude by staying upright after the elbow to his face, but it would have weakened him. Besides that, I had a gun and he didn't.

I pulled the revolver out of my pocket and pointed it at his chest.

'Your choice,' I said. 'You can die here for a man who'll be dead himself in five minutes, or you can go home. All the same to me.'

His eyes flicked up to the warehouse, then back to the gun. I thought he was going to go down fighting, doing his duty, but he turned and ran, up the road and around the corner. A wise man. Rarer than you'd think.

I looked up at the black timbers of the warehouse. A classic problem. How to extricate an enemy from an entrenched and presumably fortified position.

Option one, the head-on attack. Invariably the worst option. Even though he'll try to remind himself you're not stupid and hence you're unlikely to take the direct approach, your opponent will set himself up to defend it. He'd be a fool not to. He'll point his gun that way, and orient his body towards it. Waiting for the knock at the front door. The run across no-man's-land. If you take that route, you'd better be prepared to encounter heavy fire. And if you fail, you've only got yourself to blame for your lack of imagination and planning.

Option two, make him come to you. Make his current situation so untenable that rushing out into a hail of your bullets becomes his preferred option. Let the artillery bomb him out of his foxhole. An attractive option for the man in the trench, but proven time and again to be futile. Nevertheless, worth considering. I could burn him out, let the car bomb do its job. The timber building, black with tar, would go up instantly. But then he'd be in control of his reaction. Once I set things in motion he'd be on his guard, probably sneak out the back door and come at me from down the road, out of the shadows.

Which led to option three, let him think he's in control. Let him know where you are, and let him think of a way to outflank you, to surprise you. Then disrupt his plan once it's in motion. The best option, if you can outsmart your opponent. The worst, if it turns out he's smarter than you are.

I went with the front door. If in doubt, go with simplicity. Not the first time I'd walked through a door into a hostile situation. I hoped it wouldn't be the last.

88

I pushed open the outer door and stepped carefully into a small lobby. I was taking the expected route, but that didn't mean I'd give up on the basics. I listened carefully, but couldn't hear anything.

Dusty black work coats hung on hooks. An open door in front of me revealed a cavernous space beyond, crates stacked in towers but a lot of empty space in between. Either Lawrence was deliberately drawing down his inventory, or he was between deliveries.

From the warehouse space, a staircase led up, fixed to the wall and open on the side. Above, a gallery ran along the wall, with doors to what were presumably offices or living quarters. One door had a light shining through its window. No way to approach with any degree of surprise. Option one was looking more and more foolhardy.

The stairs creaked under me, nothing I could do. I was expected anyway. I walked along the gallery, listening. I heard a voice, but it was distorted. A radio transmission.

Lawrence was alone. He had his feet up on a laminated desk littered with newspapers and food wrappers. He had the wireless on. Radio Hamburg. Lord Haw-Haw, gleefully predicting the imminent arrival of Nazi parachutists over Kent and Sussex.

He seemed pleased to see me. He gestured to me to come in, and looked behind me to check I was alone.

'You didn't do too much damage, did you?' he asked.

'Nothing brown paper and vinegar won't cure.'

'That's a shame,' he said. 'Nice guy. Nice wife. Couple of nice kids. The lot.'

'In my experience there aren't any nice guys out on the streets at three o'clock on Sunday morning.'

'What are you drinking?' Lawrence asked, leaning back and pulling a bottle of whisky out of a crate.

'I'm not here to drink with you.'

He opened the bottle and poured generous measures into two glasses. He raised his own glass to the light, then drained it.

'Take the weight off,' he said, gesturing to a chair in front of the desk.

I took the whisky but stayed standing. I wanted to make it clear this wasn't old friends catching up.

'Been in the wars, have you?' Lawrence asked, genuinely curious.

I could only imagine how I looked from his point of view, still covered in a mix of dust and blood, now dried solid in a black mess.

'This is about all that's left of Baxter and his friends,' I said.

'Who's that again?'

'The man you've been keeping supplied with young girls,' I said, watching for his reaction.

'Girls aren't really my line of business.'

'I think they're exactly your business,' I said.

He shrugged. 'I'm not going to lose any sleep because I helped a few girls get berths in mansions instead of rat-infested slums.'

'You were always good at telling yourself stories.'

'You think they're any safer in the places they're meant to end up?' he asked. He laughed. 'I forgot, you're a believer in the poor.

Salt of the earth the lot of them, isn't that right? You should have a look for yourself. It's not all scrubbed doorsteps and singing round the piano. Besides, everyone's for sale, you know that.'

'I've come to ask you to stop,' I said. 'I don't expect you to agree with me.'

'You used to have more of a sense of humour,' he said, pouring himself another measure of whisky. He held up the bottle to me and I let him refill my glass.

'You used to have a sense of right and wrong,' I said.

'Did I?' he asked. He gave the question serious thought, sipping his whisky. 'So now what?' he asked. 'Pistols at dawn? Fist fight? Dominoes?'

He leant back in the chair and scratched his leg. Suddenly his hand appeared, holding a gun. He rested his hand on the desk, keeping the gun aimed at me. Throughout this move, his eyes never left me.

I'd matched his move, bringing my cut-down revolver out of my pocket, trigger guard filed off. Dangerous carrying a gun like that. More dangerous drawing a gun that isn't ready when you need it.

'You've been practising your draw,' I said. He'd modified his gun in the same way. We'd both learnt from the same teachers on the streets of Hong Kong.

'Are you going to shoot me?' I asked.

'I'd rather not,' he said. 'You're a useful chap. You should join me. Us against the world, like old days.'

'It's a tempting offer,' I lied.

'Looks like we've got the same supplier,' he said. His gun was a Webley. Brand new apart from the modifications. Identical to mine.

'They're brothers,' he continued. 'Forged in the same production line. Honed by the same man. Put into the same box and sent across the sea.'

Without taking his eyes from me, he used his foot to push a crate from under the desk. I glanced down at it. It was covered with shipping labels. I couldn't be sure, but it looked like it was from Margaret's delivery.

He was trying to rattle me. He wanted me racking my brains trying to work out who my mole was. He'd only need a second.

'I know who sold them to you,' I said.

He looked inquisitively at me.

'How do you feel about that?'

'I'll live,' I said.

'Well, one of us will,' he said.

Then he did something that surprised me. He lowered his gun and put it on the desk. He took his hand away from it and picked up his whisky glass.

It was a ploy. I give you something, you give me something back. Reciprocity. He wanted me to lower my gun, to take him out of the crosshairs. Presumably I was meant to buy into some kind of idea of truce. Of brotherhood. But Lawrence would no more take his gun off an opponent than he would throw himself off a cliff. The gun on the table was an illusion. Which meant there was another gun, still on me, waiting for me to react.

I stepped backwards sharply. The back of my head hit something metal and there was a hurried shuffling noise as the man holding it tried to react to my move. I was being marked from behind. Point-blank range, no risk of missing. Lawrence watched me take the step and grimaced. He knew what it meant. His plan hadn't worked. I'd die, but so would he. The only man who'd walk away would be his man behind me. A failure, in terms of strategy.

'Worth a try,' he said.

I had the advantage, even if the other two men in the room didn't know it. The man behind me reported to Lawrence.

If he pulled the trigger, I'd still get off a shot and his boss would be killed. Perhaps that was all right with him. Probably wouldn't lose any sleep. But a tiny barrier to action, nonetheless. Added to that, I was betting he was a follower. Used to being told what to do. Probably generations in his past of people being told what to do. Thinking for himself didn't come naturally. Another tiny barrier. Fractions of a second perhaps. Enough for me to get the upper hand, perhaps.

I dropped to my knees, clearing my head from his line of fire instantly. As I fell, I reached around and grabbed his arm. I hung on, and let gravity pull him down with me. The gun fired, loud in the small office, and as he landed on me I heard an even louder noise, an explosion. The car. The room was lit up as an orange fireball rose up past the window.

My assailant was quick. Before he even landed on me he was pivoting, ready to roll away, giving him clearance to bring his gun arm back into play. I matched his movement, grabbing him and rolling with him, both of us pushing in the same direction. He fought the momentum but I pushed with it, rolling us towards the desk. I grabbed his head and pushed his face into the sharp corner of the desk leg, pushing further as the square leg found the depression between his cheek and his forehead. His eyeball burst, and I felt its wetness on my fingertips. He grunted with effort as he tried to pull his head back, but my arm was stronger than his neck. More leverage.

I heard the scrape of the chair as Lawrence got up and hurried behind me. I fired blindly back over my shoulder, tracking the route I thought he'd be taking to the door, discouraging him from trying to grab me from behind. The door slammed. He'd remembered his training. You win every fight you don't have.

My assailant let go of me so he could bring his hands up to his face. Suddenly the thought of fighting me had been pushed down the order of priorities. I rolled away, ready to chase after Lawrence. But I couldn't leave an enemy behind me. Too much that could go wrong with that, so I gave him a kick to the head that put him out. He'd probably burn with the building if the fire from the car caught hold, but that was a result of his own choices, not mine.

I opened the door to follow Lawrence and was hit by a wave of heat and thick smoke. I was inside an old wood building, dried by the sun and sea air, painted with tar and creosote, then ignited by a spray of burning petrol from my improvised bomb. It was on its way to becoming an inferno.

89

I stood on the landing and assessed the situation. Always worth taking a second to plan. I looked out over the warehouse space, through thickening black smoke. I couldn't get out the way I'd come in. The inside of the front wall was a curtain of fire, flames licking up from the door to the lobby, sheeting up the wall like a waterfall in reverse.

I ran down the open staircase towards the ground floor, but the heat from the burning front wall forced me back. I was about halfway up, about eight feet down to the concrete floor. I climbed over the banister. There was a pile of crates six feet away. I threw myself towards them and landed awkwardly on my stomach, the top crate digging into me painfully. I let myself down, landing on the floor. As I did so I heard the scrape of wood on concrete.

On the far side of the warehouse, Lawrence was pulling a large crate into the open. He saw me land and raised his gun, firing at me. The banister exploded next to me and the left side of my face was peppered with splinters. I threw myself on the ground and sheltered behind a crate as his next bullet disappeared harmlessly into the burning wall behind me.

'Not too late to change your mind,' he shouted. 'My second-in-command's just been let go. I'll be looking for someone to take his place.'

I heard the clatter of metal on concrete and then a wrenching sound. The scrape of a crowbar, the scream of a wooden lid being levered off, nails complaining as they bent and slid against fresh pine. I wondered what was in the crate that made it so heavy and so valuable to him.

My answer was provided immediately by the metallic crunch of a full magazine being loaded onto a Bren gun, followed by two snicks as the built-in tripod legs clicked out, ready for one-man firing, braced on a steady surface.

I threw myself to the ground behind my crate as he fired. In the enclosed space the sound was deafening. Eight rounds per second, .303 calibre, capable of piercing the armour of a light tank. He ran through the 50-round magazine in seconds. I risked a look over my protective crate, now partially destroyed, and saw him grab the gun, meaning to take it with him, but the super-heated barrel seared his hand with a hiss and he bellowed with rage and pain.

Behind me, the front wall collapsed, heavy roof timbers crashing down in a shower of sparks. I could see the street beyond and the burning shell of the car. There was a chance I could hurdle the burning timbers. A slim chance, but a chance.

Lawrence had his hands in the crate, struggling to get another magazine out. The crate itself was smouldering and as I watched, the flame caught in the air above, igniting the gases boiling off from the fresh pine. Lawrence ignored the flames and leant into the crate, submerging his chest and arms in the fire. He roared in frustration as he finally yanked a magazine out.

'Lawrence!' I shouted.

He looked at me, and at the mirage of the street behind me. It would be an admission of defeat, a path he wouldn't take.

He grabbed the gun again and I heard the hiss of seared meat as his hands became one with the metal. He slapped the magazine into place and raised the gun to his shoulder.

I turned to the gap in the burning wall, sprinted towards it and leapt through the glowing wreckage. My clothes ignited as I passed through the curtain of fire and I felt my face searing in the fierce heat. The Bren thundered behind me. A distant corner of my mind worried about getting hit, but I didn't give it much thought. The fire was going to kill me before the bullets did.

90

I landed in a pool of melting tar and rolled forwards, into the street. I heard shouting and felt men kicking me. I let them do it. I didn't have the strength to fight back. They rolled me, stamping on my back. They weren't kicking, they were putting out flames.

I rolled over and retched, and threw up a sour mix of smoke and dust.

Then I heard the click of a hammer being cocked.

I looked around at the men. Some held revolvers. One wore a steel helmet from the last war. Lawrence's men, but Lawrence was lost in the fire. Now they'd have to work out who was boss.

There was a roar of flame and we all turned to watch in awe as the building collapsed in on itself with a crash. If Lawrence wasn't dead already, now he had no chance. Nothing could have survived.

'Leave him,' one of the men said. It was the sentry I'd let walk away. He nodded to me. Seemed like he was the next in command. A battlefield promotion.

A church bell was ringing, and I assumed it was an alarm for the fire.

Another church bell joined the chorus. This one further away. Then another. Quite a cacophony. Every church in Brighton must have been getting in on the act. I realised why I found it so strange. There hadn't been any church bells since the start of the war. It was forbidden. They were only to be used to sound the alarm for the start of the invasion.

91

I walked down Ship Street, towards the sea. Lawrence's men followed. The sky was lightening. It smelt like a warm day ahead. It felt like a holiday, the seagulls overhead and the sound of the waves crashing on the beach ahead of us.

Every church bell was tolling. People were sliding up their windows and opening their doors, peering out, wondering whether to run or hide or fight. As we passed the pub, the landlord hurried out, wearing his slippers, feeding shells into a shotgun.

I reached the seafront, now at the head of a growing band of people. I crossed the road to the promenade, and stood at the railings, looking out to the grey sea. To my left, the sun was coming up, and the sky was almost clear of clouds.

The beach was a mess of barbed wire. A solitary Home Guard sentry stood down by the sea, like a boy debating whether to go for a paddle. I looked around me. Perhaps ten of Lawrence's men, each with a gun, about thirty more civilians with a motley collection of decorative or hobby weapons, and about a hundred women and children hanging back, come to see the end of the world.

I looked out to sea. If I was running the invasion, I'd have had battleships moored halfway across the Channel, firing heavy guns into the coast. I'd send waves of bombers overhead, taking out embedded positions and softening up any defensive forces. I'd have regiments of paratroopers falling out of the sky, probably further inland, to attack the defensive forces from the rear.

But there weren't any shells thudding into the promenade, or bombers droning overhead, or paratroopers falling out of the sky with knives between their teeth. Just us, and the solitary Home Guard in the surf, and the tolling bells.

'There's a boat!' someone shouted. We all scoured the sea. A collective effort. We all saw it. A distant speck in the grey expanse. A small fishing boat, slowly growing larger as it came towards the beach. But it couldn't have been a fishing boat. They were banned from this section of the coast. They knew their lanes and they stuck to them.

As the boat grew closer, more appeared on the horizon. One of them was trailing a thin column of smoke. None of them looked like much of an invasion fleet.

I walked down the steps onto the beach, pebbles crunching underfoot. Lawrence's sentry followed me. We threaded our way through the barbed wire, down to the shoreline.

The Home Guard sentry looked at us wildly. He looked about thirteen, and he was terrified. He held his Lee–Enfield rifle up to his shoulder, ready to fire. I pushed the barrel of the gun away, towards the sea.

'What do you see?' I asked him.

He looked out to sea, peering through his gun sight.

'Four, five boats,' he said.

'Have you taken any fire?' I asked.

'No,' he said.

'Seen any bombers?' I asked.

He shook his head, scanning the sky in an ineffective jerky motion, waving the gun as if he were going to shoot down a bomber at twenty thousand feet.

'I thought I heard one,' he said.

'Lower your weapon, private,' I said.

He lowered his gun and looked at me in relief. He'd done his job of protecting the beach until a superior officer arrived.

'Good job, soldier,' I said. 'What's your name?'

'Guthridge, sir.'

'Where's the rest of your unit, Guthridge?'

'Blowing up the pier, sir. And the rest are spread out along the beach. We've got one section each.'

'Any backup on its way?' I asked.

'Don't know, sir. I don't think so. I think we're it.'

A shot rang out from behind us, followed by a whiz as the bullet tore the air above our heads.

I turned back to the crowd on the prom.

'Cease fire!' I shouted. Full command voice.

Thankfully, nobody else fired. I didn't fancy our chances, standing a hundred yards in front of a group of amateur marksmen.

The first boat was nearing the shore, making for our section of the beach. The others followed close behind, with more on the horizon.

Guthridge raised his rifle again, squinting through the sights. He kept it trained on the first boat.

'What do you see, Guthridge?' I asked.

'Soldiers,' he said.

'How do you know they're soldiers?'

'They're wearing helmets, sir.'

'What do the helmets look like?' I asked.

He peered through the gun sights, even though they were just raised bumps on the rifle stock. I presumed they gave him the sensation of focus.

'I think they're Tommies, sir.'

He lowered his rifle.

I walked into the surf, and Guthridge followed. We reached the boat as its keel grounded on pebbles with a loud scrape. The boat tilted and settled as the wave it had ridden in on receded with a sucking sound. A small fishing boat, not much larger than a rowing boat, with a wheelhouse big enough to shelter one man from the worst of the elements. The boat was crammed with soldiers, lying huddled together, listless and bleeding.

The boat's pilot, a soldier with a bloody bandage wrapped around his head, pulled his hands off the wheel and jumped over the side. He sank to his knees in the water and muttered something inaudible.

Guthridge and I grabbed the soldier and helped him to his feet. There were shouts from the men in the boat as a sergeant major roused them, and soon they were all climbing out, into the water.

We helped the soldier up onto the beach.

'What happened?' I asked.

He shook his head.

'It's over,' he said. 'They've got France.'

A second boat slid onto the gravel, and men jumped out, whooping and cheering as they sank to their knees on the beach.

Lawrence's sentry pulled a whisky bottle from his pocket, cracked the seal, and held it out to the soldier. The soldier took it gratefully, took a swig, and then handed it back, nodding his thanks.

'Churchill told us to hold Calais until the last man,' he said. He shook his head again. 'Fuck Calais, and fuck Churchill.'

'Well, you're home now,' I said.

The soldier looked up at what he could see of Brighton from down on the beach – the tops of the seafront buildings in front of us, and the pier further down the beach.

'We've got to get ready,' he said. 'They'll be here soon.'

I looked back at the crowd on the prom, with their shotguns. Another boat slid onto the beach, prompting an exhausted cheer from its passengers.

I looked out to sea, picturing it thick with German battle-ships and landing craft.

We weren't ready. We'd known this was coming for years, and we'd wasted our opportunity to prepare.

I had a lot of work to do.

We all did.

92

The Spitfire came out of the South, where the Downs were silhouettes against the deep blue of the evening sky. I watched as he cleared the oak at the bottom of the meadow. Probably didn't see me in the dusk, I told myself, but as he passed overhead he waggled his wings, to the delight of the children, who waved back.

Frankie ran across the meadow and Elizabeth walked carefully behind. He'd promised to show her the rabbits. I'd taken him to see a warren on the far side of the meadow, and now he was proudly passing on his knowledge, like a lord showing off his lands to a visiting dignitary.

She held herself carefully. She'd be recovering for a long time, Doc said. Not just physical damage. Like shell-shock, he said.

They said Doc had brought her back. After I'd left her for dead, he hadn't given up. Something he'd read in a journal. Thought it was worth a try. His way of deflecting the attention. He couldn't save the baby, but he saved her. Funny how the quiet ones turn out to be the heroes.

Margaret got up from the blanket we'd spread on the ground. She brushed off the crumbs from our picnic dinner and followed the children. She didn't like to let Elizabeth get too far out of sight.

The news was full of the evacuation of Dunkirk. Hundreds of thousands of men. Thousands of boats. They were still coming, landing on every beach and harbour from Folkestone to Portsmouth. They were calling it a victory, and the press were falling over themselves to play along. A triumph of the bulldog spirit. One in the eye for Hitler.

Or, if you looked at it another way, we'd just demonstrated how feasible it was to move an entire army across the Channel under heavy fire. I could only imagine what Hitler was thinking now he'd seen it done. If I were him, I'd be rounding up every fishing boat and barge I could get my hands on.

Margaret stopped halfway across the meadow and looked back at me. It was too dark for me to see, but I knew she was smiling. I stood up and walked to her. I took her hand and she pulled me into a kiss. Just a brush of her lips, enough to get me thinking about what might come later, then breaking away, pulling me towards the children. Quite a family, I thought, as I let her lead me through the long grass.

The invasion would happen, that much was clear. Hitler had Europe. He had the most modern, mechanised army the world had ever seen. And now he had our artillery, our tanks, and our weapons, everything that couldn't be stuffed in a man's pocket and carried onto a fishing boat. They would come by air, and by sea. The sky would be black with parachutists, and the sea would be thick with troop carriers. They'd soften us up with bombers and long-range artillery, and then they'd make their move.

Let them come, I thought. Let them roll through my farm and my town. I'd surrender, and I'd say my 'Heil Hitler' along with everyone else. I'd survive and I'd make sure my family survived. And then, when their generals had gone back to Bavaria to plan the invasion of Russia, I'd be ready. Ready to do my bit. Ready to get the job done.

Author's note

First of all, my apologies to the people of Uckfield and the surrounding countryside for taking creative licence with the geography when it suits the story. Even though I've spent half my life in Uckfield, when I found myself sitting down to write this book, I let my imagination run rather loose when it came to creating roads, or stately homes, or pubs. So please don't go looking for The Grange, The Cross, or Cook's farm. Apart from anything else, Uckfield has changed a great deal since 1940 and most of the farms, fields, and stately homes are now long gone.

I was inspired to write this book while reading *The War In The West*, the first volume of James Holland's excellent history of the Second World War. A brief mention of Auxiliary Units combined in my imagination with boyhood memories of exploring the countryside around Uckfield, and I could instantly imagine John Cook, tramping around the fields and woods, ready to get the job done.

This book is a work of fiction. Part of the joy of writing historical fiction is learning about the period and using those details to provide a sense of realism. This approach comes with risks – too much history will get in the way of the story, while too little will do a disservice to the people who lived through the events depicted. This tension was never far from my mind when writing this book. I felt a sense of responsibility to those who lived and fought at the time, and I wanted to get the details right where possible. I have invariably made many mistakes and, indeed, sometimes I have chosen to err from fact when I felt fiction would make a better story.

I've tried to be accurate with key dates. It's easy to find when a battle took place, but it's harder to find when that news reached the average person in England. In the story, I have Cook watching newsreel footage of battles only days after they have taken place. It's likely it would have taken much longer for such footage to reach the public. The wireless (radio) was the way that most people in Britain got their news. The BBC was the only provider of radio programming that people were allowed to listen to, although in fact many did tune in to broadcasts from the continent because, as Cook's Mum observes, they had better music. In the early years of the war the BBC struggled to find the right balance between entertainment and education.

Although Bunny, Cook, Lady Margaret, Eric and Cyril are fictional characters, there were indeed groups of resistance fighters (called Auxiliary Units) formed by the government, given weapons, and told to stand by. I learnt a lot about these units from the excellent website (*www.staybehinds.com*) maintained by The British Resistance Archive. There are also a number of books on the subject, and I found *The Last Ditch*, by David Lampe, and *With Britain In Mortal Danger*, by John Warwicker, very useful. The men (women were not allowed to sign up for combat) who served in these groups did indeed have a life expectancy predicted to be counted in weeks if the Germans invaded. It's a matter of lively speculation as to whether there are still caches of weapons buried in woods and fields around Britain.

Some of the things that Cook thought of as 'common knowledge' at the time are now known not to be true. For instance, it was generally believed that on the first day of the war, the Germans would drop gas and bombs on the major cities in the UK, killing 200,000 people. With the benefit of hindsight, we know that this didn't happen straight away, but think of how worried people were in the days leading up to the outbreak of war. Many people had their dogs put down, for instance, because they wanted to save their pets from the agony of suffering from gas attacks. It was also assumed that Hitler's plans were to invade the UK after France, but now some historians think such an invasion was never a priority.

I grew up in Uckfield in the 1970s and 80s. At that time the Second World War seemed like ancient history, even though it was in living memory for anyone in their forties or older. Echoes of the war were felt particularly in the films that we watched, and even in the games we played. Yet when I started work on this book, I realized how inadequate my knowledge of the period was. Did they have telephones? When was rationing introduced? How much was a pint of beer? Clearly, a childhood of watching *The Great Escape* had not given me a well-rounded understanding of life in Britain in the 1940s! I was lucky to find a number of diaries of life on the home front. In particular I recommend *Betty's Wartime Diary 1939–1945*, edited by Nicholas Webley, and *Despatches (sic) From The Home Front – The War Diaries of Joan Strange 1939–1945* which is especially relevant as Joan lived on the Sussex coast. For an overview of the wartime experience, I recommend Juliet Gardiner's *Wartime Britain 1939–1945*.

Life on the home front in the South-East, especially near the coast, also involved many additional regulations designed to maintain security in the predicted invasion zone. Sometimes there are disagreements between sources about certain facts, such as when Brighton beach was closed to the public. I've seen photos and read diary entries of people on the beach in June 1940, but other sources suggest it was closed by then. *Brighton Behind The Front*, published by QueenSpark Books

& the Lewis Cohen Urban Studies Center at The Brighton Polytechnic is an excellent source of personal memories and photos. The idea of flooding the sea with burning petrol to deter invaders is not fiction, although the aquarium was not used as a storage tank – the actual tanks were set up nearby.

Uckfield's position in the predicted invasion zone is clear from the many defensive pill-boxes that dot the surrounding countryside, in addition to concrete tank traps that can still be seen by roadsides. *German Invasion Plans For The British Isles, 1940*, published by the Bodleian Library, is a fascinating resource. When I was a child, decades after the end of the war, many villages in Sussex still had collections of Nissen huts and other abandoned military buildings, either staging points for troops awaiting the D-Day invasion or POW camps. The airfield on Ashdown Forest is still marked on some maps, although it is not believed to have been put to use.

There are of course many excellent books and films about the evacuation scheme. While overall a success at moving a large volume of children out of the cities, it is now understood that it exposed many children to harsh conditions and even abuse. However, there is no suggestion in any of the historical sources I've seen that there was deliberate abuse on the scale this book suggests – that part of this story is created purely for dramatic purposes and I hope it doesn't upset any readers who have treasured family memories of the evacuation.

Despite growing up in a small town on the edge of the countryside, I have never worked on a farm. I found the BBC television series *Wartime Farm* fascinating, along with the companion book by Peter Ginn, Ruth Goodman and Alex Langlands. For first-hand information from the period, several books by A.G. Street were informative reads – *Round The Year On The Farm, Farmer's Glory*, and *Harvest By Lamplight*.

Cook was largely defined by his experience in the Great War. Nick Lloyd's recent history *The Western Front* was invaluable, and for a primary source, Edmund Blunden's memoir *Undertones Of War* was fascinating, particularly as he came from a small village outside Uckfield, and served with the Royal Sussex regiment.

There are very few resources detailing the kind of experience Cook would have had on the North-West Frontier. I relied on *Afghanistan 1919, An Account Of Operations In The Third Afghan War,* by Lieutenant-General G.N. Molesworth, CSI, CBE.

Planes did come down frequently across Sussex, and there were many bombings. *The War In East Sussex,* a pamphlet distributed by *The Sussex Express* in 1946, is an excellent resource, as is *Battle Over Sussex 1940* by Pat Burgess and Andy Saunders. The first bombs to fall on Uckfield were dropped on 15 August 1940 at The Rocks Estate, near the fictional location of Cook's farm. Over the course of the war, there were 723 bombing incidents in the Uckfield district, with 23 houses totally destroyed and 31 people killed (not counting military casualties). Some bombs were High Explosive (HE) like the one that destroys The Grange, many others were incendiary devices. In addition, many Sussex towns were victims of what were called 'tip and run' raids, where German fighters would fly over a town at low altitude, shooting and bombing, before flying off.

My grandmother Bessie was an Air Raid Patrol (ARP) warden during the war, and I regret that I didn't get to talk with her about her experiences. John Strachey's book *Post D – Some Experiences Of An Air Raid Warden,* published in 1941, is a fascinating first-hand account, including the process and experience of digging out bombed buildings.

I hope you've enjoyed spending time with Cook and Lady Margaret, in their corner of wartime Sussex, as much as I have. Please do consider leaving an online review, and look out for the next in the series, coming soon.

Acknowledgements

A book starts out as one person's work, but quickly becomes a team effort.

I had the good fortune to have a number of people read early drafts. Every person gave great comments, and all contributed to the book becoming what it is. Thanks to Brian for reading it twice (on his phone), to Lisa, Danielle, Jan, Paul, Steven, and Mum. Thanks to Joanna Barnard for providing an initial edit and for the unflagging enthusiasm ever since.

When I had the manuscript finished, ready to go out into the world, I took an excellent online course with Curtis Brown Creative – Edit and Pitch Your Novel. This was invaluable both for everything I learnt (mainly, that your novel is not ready when you think it is!), and for the community of readers and writers it introduced me to. Thanks in particular to the Pencil Pack – Naomi, Joanne, Diane, Sarah, Polly and Jude. Special thanks to Patrick, who gave many detailed notes on the book, and was my adviser for all things military. All of the mistakes are mine, not his (many of the departures from military and historical fact have been debated between us many times!).

Thanks to Dad, for the countless walks in the countryside around Uckfield, and for inspiring me to write, to Graham, for the lifetime of bookish talks, and to Helen and Sarah for the encouragement and enthusiasm!

As any writer will appreciate, one of the big stepping stones towards traditional publishing is getting an agent. Many thanks to Elane and Sarah and their organization I Am In

Print, for providing me the opportunity to meet with potential agents. For any unrepresented authors, I highly recommend their agent 1:1s.

Jordan Lees is my agent, and from the minute we first met he's been an enthusiastic supporter of John Cook. Every note he's given me has made the book better. Thanks to Jordan and the awesome team at The Blair Partnership.

Thanks to everyone at Hodder & Stoughton, in particular Morgan Springett, my editor. I couldn't ask for a better thought-partner. I am confident this is the beginning of a long and fruitful partnership.

Finally, of course, thanks to Danielle, Lauren and Charlotte, for everything.